Niki Valentine is an award-winning writer who, under a pseudonym, has been published internationally to huge acclaim. When she isn't working on her next psychological horror novel, Niki teaches Creative and Professional Writing at Nottingham University.

Visit her website at www.nikivalentine.co.uk.

THE
HAUNTED
NIKI VALENTINE

sphere

SPHERE

First published in Great Britain in 2011 by Sphere

A CIP catalogue record for this book
is available from the British Library.

ISBN 978-0-7515-4508-1

Typeset in Caslon by M Rules
Printed and bound in Great Britain by
Clays Ltd, St Ives plc

Papers used by Sphere are from well-managed forests
and other responsible sources.

MIX
Paper from
responsible sources
FSC® C104740

Sphere
An imprint of
Little, Brown Book Group
100 Victoria Embankment
London EC4Y 0DY

An Hachette UK Company
www.hachette.co.uk

www.littlebrown.co.uk

Acknowledgements

Special thanks to Luigi Bonomi, Cath Burke and all at Sphere. Also to Richard Pilgrim, Maria Allen, Chad, Mum, Dad, Deborah, Paul, Adam, Danielle and Natalie, as well as all my family. Finally, to my students at Nottingham University, with whom I learn as much as I teach.

For my parents

1

On the night she arrived in Fort William, Susie dreamed of weddings.

She used to dream about weddings often. Mostly her own wedding in the big, dark Catholic cathedral; the white designer dress she'd worn and the single white rose she'd carried instead of a bouquet. She'd had a recurring dream where the thorns dug into her hands and she bled until the dress turned red. There was another nightmare, one she'd had when she was first engaged but still came from time to time all these years on, about her engagement ring. In this one, the stones came loose from her ring and scattered on the floor. She got down on her hands and knees, searching with her fingers for the diamonds and rubies, then trying to shove them back into their settings, watching them fall and bounce on the floor again, getting increasingly frantic. It always worried her that these dreams might be some kind of portent. She believed in that kind of thing even if Martin dismissed it all and found her rather silly.

In Fort William, though, she dreamed of a friend's wedding, a man she knew well called Tom who had married years ago. In the dream, it was the same bride and groom but it was in the present day. Susie had on a pink suit with a white carnation for a buttonhole. The perfume from the flower struck her powerfully: the smell of weddings. She walked into the church smiling, but then the breath was knocked out of her. Tom was standing at the front in a black dinner jacket, looking suitably nervous, but the church wasn't set up the way she was expecting it to be at all. Instead, a funeral was to take place. The coffin lay in front of the altar on a trolley with wheels.

Tom walked down the aisle the wrong way, towards Susie. He was talking, garbled words coming out of his mouth the way they did when he was distressed. His wife had died suddenly, he told her, but that was okay because the priest had been so accommodating, really he had, and managed to arrange a funeral instead and wasn't that good of him? And, really, no, it was all right, because it had to be done, his wife needed to be buried if she'd died and it was good of the priest to fit them in this way and at least all their friends were here. His cheer was fake and very disturbing, the smile of a horror-movie clown.

The scene cut then, the way it only does in dreams or films, and she was in a small room on her own. There was a wooden cabinet standing in front of a set of French windows and it was the smell of polished wood that filled her senses now. She opened the doors on the front of the cabinet and examined its contents. There were urns inside, filled with ashes and with a small, brass plaque on the front of each to say whose remains they were. She had realised she was dreaming some time before this, and was looking for significance in the names on the plaques; for someone she knew, perhaps even her own name. None of them meant anything to her. Amongst the urns was a bucket. It stood out; it was brightly coloured like the kind you might buy at the seaside. She knew immediately that it contained the ashes of a child. She rushed to shut the door but the cabinet was unsteady and it rocked. The bucket had no lid and it tipped over, its contents spilling on to the floor. She grabbed at the dust, pulling it up from the floor in a panic, feeling dreadful guilt. The ashes flowed through her fingers like sand on a beach and she felt bits of bone, rough against her skin. Then she woke up.

She was hot with fear and her arms were aching. The alarm clock said it was five past seven but some light already seeped in under the curtains, thanks to the recent change back an hour to Greenwich Mean Time. She remembered her wedding day ten years earlier had lasted an hour longer for the same reason. She turned and saw Martin, still fast asleep and snoring. His blissful peace seemed impossible. She could hardly believe he wasn't attentive to her terrors, that he hadn't realised something was wrong and woken up to comfort her. How could he sleep right next to someone night after night and not be in touch with their soul? She was almost certain she would have woken with a start had the situation been reversed. She got out of bed and shrugged on her dressing gown. She walked over to the window and peeked out, careful not to move the curtains too far for fear of letting in too much light and disturbing her husband.

She needn't have worried so much about the light. As usual, Fort William was shrouded in cloud. The rain dripped relentlessly on to this cold, damp corner of the world. Even through the mist, though, the view was magnificent. Looking at the spectacular curve of ben to loch, the dramatic etchings of long-gone glaciers, it reminded her of their honeymoon, when their marriage was new, and she smiled. That was the point of coming here, after all.

She remembered the conversation they'd had the previous evening about taking a trip to the bothy. This was a crofters' hut in the middle of nowhere, a place for walkers and shepherds to put up for the night, that Martin had visited on a holiday with his parents when he was young. He said now that he'd tried to persuade her to go there on their first trip to Fort William but that she'd been dead against it. She didn't remember this at all but she didn't argue about it. She had no idea why he was so keen to rough it in a hut, and it wasn't her usual style, but she was happy to indulge him. It would be an adventure and that was what this holiday was about.

A loud snort came from the bed, making her start and spin round to look at her husband. He turned on to his side and made snuffling noises, then settled down into a deep sleep once again. She watched him as he slept, wondering if she'd be able to get a coffee from downstairs. She didn't want to boil the kettle in the room and wake him. She smiled gently to herself. Every marriage had its problems; working through them was the thing. She wished she could remember why she hadn't wanted to go to the hut on their honeymoon but the details completely escaped her. This time, though, when he asked her to take that adventure with him, she had said yes. They would walk together in the fresh Highland air and find the bothy. They would burn a wood fire, and lie close to each other in the dying light and it would be perfect. It would be like turning back the clock and starting everything again.

The feeling from the dream washed over her and she shuddered. There had been something about the dream, something different but difficult to define. She'd had these kinds of dreams before and they often meant something. But it was just an ordinary nightmare, she decided. She watched her husband's chest rise and fall and felt some comfort in how clear that movement was from under the sheets. Then, like a miracle, he woke up as she watched.

'Hey baby,' she said, as he came to. She loved to see him wake in the morning, never tired of this ordinary magic. Previous experience had taught her that such things could not be taken for granted.

He mumbled something in reply, still under the deep spell of sleep. She walked back over to the bed and lay down there next to him. She nuzzled in and they began to kiss. Even after all these years, his kisses left her slightly high sometimes, with that heady feeling of loving and being loved. She'd thought this would pass, had been told it would, but this wasn't her experience.

Susie relaxed, placing a hand on his shoulder. They lay there like that, face to face, neither in a rush to move, just seeing the day in together.

Susie felt conspicuous at breakfast. The room was so quiet that even the clinking of their pots felt like a deep disturbance of the peace. This hushed them for a few minutes but then the excitement of being on holiday and planning an adventure together broke through and they were chatting animatedly. The day was looking quite bright now and there was a big picture window in the dining room to show it off to its best effect. Susie felt happy to be alive and married and here with her husband.

Martin's mouth was still curled upwards from the revelation that there was black pudding on the menu and he looked very satisfied with himself as he lifted a forkful. She watched him feed and pushed cereal around in her bowl. She'd only had a few spoonfuls; she was never hungry in the morning. Martin poured them both more tea.

'The waiter here's good,' Martin said, through a mouthful of food. 'I mean, he's attentive, and over at the table when you need him, but you don't really notice him when you don't. Exactly the right balance.'

'Yes,' Susie said, smiling. It was good to see her husband so content and she was pleased they'd managed to find a decent hotel. She sipped her tea, which was a tad too milky, but it didn't matter. All around the room there was the sound of good pots and cutlery. This was certainly a rather better hotel than the one they'd stayed in on their honeymoon. Of course, Martin had been just an ordinary class teacher then, and Susie's job had been at entry level in social work, and their wages hadn't been that great. They'd both had lots of promotions since. Susie had been able to take her career as seriously as Martin did his; it was one of the upsides of not having kids, he often reminded her.

With a final scrape of knife against crockery, Martin finished his food, then pushed the plate away. He smiled Susie's favourite crooked smile and wiped his mouth with a napkin. 'So what do you fancy doing today, Sue? Shall we make out for the bothy like we talked about?'

Susie beamed at him and picked up her cup. The tea was going a little cold, though, so she grimaced and put it straight back down. 'I was wondering about the castle nearby. The one we passed on the way here, you know, the one you took the photo of from the road. I think that would make a lovely day out.' She wasn't sure why she was stalling except that, now it came down to it, something about going to the bothy rested heavy on her heart.

'Yes, no doubt it would,' Martin said. He took a sip of tea himself. 'Cold,' he said, pulling a face.

'Or there are some fabulous short walks around and about.' Susie picked up her handbag and pulled a leaflet from its folds. 'The one to the waterfall looks divine.'

Martin grabbed the leaflet, gave it a perfunctory look over, then dropped it on the table beside his greasy plate. 'A little bit lightweight for my tastes, Sue.' He grinned at her and his eyes glowed with enthusiasm for his planned trip. It was a look that meant she couldn't refuse him and she began to melt even before he spoke again. 'We've only got a few days in Fort William before we head west and who knows if we'll ever come back here. If we're going to spend a night sleeping rough then it'd seem tonight or tomorrow would be the time to do it.'

Every aspect of what he was saying made sense, as ever. Martin was nothing if not logical. Susie wasn't at all sure what was holding her back. She'd felt excited about the trip earlier. But something about his eagerness to go jarred with her. She couldn't explain but she felt his draw to the place was unnatural, creepy even. She had a vague sense of remembering now why she'd said no on the honeymoon. That feeling from the dream came back, the fear, and she tried to dismiss it.

Martin's face softened as he smiled at her. 'Come on, Susie-Sue,' he said, his old name for her, the one he had used all the time when they were first together and she liked because it reminded her of those times. 'It'll be fun. We can cosy up together in front of the fire and tell ghost stories; you'd like that. And we can get cosier than we have in a while, if you know what I mean.' Martin winked at her, and Susie couldn't help but smile at this. They never did seem to find enough time to get close in their busy lives and she missed the physical side of their relationship. The idea of the two of them curled up warm together against the night really appealed.

'Do you even know anything about this bothy? Where it is? Whether it's actually usable? It's a long time since you were here with your parents, honey.' Susie spoke carefully, with a deliberate cheer in her voice.

'I know about all that,' he said. He reached to the floor and picked something up, placing it on the table away from his dirty plate. It was a transparent plastic case and inside were printouts of what looked like a website. There was also a map and compass. Susie took hold of the package and pulled papers from inside. Martin had certainly done his research and she wondered why this would come as a surprise to her after all these years. There was a picture of the bothy, and some information about its registration with the Mountain

Bothies Association and its state of repair, which was detailed as 'good'.

Susie looked at the printouts and remembered watching her husband sleep, the peace across his brow. She wanted to make the man she loved happy. She remembered the way she'd felt that morning, excited about an adventure together and ready to try something new. It had been years since she'd done anything she would describe as genuinely exciting.

'Okay,' she said. 'Let's go to the bothy today.'

Susie had turned the temperature high on the shower so that it steamed up the bathroom. She enjoyed the feeling of her pores opening and her bones heating up. She knew the shower was a luxury she could forget now for a couple of days, even though they would still be paying for the posh hotel room, so she made the most of it while she could. Her skin was welting red under the water. She breathed and ducked under the spray, scrubbing at her face as if it had been covered in mud. Beneath the rush of the water, she could hear Martin moving around in the room next door, packing.

She continued showering until she felt too hot, like she might faint, and the skin on her fingers had begun wrinkling. She stepped from the bathtub into the cold of the room and wrapped herself up in a soft, warm towel. She thanked God again for being able to afford such a lovely hotel. It was madness to be leaving it to stay in a shepherds' hut in the middle of nowhere with no shower or bed and definitely no soft, warmed towels to wrap herself up in. But how wonderful would the shower feel after all that roughing it? It was worth the trip out into the mountains just to come back. She dried herself slowly and decided that she would imagine how this shower was going to feel when they got back here if she ever felt cold or uncomfortable on their adventure.

As she emerged from the en-suite, she saw Martin had unpacked and was now repacking a rucksack. He was throwing items back in rather roughly and she knew from his body language that he was frustrated with how long she'd taken in the bathroom and keen to get on their way. She hadn't meant to take so long. It had just felt so nice under the heat and steam. She hurried now to get ready. Martin must have noticed this, as his movements seemed to calm. She glanced over to see him packing one of his purchases from Fort William. It was a hunting knife. Sharp and vicious, it glinted at her across the room. She didn't really get why

13

they needed it. They didn't go hunting. Martin had just wanted it, though, another boy's toy, and she had no real reason to object to that.

Susie's hairdryer was at the bottom of the suitcase and she virtually had to unpack the entire bag to find it, but she preferred it to the one the hotel supplied. She plugged it in and switched it on. Martin was talking to her but she couldn't hear his voice. She stopped the dryer for a moment.

'Is that really necessary?' he said. 'We should get a move on and set out.'

'I can't go with wet hair,' she told him. 'Walking on those hills at the beginning of November? It won't be much fun at the bothy if I've got a cold.'

He nodded and began to say something but Susie had the dryer on again and couldn't hear.

Martin had brought a slightly smaller rucksack with them for Susie to carry on treks. When she'd finished drying her hair, she packed this second bag with some of the lighter items they needed, the way they'd agreed. Her mobile phone rang. She looked at the display and saw that it was work, probably a colleague with a question. 'I'll have to take this,' she told Martin, but he didn't seem to be listening.

It was Coral, asking about a client file, and Susie gave her the information. Martin was talking to her as she spoke on the phone, something about a torch, but she wasn't taking it in. If he really wanted her to hear something, he should wait until she was off the phone. Susie didn't make a special effort to work out what he wanted and she discussed a couple of other issues with Coral before hanging up. She zipped up the rucksack.

Martin was sitting on the bed with his arms crossed on his chest and his coat on. 'Are we going, then, or are you going to find something else to hold us up?' he said, teasing her.

'Sorry,' she said. 'I didn't mean to be so useless. I just got a bit wrapped up in my shower.'

Martin smiled, and patted her bottom playfully. 'You're a nuisance sometimes but you're worth it,' he said. 'Shall we get off?'

Susie grabbed the smaller rucksack and hoisted it on to her back as an answer.

2

Despite his apparent keenness to get on the road, it had been Martin who had insisted on having lunch before they go. They found the nearest café and sat down. They both ordered a big roast dinner. Susie's appetite was building now and she wanted to eat good, hot food while she still could. They had packed a small gas stove and tins but meals would be basic at best for the next couple of days. She didn't mind; it was part of the adventure, but she was still going to make the most of civilisation while she could.

The meal took longer than they'd expected, and as a result it was nearly two before they set out. The sky was big and grey above them; a massive cloud reached across and over the hills as far as Susie could see. The air was damp but it wasn't raining. 'Maybe tomorrow would be a better day to go,' she said, worried about how soon it might get dark.

Martin looked out to the horizon, a slight grimace on his face. She could tell he was weighing up the hours they had left of the light and how long the walk might take.

'We'll be fine,' he said, after considering this for a moment. With that, he set on his way and Susie followed. She couldn't quite shake the feeling that something wasn't quite right with what they were doing but she tried focusing on the walk, the fresh air in her lungs and beauty of the scenery spreading out in all directions.

Needle pricks of moisture burst on to Susie's skin as she walked. The air was infused with dampness, a stage up from mist. Susie lifted a hand up to her hair and found it already wet through again. The chill from the moisture and wind made her cold to the bone. Martin was moving fast away from her now. All of a sudden, staying in a cold, damp hut seemed a very bad idea. She toyed with a picture of herself heading back to the hotel, leaving him to have the adventure by himself, but this was followed almost immediately by another image: mountain rescue, helicopters, a man halfway down a cliff dying from injuries and exposure. The truth was, she just didn't trust Martin to look after himself. She felt it keenly; despite all his bluster she was the stronger one. She could save them both if she needed to.

'Should we perhaps tell someone at the hotel where we're going?' she said.

Martin kept striding forward and Susie wasn't sure whether he'd heard her. All she could hear was the wind in the glen, whistling and howling at her like a warning.

She repeated her question. 'Martin, shouldn't we tell somebody?' She was sure she'd seen this advice when she'd read about hiking in remote places where you could be hours from civilisation, or even mobile phone coverage. Martin's footsteps made dull thuds against the path as he trod onwards, determined to lead them on an adventure.

'It's not the bloody Arctic, Sue,' he said, then upped the pace so that she had to double step to keep up.

The tense feeling Susie had been having let off for

a bit, and they made their way along the path side by side. It was firm and well maintained, an easy stroll, and this was part of what had lightened her mood. The hills and glens ahead of them looked dark and still, but they were in the future and, for now, they both enjoyed the walk. Martin had a swing in his step, but he wasn't stomping ahead the way he had before. Susie felt comfortable walking next to him and had even begun to look forward to being out in the wilds together, remembering the way he had described it back at the hotel. It would be like the many good times they'd had together, and those were what held her to him.

'Maggie at work's having a baby,' Susie said, making conversation. It was the first thing that came into her head.

Martin let out that laugh he had for these situations, the snort of derision that anyone would be mad enough to ruin their lives this way. They had discussed it at length themselves, back when it would have been the next natural step. A baby was the end of everything. It would be the ruin of Susie's body and her career; she would never recover from it. Susie had always agreed. Except that for Susie, more and more, this agreement came with a sigh, a sad letting go, resignation. She often wondered what kind of woman she would have become if she had been a mother. She'd asked Martin what he thought about this once, whether it ever crossed his mind, but he had looked at her as if she were crazy and said 'but you're not' in a confused voice.

'They're all at it,' he said, leaving enough of a gap for Susie to wonder what he was referring to. 'Reproducing. Like they don't understand what'll be left to inherit. I wouldn't wish it on my worst enemy, never mind my own flesh and blood. Always the worst, the vainest of people who reproduce, too. One of the flaws in the process of evolution at this advanced stage.'

Susie shrugged. She'd heard most of these arguments before. It didn't stop her, though, sometimes seeing a little child being held by its mother and feeling a jerk of pain, deep inside her belly. It didn't stop her waking up in the middle of the night, gasping with fear and the feeling she'd forgotten to do something important. And all of this was strange, because she didn't want a child. Honestly, she didn't.

'The weather looks like holding up,' Martin said.

Susie looked into the distance. The huge, grey cloud still stretched over the glen and she wondered if Martin could see it at all. 'Maybe,' she said. She changed the subject to something she was more comfortable with. 'Mary Bradham's writing a book,' she told him with a little laugh. 'Mum says it's about her life and travels, even though she's never been further than Clapham Junction.'

Martin laughed at this idea too. Mary was a friend of Susie's sister who Martin had always found a bit ridiculous. She drank too much and would flirt with anyone that breathed. She'd never managed to hold down a job or a relationship. 'I don't know what your sister sees in that daft cow.'

'Martin!' Mention of Mary always brought out the judgemental side of Martin's personality. Susie played it like she disapproved but it was an open secret between them that she talked about Mary because she enjoyed his reaction.

'What? You brought it up!' He grabbed for Susie's hand and swung it.

'I know, but you really are mean to people sometimes.' Her voice carried a smile with it, though.

'Ordinary women have a lot to live up to with the examples I have to compare them with,' Martin told her. He was still swinging her hand to and fro. She caught his eyes and they both grinned. He knew just the right thing to say sometimes. 'You should get on and write that book you've always talked about,' he said.

Susie hadn't thought about this for years. It was an old dream, one she'd never been that serious about. She considered it now. 'I think I'd rather live life than waste my time trying to make things up.'

'Quite right,' Martin said. 'Good for you.'

Something bubbled up inside Susie then, a real enthusiasm for what they were doing. 'We should do more things like this, have adventures,' she said.

He turned and grinned at her. 'Perhaps we should. Let's start with this one and see how it goes.'

'How old were you when you went to this place before?' she asked him, trying to picture Martin as a child. He was one of those people who it was hard to visualise as a kid, the kind who you imagine being born grown up.

'About nine. Before everything went really pear shaped with my mum and dad.'

Susie squeezed his hand. 'One of your last good holidays together,' she suggested, assuming that this was why he wanted to relive it.

'Actually, it was a bit weird. I've always wanted to

come back to the place and get my head round it, replace my memories there with something happy.'

Susie turned to look at him, surprised. It amazed her that she'd been married to him all these years and there were still things she didn't know about his life before she came along. Sometimes she forgot he even had a life before her; the connection between them seemed so permanent. 'So it was where it all went wrong?' she said.

'It was complicated, Sue. It was never one thing. But it's the first time I remember seeing them row.' He let out a lightly amused sound. 'I suppose that was natural. I mean, there's just two rooms and so you can't miss anything, not like the space we had at home.'

He was making light of it but Susie could tell his stay at the bothy had affected him deeply, and not in a good way. It was not like Martin to want to go back to somewhere in these circumstances. He was usually much more logical than that. It all made Susie feel a little ill at ease.

They walked without talking for a few moments, the sound of their boots scraping the path and competing to be heard against loud, ugly bird calls: crows or ravens or similar, Susie wasn't sure. She studied the path as she walked, focusing on the hard ground ahead of her.

'Babe, I'm thinking of applying for a headship,' he said, as if it was the same sort of small talk as the weather, or her sister's slightly insane friend. 'It might mean a move.'

'A move of school?' Susie said.

'Well, yes, obviously that,' he said, as if she'd said something ridiculously evident. 'But perhaps also a move of location, of town. You wouldn't need to come with me straight away, of course. I'm just giving you a heads up, so to speak.' He looked pleased with himself, at the pun, although it was probably not intended and not especially funny. Susie turned and watched his face as he walked. She thought about what he'd said; what a funny time to mention it. Like the way some people start serious discussions in a car when you can't get away.

'Okay,' Susie said. 'I consider myself briefed.' She didn't know what she thought about his news yet. There was a time, not even that long ago, when she would have been derailed by the idea of living apart from Martin, even on a temporary basis, and would have been riled by his lack of consideration towards her life, her career. But none of these emotions came. There was a blank, empty space where these feelings should be.

It was raining now, coming down in fat, heavy pellets, not fast but relentless. Susie didn't think she could get any wetter. She walked, and the trail ahead looked darker. The whole event of their hike out into the middle of nowhere was turning damper by the minute. The path became muddy and their brand-new walking boots stuck occasionally in the boggiest parts. Susie noticed Martin's breathing had become heavier. She heard her own, too; flowing with the rain over the deserted land. Whose idea was it to come to Scotland anyway, in the winter? She couldn't remember who had suggested the reliving of their first trip here, but knew for a fact that spending the original honeymoon here had been Martin's idea. He had thought they would save money that way but this hadn't turned out to be the case by the time they'd invested in all the walking gear and paid for hotels and bed and breakfast last minute, by the night instead of part of a package.

They passed a small wood to their left. It was letting off a damp, musty smell, the odour of leaves mulching and decaying, but not altogether unpleasant.

Susie breathed it in deeply and her spirits lifted; now she knew she was in the country, getting fresher air. Ahead she could see a steep incline and what looked like the end of the path. Susie turned to Martin, waiting for direction, but he continued to tread boldly towards the slope.

'It's just a small scramble,' he said, as if he had read her mind.

'A scramble?'

Martin stopped and turned to face her. 'You've done harder than this on strolls around Derbyshire, Sue,' he said, sounding reasonable. 'Come on.'

She took a deep breath and bit her lip. Scrambling was only a step from proper climbing as far as Susie was concerned, and for much more serious hikers than herself and Martin. She knew he thought that all of this was fine because he'd done it before and come to no harm, mostly on trips when he was a boy. He ignored the fact that those previous times were always as a part of groups, with instructors who knew what they were doing, and that he was by no means an expert. She turned to look back the way she'd come. She wanted more than anything to head back in that direction. It didn't bother her that the walk would be by herself, along a lonely path. She saw that picture again, though, of Martin in trouble and helicopters winching him from the side of a steep hill. She couldn't leave him to carry on alone and she knew that his determined nature meant he wouldn't turn back, no matter what she decided, not at this stage.

Martin had stopped and was watching Susie. As soon as he saw her hitch her rucksack on her back and steel herself to go forward, he took it as a signal and was off. He clambered on to the hillside and climbed it like an animal, using his arms to steady himself and provide leverage. He moved fast, like a rat over rubbish. Susie followed, keeping up the pace. It wasn't so bad. She knew that she mustn't look down. The ground was mushy underfoot but not slippery yet and she made good progress.

She had almost reached the place where the ground levelled out when she forgot about not looking down and turned to the hillside behind her, still clinging to the side of the mountain with arms and legs. At first it wasn't a problem, and she stood admiring the view, which took her breath away in a good way. When she decided to continue forward, though, she found she couldn't move at all. It felt like the mere twitch of a muscle would cause her to fall right off the side of the hill. She reminded herself that it was not sheer cliff. She had scrambled up and, if she did fall, which wasn't exactly likely, she would just roll to the bottom. But she thought about turning over and over as she spun down the hill, out of control, the trees and boulders she might hit at speed, and these thoughts paralysed her.

Her breathing became heavy and she tried to control it in rapid, deep snorts, in and out, to stop from hyperventilating. She could see Martin, still making fast progress ahead of her. She dug her hands into the mud of the hillside and told herself she would spring off forwards. She pictured herself, continuing up and coming over the top of the steep incline on to the ledge that she could see above her. But other pictures invaded, images of falling through air and landing hard on the ground below. She shouted, loudly, up the hill. 'Martin!' He did not turn and soon disappeared from sight. She shouted again, and again. Shouting his name took her mind off her breathing, which returned to normal, but she still couldn't bring herself to lift a hand or foot and move onwards. Instead, she dug her hands deeper into the cold earth as if she needed to cling on.

It seemed a long time that she was standing on the hillside, although it could only have been moments. Then Martin appeared above her. 'Come on,' he said, gently. He reached out a hand. Something about his firm grip quelled the fear inside her. As she calmed she realised she had been shaking. Now, stillness rushed through her and she remembered why she loved her husband.

They reached the top together. Once Susie was there, she couldn't understand why she'd felt so scared. Martin headed straight onwards, hardly pausing for breath. He didn't say a word about her panic and even smiled at her, a gently encouraging gesture. He held out a hand again and she took it. His grip felt warm and strong. Susie was glad, but she couldn't help worrying that he might find her a bit pathetic for panicking like that. More than anything, she wanted him to respect her, think her strong and capable and not silly like Mary Bradham.

The walk was more or less flat from there on, and there was no more scrambling. After a while, Susie let go of Martin's hand, not because she didn't feel like holding it, but it was easier to go at her own pace. Being attached was not the best method for walking.

They made their way up and down slight hills and

over land that was springy, verging on boggy. Martin said that there was a track just a little further along, and checked the map and compass a couple of times on the way. Susie's spirits began to lift at this point and she was feeling good. Although they were no longer physically touching, she felt closer to Martin than she had in ages.

When the sun went down it was sudden, and the Highlands went very dark around them. It was as if a curtain had fallen over the hills. Even when their night vision kicked in, the dark around them was consuming. They hadn't even made the loch path yet.

Ahead of them a black hill loomed. They stopped a moment. 'Should we go back?' Susie said.

Martin appeared to consider this. 'We couldn't do the scramble down in this light,' he said, at last.

'No, we couldn't,' Susie owned. All of the good feeling drained through her toes and into the ground.

Martin pulled a torch from his pocket and switched it on. 'You brought the spare one like I said, right?'

'The spare what?' Susie said.

The whole of Martin drooped with the disappointment. He breathed deep then said, 'You brought the spare torch?'

Susie thought about this, then pulled her rucksack from her back. She vaguely remembered a conversation, but the memory was as misty as the day. She dug in the bag and hoped, but she was feeling cold all over. After rummaging for a few minutes to the sound of Martin's deep, stressed breathing, she finally gave up. 'I don't have it,' she said. 'I don't know how I managed to forget it.'

'Neither do I,' Martin said. He turned from her and began walking fast. He was muttering to himself.

Picking up her pace to catch him, Susie felt a bit annoyed. If he'd thought the torch was so important he should have packed it himself or, at the very least, made sure it got packed. The trip had been his idea, as had going for lunch, and she had mentioned that it was a little late to set out after that. She had said it might get dark and he had dismissed her opinion. They weren't in this mess just because they only had one torch. She found she was double-stepping to keep up with Martin but it made her feel good to walk fast. She overtook him, and walked faster.

As usual, Susie's anger lasted all of five minutes. She wondered if that was one of her problems, that she couldn't stay mad, couldn't hold that kind of negativity inside herself long enough to do anything about it. Her sense of empathy was too strong and she found it far too easy to see the other point of view. After all, that was usually the point of view of the man she loved.

She turned around to look for him then. He was nowhere in sight.

3

The rain was still dripping like a tap and blusters of wind sent it sharp into Susie's face. Her jacket swelled and buffeted as she walked. She dug her hands deep into her pockets and moved, one foot then the next. She was alone, exposed on the hillside in the middle of winter and in the dark, the most dangerous situation she'd been in for years. She couldn't feel the danger, though. Even when she considered she had no torch or map, no idea of the way home or on to the bothy, it still felt as easy as waiting a few hours for sunrise. She had food in her rucksack, although Martin had the stove, and she had a sleeping bag rolled up and attached to the bottom. She only had one bottle of water because Martin's research had told them there was a stream near the bothy. That was okay; she wouldn't die of thirst overnight. She didn't even feel hungry. In fact, a slight nausea settled over her at the thought of food. She figured this was a sign that she was stressed, even if she didn't know it.

The cold against her wet skin and clothes was beginning to grind her down. She walked fast. She moved in wheel spikes, away and back from the place she'd found herself alone. She called out her husband's name – 'Martin!' – and then, a little louder – 'Martin?' When he didn't answer after she'd called for him a few times, her movements became less focused, more jerky and manic. She breathed deep and refused to panic. She was a survivor, she told herself.

She was beginning to think she should give up calling for him and settle down for the night. She looked for a bush or tree, somewhere that might provide a little shelter, but it was too dark to see anything clearly except the ground right next to her. She thought then she would wait a little while longer, see if the rain settled so that she could uncurl her sleeping bag without getting it wet. If it did calm down, she could switch straight into survival mode and wrap up for the night. She was tired. She would fall asleep easily, despite the situation.

A presence behind her made her stiffen. A hand on her shoulder. She let out a sharp sound, then turned. Of course, it was just Martin. She found she did not feel that relieved.

'What's wrong?' he said, as if they'd been at home and he'd just nipped into the other room. She hated the way he made her feel like she was being hysterical.

'What do you mean what's wrong? You disappeared.' Susie tried to control her voice but the words came out squeaky.

'Oh, for God's sake. I was taking a leak. Why do you have to turn everything into a drama?'

She looked at his face. His eyes were blank, his expression completely normal, and if he was lying, there was no way to tell. But he'd been gone ages. What he was saying did not add up. She thought he must have wanted to scare her. He had walked away and stayed just long enough to get the effect he wanted. It struck her then: maybe the route they'd taken had been planned that way, too; the scrambling, the dark coming down in the middle of their journey all carefully arranged to freak her out. What if it was all one big game to him? She wasn't enjoying playing at all.

After trekking over rough ground for another ten minutes, they found the track that led alongside a loch all the way to the bothy. The relief at finding the worn path felt to Susie like safety and she had to remind herself that they were not there yet. If the bothy wasn't habitable, or if it was impossible to reach over boggy land, they would have to turn back or sleep in the open, neither of which was particularly appealing.

It was clear that Martin felt surer of himself once they were on the track. His back straightened, his pace quickened. It was only when she noticed this that Susie realised he'd been worried too. Doubt crept in then about the thoughts she'd been having. Martin had told her she was paranoid before and maybe he had a point. She wondered if she had imagined everything. She had to step quickly and add the odd little skip to keep up with his new pace. She tripped a couple of times on dips in the path and stones she couldn't see and Martin reached out a hand to her. She grabbed it, holding on tight, and it helped her to walk steadily. They followed the shoreline of the loch, which was just discernible as a greyish black.

'How far is it now?' Susie asked.

Martin hesitated before answering, as if he had to think about it, but the accuracy of his answer when it came gave away that he was faking. 'Another two and half a kilometres.'

Susie didn't take in the numbers at first, and had to ask for confirmation to check she'd heard properly. She took in the distance he was talking about, thought about how long that would take to walk.

'You can't possibly have thought we'd arrive in daylight,' she said.

Martin shrugged. 'I guess not. But I knew this last bit was flat track alongside the water and would be plain sailing,' he said. He hesitated, then continued speaking. 'I thought we'd have a spare torch, to be fair.'

Susie's face flushed with heat. She let go of Martin's hand. She was really annoyed that he'd needed to bring this up again. They'd both made mistakes today. She knew that forgetting the torch was a big error but they wouldn't have needed to walk in the dark in any case if Martin hadn't insisted on setting out even though it was blatantly too late. She thought about saying something, standing her ground with him. There would be a row if she did. She could tell by Martin's demeanour that he was as tense about this situation as she was. She remembered what it had felt like to be by herself on this dark, lonely hillside. She shivered. It was definitely not worth making an issue of anything. Besides, they were supposed to be bonding and making the most of each other, having a second honeymoon.

They trudged together for a while. Susie found she was tripping more often. The path was becoming a little slippery. She was falling behind her husband. She watched him, the way he continued forcefully on his way, not slowing for a moment for her, not even checking on her progress. He was switching the torch on then off as he walked, making a show of how he had to save the battery because of the mistake she'd made. He could be like this; it was the other side of that judgemental part of him that she enjoyed when it was directed at other people. When he behaved this way towards her, though, Susie felt she had married the wrong man. She checked herself. This could ruin their holiday if she didn't pull it together for both of them. She was responsible for them connecting and having a good time too. And she had been a bit thick about the torch. She would make an effort to make amends now, perk up and bring them back together. As soon as she had decided this she felt better. She found she was walking faster and tripping less.

Soon she was walking level with Martin again. He turned and offered her his hand. She smiled, unseen in the darkness, and took hold of him. Her body relaxed as they walked and tripped together on the uneven path and she wondered how she could ever let any bad feeling build towards her husband.

'It's not much farther. Just the other side of the burn,' Martin said as they approached the flowing water they'd been able to hear for quite some time. It was nothing more than a small stream on the map but rain had made it swell and it looked black and cold in the dark. It was loud and sounded fast-flowing.

They found the edge of the water and Susie looked doubtfully over it. 'Is it passable?' she said.

'There's only one way to find out.' Martin was rolling up his trousers.

'Be careful,' Susie said. 'It sounds very flooded.'

'I'm sure it sounds much worse than it is.'

'Try not to get too wet. It'd be very uncomfortable if we had to walk back,' she told him.

Martin was still bent over, arranging his clothing, but in the torch's light she saw him give her an upward glance. 'We won't have to turn back,' he said, confident as ever.

Then he was off across the river, striding through the rapidly flowing water. Susie took two steps forward to watch, going as close as she dared to the stream. According to the details Martin had downloaded there were normally stepping stones, but these weren't visible in the dark and with the water at this level. It would have been more dangerous to try to pass across slippery wet stone anyway. Martin didn't mess around but flung himself through the water, striding wide and splashing loudly as he went.

Just for a moment Susie watched him and felt conflicting emotions. On one hand, he looked like her superhero, striding bravely through the fast flow of the river. On the other, she found his confidence a bit galling. She couldn't help wondering if he was a little dangerous, in a way. He couldn't perceive of a single situation he couldn't handle. She was pretty sure there were plenty of things he wasn't an expert on, especially to do with the great outdoors, but there was no way he'd ever let that stop him. She worried a little that his overconfidence could get them both into trouble. There was part of her that thought it'd be good for him if he did come a cropper. Not in any serious way. She wouldn't want him to get hurt. She just wished something could happen to make him get real. She shook these thoughts away. Even having them made her feel disloyal.

It felt like an age had passed as she waited for Martin to explore what was on the other side of the river and come back. Susie was cold, and pulled her coat around her. She thought how it would serve her right if something happened to Martin now after the horrible thoughts she'd been having. She shivered. Then there was the sound of heavy, wet stamps coming towards her. She stepped backwards from the edge of the burn. Martin emerged in a spray of water like some kind of sea monster. He was smiling and it made him look sinister.

'I thought we were fucked there for a moment,' he said. 'I wasn't sure I'd be able to get across.'

'You're soaked.' It was all she could think to say, and she shivered again.

'It's okay. There's shelter and we've got a gas stove. We can dry off and drink tea.'

Tea sounded good to Susie but she looked at the swollen burn in front of her doubtfully.

'I'll help you across,' Martin said, reasonably, as if he'd read her mind.

'Okay.' She bit her lip.

His arms went about her then, and as best they could around her rucksack, and Susie grabbed Martin back, holding on tight. It struck her that she used to hold on to him this way, cling to him, when they were first together. She would do it at emotional moments. When they'd just made love, or were about to go their separate ways for a few days. She couldn't remember the last time she'd clung to him like that. She held on tight now and he moved forward fast. She braced herself for the cold. She knew that Martin was no-nonsense that way; he believed in pulling off the sticking plaster in one swift movement.

Then they were in the water. It was so cold Susie found she was shaking all over, hyperventilating. She was glad of Martin's solid stride as he pulled them both through. Water had got into her shoes and between her toes. Her foot stuck behind something. She tried to call to him to slow for a moment but the noise of flowing water was too loud and drowned everything out. She was pulled forward and one arm went into the water. She felt the freeze leak into her clothes and cover her forearm, then elbow, then her armpit. She squealed but that was lost in the air too. The force of Martin came from underneath her. He bent again and pushed her up and out of the water. He almost submerged himself to keep her standing upright.

Steadying herself, the thought entered Susie's head that she wouldn't be able to make it across. She could feel a panic rising in her throat about this, and then she could feel the strength of Martin forcing her onward. It seemed he didn't care how wet he got so long as they both got across the water. Then she was stepping out, carrying what felt like a tidal wave with her. She stood, winded, on the other side of the burn. She bent down and leaned on her knees to catch her breath. She turned towards Martin, who was also breathing heavily. They were both soaked to the skin. It was all so ridiculous she felt like laughing, a comic, evil laugh that would wrack her body and have nothing to do with anything being funny.

Eventually, Susie could stand up straight. Martin had recovered too. They looked at each other for a long time. Susie held out an arm and Martin grabbed it, pulled her to him. He held her firm against his strong chest. Susie was comfortable there; she felt like she could rest there listening to his heartbeat forever. She looked over his shoulder and she could see the bothy, a dark, squat shape in the moonlight, stuck to the side of the hill. It hardly looked warm and welcoming but that would change once they'd lit a fire and unrolled their sleeping bags. It was a cold, empty building battered and rattled and exposed on the side of the loch but it was shelter after a long, hard walk.

Inside the bothy it was dry and dark. It smelled woody and natural, like the forest. The couple shivered as they changed into the dry set of clothes they'd brought with them. They'd almost decided at the last minute not to bring spare clothes, to cut down on the weight in their bags, and Susie was thankful that she had insisted. She thought about her husband. She felt silly now, and paranoid. No marriage was perfect but Martin wasn't setting out to play with her head. She knew that now, and was glad that she had kept her peace about these crazy feelings.

Martin had changed and he smiled at her, telling her

he was just having a quick look around to scope the place out. Susie pulled on her dry sweater and was almost warm. She pulled her still-wet coat over the top. The waterproofing was good and the inside still dry so that the effect was only slightly dampening. She dug in her rucksack for the small pan they'd brought with them. She pulled it out, and took the torch too, going outside to fill the pan with water from the burn. The chill hit her even through the dry clothes and she moved fast. As she turned back towards the bothy she saw Martin, a flash in her peripheral vision that she caught with the torch as he went back into the hut. She watched the door slam behind him and walked back towards it. When she got there and tried to open it, though, it was jammed shut.

Water was spilling from the pan as she pushed on the door, so she placed it down on the ground. She pushed hard with all her weight against the door, ramming it with her shoulder but it didn't give. She pushed and pulled and rattled the door, but still nothing. She tried again, and began shouting to Martin. 'Come on, love. Let me in!' she said, and battered on the door with both hands.

A hand on her shoulder. Susie jumped a mile and

turned. But it was just Martin. She stared at him, confounded.

'What's wrong? You look as if you've seen a ghost,' he said. He was smiling but she couldn't help thinking that there was something wrong with the smile. It looked devious, plotting.

'That was weird,' she said, bringing a hand to her chest. 'I could have sworn I saw you go through the door and it's jammed shut. Oh . . .' she hesitated. 'Do you think there's someone else staying here?'

'I wouldn't imagine so. There weren't any signs of life when we got here.' He pushed against the door and it opened easily. He gave her that look he did sometimes, like she was a silly little girl. She turned away from him. She wasn't sure what was going on but she knew she'd pushed hard on the door, and pulled it too. She could only figure that she was confused, exhausted and stressed from the trek in the dark, and from crossing the water. She was letting the situation get to her.

Inside it was quiet and empty, the way they'd left it, and Susie's eyes searched the hut for any small movement. It was dark enough that someone could have hidden. Martin shone the torch around the room, illuminating it for Susie to see. It wasn't big and there was nothing to hide behind. Aside from the wood store in the corner, which was piled high, it was definitely empty. Martin walked through the door and into the back room, shining the torch around that too.

'Nobody here, not a soul,' Martin said. His face was lit by the torch, and with how daft he thought his wife was being. She saw and noted the expression he was giving her. 'You're probably overtired after that walk,' he said, closing the door between the rooms. He busied himself then, taking wood from the store and piling it into the fireplace. There was also kindling and even a few firelighters. As the room lit up orange, he walked over to Susie and ruffled her hair, then put his arm around her shoulder and pulled her to him.

Susie let him hold her but didn't grab him back. Her eyes darted about the room. She told herself she must have imagined the man walking into the hut, and that the door must have stuck on something. But she was unsettled. A feeling began in the pit of her stomach, a dull, familiar ache. She shivered. 'Someone walked over my grave,' she said, and Martin pulled her closer.

'Come on,' he said, 'let's go to bed.' There was a

playful edge to his voice and plenty of warmth there. It made Susie settle, feel like everything was normal after all. She put her arms tight around her man and looked up at him. The light from the fire warmed his face and made his eyes glow. She couldn't help but kiss him and he responded. Then they were kissing passionately.

They moved with practised coordination towards the nest they had made with their sleeping bags. After all their years together they were so in tune that it was like they were well-established dance partners, instinctively one foot moving and the other in sync. Martin lifted Susie's fleece up and over her head. She didn't feel the cold and it seemed that Martin didn't either as she pulled clothes from him. She felt strangely passionate, hungry for him in a way she hadn't in years. Perhaps it was the fresh air or the danger; those things can be aphrodisiacs. She couldn't remember feeling like this about anyone for a very long time, since her university days if she was being really honest. The intensity of the sudden passion took her a little by surprise.

Something seemed to take over Martin too, as he pulled off what remained of his own clothes quickly and threw her on to the sleeping bags. They made love quickly, frantically. Both of them came fast.

Afterwards they lay together on sleeping bags, having a slightly awkward moment. Susie felt a little embarrassed by the strength of her desire, how wanton her behaviour had been. She suspected Martin did too. She still felt warm from it, though, a contented afterglow.

Martin laughed lightly. 'It's moments like this I wish I'd never stopped smoking,' he said. 'Oh, the pleasure of that cigarette after sex.'

Susie let out a sound at this, part contented sigh, part laugh. They turned on their sides and faced each other, kissing again but gentle, post-coital kisses.

'You were my hero on the river,' Susie told him. She kissed him again and could feel his smile against her lips.

'Glad to be your hero,' he said, sounding sincere.

Susie pulled the sleeping bags up and around them and snuggled in close to Martin, wrapping one leg around him. It was a position she couldn't imagine sleeping in but it felt pleasant for now.

The glow from the fire lit everything in warm tones and made Susie's spirits swell. She looked at the face of her husband glowing back at her.

'I'm glad we came here,' she said. 'I have a feeling it's just what we needed.'

'Me too,' Martin said, sounding sleepy.

Susie was surprised to find she was feeling sleepy too, drifting off despite the way she was lying. She surrendered to the feeling and let herself slip away.

4

Susie woke up early the next morning, a combination of the effect of being in a strange place and early morning light. She didn't feel tired, though. The fire was just embers now, although they still glowed nicely. She got up and poked at the ashes gently, careful of making noise as Martin was still sound asleep. She added some wood. The air was chill and damp but not altogether unpleasant. Outside looked dull and set for more rain, but then that was Scotland, especially this far north.

She carried the gas stove outside the hut and breathed the fresh air. It filled her lungs and cooled them and she felt infused with a new kind of optimism. She decided she'd rather be on this damp Scottish hillside with her husband than anywhere else in the world. She was glad she'd said yes to the adventure this time around.

The cooking pot was still outside on the ground and had some water in it from the night before so she put it on to boil. The bottom of the pot was wet and it spat as the gas heated it up. Martin emerged from the door, rubbing his eyes and looking a little creased. It was a look that suited him, and Susie walked over to give him a kiss.

'Good timing, lover. Did you smell the water boiling?' she said, smiling.

He half smiled in return. 'I must have,' he said, watching as she bustled back and forth, pouring water into their big metal camping mugs.

The sky murmured and threatened as they drank in companionable silence. Martin suggested a walk and, although it looked like the weather might take a turn for the worse, Susie agreed. She went inside and set their clothes from the previous evening by the fire to dry, just in case the rain really came down again. It would be no fun even snuggled up in front of the fire if all their clothes were soaked. Martin grabbed the cooking pot as they left, planning to go to the burn to fill it.

From where they were sitting they couldn't see the river; it was to the back of the hut. Susie could hear it, though, the rush of its flow. It sounded nearer than she remembered it being.

They walked first out towards the bog but didn't venture too far in that direction. It was too obviously sodden, glistening with water, and neither wanted to get themselves covered in mud and wet to the bone again. They came back on themselves and towards the burn. There was a flash of lightning in the distance, which made Susie start. Martin held out his hand and she grabbed it. The rain came down in earnest, big fat globules of water that exploded on the skin. They didn't talk much then but that was fine. They were incredibly comfortable together and Susie was enjoying the fact that she didn't need to fill the air with nonsense the way she did with certain friends.

As they neared the burn, Susie was shocked at its appearance. It looked like a full-flowing river rather than the stream she was expecting.

'Wow,' she said. 'I'm surprised we got across safe looking at that.'

Martin nodded. 'I'm not sure I would have attempted the crossing if I'd been able to see it properly.'

Susie shivered, thinking about the things that could have happened. She decided not to dwell on them.

'We should get back,' Martin said. 'Hole ourselves up against the storm. It's not going to get better any time soon.' They were right beside the water now and he had to raise his voice to be heard. He quickly refilled the pot and Susie noticed how strongly the river pulled on him. It must have swollen since the previous evening, she thought, as she was sure if she'd been filling the pan the water would have taken it from her.

They rushed back to the old stone hut, not holding hands this time because it wasn't practical. Inside, Martin set the fire again, pumping it with a stick to make it glow. Their clothes weren't wet enough to bother changing. Outside, the cloud cover had sent the sky dark as night. This lent the inside of the bothy a cosy aspect and something about the rain pummelling the roof was comforting too. It was really coming down now, like water poured from buckets. Susie was glad they were inside and together.

They talked a little then, mostly gossip about people they knew. Susie told Martin about the dream she'd had in Fort William, asked him what he thought it meant. Martin joked that he really wasn't the person to probe her subconscious, but it was a good-humoured comment. Their conversation ran out of steam in the end and they reverted to the comfortable quiet. The peace was like a holiday.

With their bodies tangled and warm in front of the orange glow of the fire, Susie thought again how perfect this was. *Too perfect*, a voice told her, echoing in her head. *You can't believe in this. Not after everything.* But she refused to listen to that voice. *Nothing can be too perfect*, she told it in response.

The wind and rain rattled around the hut like a wild animal. Susie still felt slightly damp as she lay close to Martin, his body heat the only thing stopping her from shivering. She pulled him closer, for the warmth as much as the intimacy. Holding him close made her feel good and she let out a deep sigh.

'What?' he said.

'Nothing.' Susie smiled. This exact exchange was one they'd had regularly when they were first together and there was something comforting in its familiarity. She could feel Martin's chest moving as he breathed, a steady rhythm that made her sleepy. She was drifting away when Martin's voice cut through the air, jerking her awake.

'Ten years. Can you believe it? It feels longer and I'm not sure if that's good or bad.'

Susie knew what he meant. She tried to pin down what made it feel that way. 'We've been through a lot together,' she said.

Martin's breathing quickened. He moved one of her arms away from his chest and took a deep breath, then let it drop back down towards his waist again. They had always slept like this, Susie tucked in behind him, holding on for dear life. Well, except those times when they'd been rowing. After arguments their sleeping pattern was different, facing away from each other, skin not in contact by even a millimetre, as if their bodies had to prove how angry they were with each other. The intensity of the reaction between them felt sometimes as if they were allergic to each other. When it was good, though, Susie forgot altogether the back-to-back sleeping and, when they spent time apart, she missed even that.

'All couples go through stuff together. It's the whole point, to have someone there. Otherwise being single and having your freedom would be the norm.' His voice was steady as he said this, but Susie sensed they were on difficult terrain, rougher than the scramble up the hill or the walk on an uneven path in the rainy dark.

She hesitated. 'Well, there was that thing with Jayne when we first—'

'We weren't properly together then. We've talked about this, agreed. You said that was true and we'd made no promises.'

Susie's heart was beating a little faster. She had said that, more than once, but she had never entirely believed it. It was just easier, sometimes: denial. But their second honeymoon was not the place to bring this up. 'You're absolutely right,' she said. 'But it was still a shock at the time and it took me a while to get over. Then your mum died and that was a terrible time for us both.' She wished immediately that she hadn't brought this up, either.

A silence stretched uncomfortably between them. Susie could hear her own breathing but Martin's was barely audible. She wouldn't have been sure that he was still alive if it hadn't been for his customary warmth and the subtle movement she felt underneath her left arm. When he spoke at last it was in a voice made of steel. 'Not everything's about you, Susie.'

'Well, you were hurting and so that meant I was too.' She stoppered her mouth. She had wanted to say 'you made sure I was' but that felt unnecessarily blunt. It was honest, though, when she thought about it. It was what she believed. She had wanted to go on and remind him of all the things he'd said and done during the three months following. She'd spoken to a counsellor at the time who had told her Martin's behaviour was an extreme form of normal; grief is a process and anger is one step along that. He had taken such a long time to come past that stage, though, and his anger had had such a clear direction. Susie had a strong sense of justice and she hadn't deserved what he'd thrown at her. She had tried to support him. 'We argued a lot for a while after that. The stress, I suppose, and I don't hold it against you. Not that I'm saying it was all you or anything. Nobody's fault.' She could hear herself gabbling on, sounding like she was taking so many steps backwards.

There was an unpleasant sound from Martin then, a dismissive snort. He cleared his throat as if he were making an announcement. 'You didn't respond the way I needed you to. I needed you to be the strong one, to sweep me up and look after me. You let me down.'

A deep breath. She was almost inclined to leave it at that; they'd had this discussion so many times over. She couldn't, though. She couldn't bear to take the blame. 'I didn't know you so well back then. I didn't know what you wanted from me. You were so hard to read and you appeared to be holding things together so well.'

'You should have come to me. That first week when you left me up in Harrogate on my own. You should have come.'

'I know that now. At the time I thought you would have said if you'd wanted me to come.' She paused. She was almost bored with this argument. She would have thought they'd have got over this one by now but it seemed to have a life of its own, an internal force stronger than love or a marriage or anything, really. She supposed the grief behind it amplified the memory. 'I didn't know what to do,' she told him. 'It was a new situation for me and I got it wrong.'

'It was a fucking new situation for me, too,' Martin said. 'I didn't have a choice but to handle it. I couldn't fucking curl up in the corner and pretend nothing was happening.' The edge in Martin's voice made the air vibrate. Susie moved away from him and propped herself up on her elbows. Although they'd rowed about this subject a hundred times, it was a shock to hear in Martin's voice how angry he still was about it. She'd thought it was all in the past. Maybe the stress of their journey up to the bothy had got to him as well. She tried not to react.

'We've both made mistakes,' she said, carefully. Martin didn't reply to this, just cleared his throat, but somehow his feelings about it hung in the air between them without him having to say a word. *You've made more*, the air sang. *He thinks you've made a lot more than he has.*

The only thing was to change the subject, Susie knew that. Martin was like a child sometimes, the baby she had never had, and distraction was her strongest ally.

'You're going to be a head teacher, then?' she said. She turned her mouth into a smile and tried to inject the right tone into her words. She aimed for an appropriate mix of proud and happy. She was proud and happy too, but there were other feelings there, to do with his expectations of her to fall in line and his sense of priority and entitlement about his own career. These feelings carried on her voice.

'What are you bringing that up for?' Martin said,

immediately hostile. 'We'll deal with it when it's an issue. For God's sake, don't start, woman.'

Susie was riled now. Martin was still speaking to her with the iron in his voice and the way he'd said 'woman' turned the word bad, made it sound like an insult. 'I wasn't making an issue,' she snapped. 'I was just making conversation. I thought you might be interested in talking about you.' The words came out sick and poisoned, the way Susie felt.

'What's that supposed to mean?'

'It wasn't supposed to mean anything. Jesus, I can't do right for doing wrong.' She breathed then, pulling air into her lungs in an exaggerated way. She had said too much and she knew she had better stop if she didn't want to bring out the very worst of her husband. This wasn't supposed to happen here. Martin turned from her and faced away, then moved so their skin wasn't touching. It was cold then. Susie's anger wasn't as good a source of heat as her husband's skin. Already, she felt regretful and couldn't understand what had made her snap back so readily. Maybe it was the damp and cold, but something about being in this place was making them both more tense than usual.

Susie turned, tried to hold on to Martin. 'I'm sorry,

baby. I didn't mean it like that.' But Martin pulled further away from her. 'Come on, don't be like this. Let's not spoil things.' She tried again to hold him, ran her hand across his back gently. He jerked away as if she'd burned him.

'A bit late for that.' Martin was getting out of the makeshift bed and standing up. Susie's eyes had become accustomed to the dim light and she could see his skin near her, dark and goose-bumped. It struck her he must feel cold standing naked on the bare floor of the hut.

'Martin!' she said. Even in her own voice she could hear the air of desperation. It wasn't that he'd go far, or abandon her; she knew her husband well enough to know he might storm out but that he would make his way back when he was calmer. She didn't want to be alone in the cold hut, though, not even for half an hour. Something about that idea was terrifying. The sleeping bags were scant protection against the November chill, she knew. She needed the warmth and comfort of his body. She wanted it. She wanted the way they had been, curled up close together like a couple in love, the way they'd been the night before. She couldn't believe she had messed it up. She couldn't understand how it had happened and what had caused the stress between them. They were on their second honeymoon and having a good time before this. It felt like it had come from nowhere.

The cold room grew colder as Martin dressed, hurriedly, every action looking furious and making Susie's heart sink lower. She knew better than to try to persuade or cajole him now. Any of that would make him even madder, even less likely to come back quickly and curl up with her in a ball, and could lead to even darker places. The spells of difficulty in their marriage had taught her one thing if nothing else: his anger hated signs of weakness. He had to pick at them; make them ooze pus, bleed if he could. Susie watched as he pulled on an item of clothing over his head; it looked like it might be his fleece. He placed a thicker item still on top, its grooves and bulges becoming clear to her as his coat. And then he was moving fast towards the door. She wanted to call out, to beg him, but she knew it wasn't a good idea. She bit her hand to stop herself saying anything.

Then he was gone. The room was silent. Susie couldn't even hear herself breathe, as if she'd been wrapped in a bubble. It was cold, so cold. She pulled the sleeping bags close around her and lay very still, willing herself to warm up. It wasn't happening. She shivered and shook. She sat up, trying to keep the sleeping bag around her shoulders. She grabbed for her coat and tried to undo it. Then she pulled her coat on, inside the sleeping bag, and lay back down.

The two layers began holding in her body heat and, after a few minutes, Susie had warmed up enough that she stopped shivering. She looked at the door. She willed and prayed for her husband to come back. She could hardly bear his being gone. She would have liked to cry, enjoyed the release of it, but she was way past crying over any man. It was as if she'd used up all those tears when she was younger over an event so bad that nothing ever quite compared. It was a shame; crying might have made her feel a little better. Instead she lay there, looking at the door. She was tired, almost mortally so, but she knew she wasn't falling under any time soon. All she could do was watch the door and listen for his footsteps.

Wind soared around the hut and battered the walls outside. It sounded furious. Susie closed her eyes. She had been lying there for what seemed like hours but she didn't even want to look at her watch and find out how long it had been. She didn't think she'd hear Martin's footsteps over the weather but she was trying hard to listen out anyway. She tried to relax. She'd been taught how to meditate a few times over the years, by counsellors or yoga instructors. Mostly, it involved breathing deeply and letting your muscles fall into the floor. When you really got it right, it could feel like floating. It wasn't happening tonight, though. Right now, she couldn't imagine it happening again, ever.

Without noticing, Susie did fall asleep, drifting off into unconsciousness for a few moments then waking with a start, overwhelmed by the feeling she had forgotten something. Her breathing came shallow and fast. While asleep she had slipped briefly into a place where nothing was wrong; a place where there had been no row with Martin. It took her a short while to come back to where she was, on her own in a remote hut, her husband God knows where but no doubt trying to get as far away from her as he possibly could.

She took control of her breath, pulling in deep draughts of air. She found she was crying after all. Not sobbing; she was making no sound and had there been anyone else in the hut they would not have noticed at all. Still, salty tears covered her cheeks and she wiped her face with a chilled hand. Her skin was sore and battered by the wind and rain. She felt old. She closed her eyes and let herself drift back to sleep again. She dreamed of walking in the rain. She woke again and thought for a moment about the walk alongside the loch, tripping along the pathway, that it all might have been part of the dream and she might still be in her bed at the hotel. The cold air against her face convinced her otherwise, though, and the clammy feeling of wearing her coat inside the sleeping bag. She wriggled her fingers and toes to try to warm herself up. It worked, but it also kept her wakeful.

Wind was scraping and howling over the roof. Susie didn't feel the least bit sleepy now. Looking around the room, all was black. She shivered. Not being able to see unsettled her and she felt paranoid; like she was being watched. She sat up stiffly and groped around the floor nearby. Eventually, she found the matches and also the small cooking stove she had used earlier to make tea. She knew it wasn't entirely safe to light it while lying in her sleeping bag and that Martin would likely make a powerful fuss about wasted resources if he saw her. But he wasn't here. They would be back at the hotel tomorrow night, anyway. Well, Susie would, whether Martin came or not. She'd had enough now of the cold and wet and something about the bothy unsettled her, although Martin would have laughed at this as a reason to leave. She lit a match, which made a satisfying scratch. The blue flame leapt from the stove and made her immediately warmer.

The room looked eerie in the tint of the blue light from the stove. She saw then that Martin had not gone that far from the hut after all. She could see his outline clearly, through the small front window. She could also see the trail of smoke from a cigarette, and the offending article itself, being wafted about by his left hand. She hadn't realised he had an emergency supply. He certainly couldn't have found a local shop and bought them, though, so he must have had a stash in his rucksack. Perhaps he just didn't smoke in front of her any more. It had been an ongoing issue between them for a while, some time ago, when he took up the habit again following a six-year break. Susie had felt cheated; she hadn't got together with a smoker and never would have. She hated it. The smell on his breath and in his hair made her feel sick. He couldn't have continued smoking in secret, she figured. She would have noticed.

He was far too lazy to go to the lengths it would have taken to hide it from her. She was confused. If that were the case, why had he brought those cigarettes with him?

Watching Martin soothed Susie. Even the rhythm of the detested cancer stick as it moved back and forth in the air, as it was finished then discarded then replaced with another, was hypnotic. It was a comfort to see the contours of the back of his head, the odd tuft of hair where it still grew. It was funny, though. If she hadn't known it couldn't possibly have been anyone else, Susie wasn't sure she would have recognised Martin from the shape of his head. It looked slightly bigger than it should, somehow, and elongated; oval.

The small room was warming slightly from the gas stove. Susie knew she should turn it off, but she was sleepy and she didn't want to feel the cold again. She watched the blue flame, straight and sleek like that on a Bunsen burner. She turned the dial down so that the flame turned yellow and licked the air. She watched this flicker for a moment then checked the stove was secure against the floor, and far enough away that she couldn't knock it over. She lay back down and pulled the sleeping bag and coat tightly around herself. She tried to relax. This time it came easier. She could feel her body falling into the ground. She remembered the sight of Martin at the window and felt sure he would come back inside soon. She fell, further, deeper, all the way into the dark.

5

The door banged shut and woke Susie with a start. The stove was still burning, casting a yellow glow across the room. Susie's vision was blurred from sleep. She could see Martin, a black shape in the warm light, and she watched as his shadowy presence made its way across the room like a spider in a nightmare. He removed clothes noisily, then noticed the gas stove, huffing and cursing about it being on. She considered pretending to be asleep, then decided to lie instead. 'I was still awake,' she mumbled. 'It wasn't dangerous.'

'Bloody wasteful, though,' he snapped back.

'Honestly, Sue, I really think we should both be more careful with our resources under current circumstances.'

It was a comment she could imagine directed at a year-eleven class, and the voice he used was the one she knew he'd honed over the years as a teacher. She resented being on the end of it but she longed for Martin's soft, warm shape beside her on the floor. This longing silenced her. She closed her eyes and said nothing, listening to the sound of Martin undressing. His breathing was a little heavy and every so often he coughed, a sound she knew so well and would have recognised a mile away.

Then Martin was beside her, curling up and moulding to her shape, the earlier conflict and even the annoyance over the stove forgotten. She opened her eyes and sighed, then watched him lean over her to extinguish the flame. Strangely, she couldn't smell the smoke on him. She wondered if she was coming down with a cold. The light faded, then was snuffed out entirely. Just in the last moment of illumination, though, Susie saw something that made her sit straight up and let out a sharp gasp.

'What's wrong?' Martin said, also sitting up.

'At the window . . .' Her voice was shaking, and it trailed off into a shiver she could not control. 'There's a man.'

'What do you mean a man? I've been stomping round outside for hours and I can tell you there ain't no one out there.' Martin's voice was firm but kind.

'But I saw him when you were gone. I thought it was you, smoking again. I thought you'd been lying about giving up.'

'Stopping,' Martin said. 'It's *stopping* smoking.' Martin was sold on a particular self-help guru and kept going on about this distinction. To Susie it felt like splitting hairs but her inability to take it on board had clearly frustrated him. He was breathing hard, as if in pain. 'Wait a minute,' he said. 'Why do you think I'd lie about it?'

The dark was pure and Susie's eyes had not adjusted to it. She sighed. 'Are you serious? Did you not hear what I just said? I saw a man with my own two eyes, smoking outside, and he was there still when the light went. I thought it was you but it wasn't, which means it's someone else. Someone who's just hanging out around here with no reason or shelter. Someone strange.'

'For crying out loud, Sue. I don't see how there can be anyone out there!'

'I saw him.' She tried to stay calm. 'I saw him clearly, standing in the window.'

'Settle down, Sue.'

'But he could murder us while we sleep.'

Martin's sigh was deep and heartfelt. 'What do you want me to do? Because it's obvious there's something and that I won't get a wink of sleep until I've worked it out and complied.'

'Whatever, Martin.'

'No, Sue, I'll do it. Whatever unreasonable hoop jumping you have lined up for me, I'll do it for a quiet life.'

She touched his arm, ignoring the barbs in his comments, trying to calm and persuade him at the same time. 'I think you should go outside,' she said. 'Find out who's out there and what he's doing here. What he wants.' Rain was beating hard against the roof now.

Martin breathed deeply, dragging out long moments that made Susie's heart beat faster. Then he said, 'Fine', and he stood up. 'I'm sure it's nothing. Just a tree casting an odd shadow or something like that.' He switched on the torch and swung its beam around the room, and then towards the window. 'See,' he said, 'there's nothing there.'

'But if there's nothing there now it can't have been a tree or a shadow. It's moved,' she said. 'Anyway, I saw it clearly. A man, smoking. I saw the outline of his hand and the smoke from the cigarette.'

'You can't possibly have seen all that detail from here,' Martin told her, his voice carrying that authority again. A voice made of steel that she imagined his students heard a lot of, that their own kids might have heard from time to time, had they gone down that route. 'There wouldn't have been enough light,' he added.

'I saw it. I'm not mad or stupid. I know what I saw.' She paused. 'He looked as real and solid as you feel right now.' She squeezed his arm where she had hold of him as if to make her point.

'It was a shadow in the window, Sue. There's no one around for miles.' He pulled her close, as if to prove his point by the solidity of his chest. She wanted to allow that to comfort her but it was impossible.

'For God's sake, stop calling me Sue,' she snapped. 'No one calls me that because I don't like it!'

There was a long, fat pause. Then Martin cleared his throat. 'Jesus, Susie, you can be so fucking petty sometimes. I've always called you Sue. Why's it suddenly a problem?'

She didn't answer right away. Then she said, 'I never liked it. I've said before but you took no notice so I dropped it. I didn't want to row.'

Static hung between them, the balance of power shifted for a moment. 'I'm sorry,' Martin said. 'I thought it was our special thing.' He sounded so pathetic, and Susie felt mean.

'You're right,' she told him, shifting that balance straight back again. 'It's really not important. I'm just tense. I'm freaked out. You weren't there and someone was standing outside the hut. Anything could have happened.'

'But it didn't.' Martin laid both hands on her shoulders, finding them easily in the dark. The gesture was more fatherly than something a lover would do and she felt it was meant to control her somehow, shut her up. 'I'm here now.' He got up then, and pulled his clothes back on quickly. 'Sharp as knives, the air tonight,' he said, hugging himself. He shone the torch into various corners of the room, making a childish 'whooo!' noise, suddenly in high spirits. He directed the light up into his face and pretended he was shaking like mad, taking lots of fast, deep breaths. 'It's only me left,' he said, manically and with an American accent. 'I don't know what happened to the others.' They'd seen *The Blair Witch Project* together, laughed about it lots at the time, although Susie wasn't sure it was quite so funny any more. She smiled, though, and batted him playfully with one hand. She liked this light-hearted side of him; she wished he could be like this more often. She took the torch from him and had a turn at trying to talk and shiver at the same time. Her performance collapsed into a fit of giggles.

Martin smiled and stood up again. He turned all business, marching towards the door. Susie could hear the drumming of rain, heavier yet against the top of the hut. She hoped he wouldn't get soaked through. It was his only set of dry clothes.

Moments later, though, Martin ducked back under the low-slung lintel of the doorway. 'It's really starting to come down out there,' he said, with a cheerful whistle. 'Well, I had a look around and I'm pretty much certain there's no one here.'

Incredulous that he had taken her seriously enough only for a perfunctory glance around, Susie tried not to speak for a few moments to prevent something bad coming out. 'Okay,' she said, at last, slowly and spreading the word out.

'What's wrong now?' Martin asked her, a new tone on his voice from before, the iron returning to it that had been there so strongly earlier.

'Nothing,' Susie replied at once. The raw feeling had passed now and, even though she was concerned about the idea of someone hanging around the hut, on balance she would rather be in danger than have another one of their rows to deal with, the way it severed them from one another. But she felt it keenly, the being silenced. The undercurrents in Martin's words were powerful enough to do what he wanted but she resented it intensely.

Martin was glowering down at her, holding on to the torch like a lifeline, and she realised it hadn't mattered that she'd kept quiet. This was going to be one of those times when she'd communicated enough for him to guess and he was going to get as mad as if she'd said exactly what she'd wanted to. 'I can see you won't be happy until I'm soaked to the skin again. You just want me to put myself out for you and play knight in shining armour, as per usual. Fine.'

'No, it's not like that at all,' Susie said, scrambling up the words. She could hear the desperation dragging her voice. 'I don't want that at all.'

It was as if Martin had heard nothing. He strode back towards the door and out of it, slamming it hard behind him. The walls of the bothy shook and Susie wondered how on earth they would dry his clothes when he got back. She felt a twinge in her stomach. Was he right? Was she being unreasonable? This was almost the hardest thing about being with Martin. Sometimes he made her feel like the worst kind of monster.

The rain was still coming down, sounding louder and more violent by the second, battering the hut and reminding Susie that the elements were more powerful than she was, and that we were all of us at their mercy whether we knew it or not. She shivered. It felt like Martin had been gone a long time and she wondered if he was stringing it out now, or perhaps he might have stormed off again and not come back before morning. It was extremely cold, even in both sleeping bags and a coat. She was very tired but too cold and upset to sleep. She had a bad feeling about the whole adventure. She should have trusted her senses about it in the first place.

She lay listening to the rain. If she hadn't been so cold and freaked out, she might have felt quite cosy. She usually enjoyed being inside and hearing the rain but, then, usually she would be in the comfort of her own bed, wrapped in quilts and covers, and next to her husband, which made it easier to enjoy these things. She hugged herself and pulled the sleeping bags tighter around her body, trying to will herself warm, but nothing seemed to work.

For a moment, Susie thought she heard footsteps outside, and the cough she'd recognise anywhere as Martin's. But the door didn't open and she decided she'd imagined it; wishful thinking. Another chill came over her then. She wasn't sure if it was a draught coming in from a gap in the door or one of the windows. She shivered and felt cold to the bone. There was the sound of an owl shrieking over the land nearby, which made her uneasy. She sat up and looked around the bothy but could see nothing. The dark was absolute. She moved her arms and legs to try to keep warm any way she could. She began to worry. Martin should have come back by now. There wasn't enough land for him to search for it to take this long. What if something had happened to him? What if he had decided he'd had enough and headed back to the hotel, left her here alone?

The air around her cooled even further. Then she felt a hand, protective on her shoulder. She started. 'Martin?' she said, thinking that perhaps she had missed him coming in, fallen asleep without realising. There was no response. The hand drifted over her back and then to her cheek, where it held her tenderly. She sensed strongly it was not Martin and her heart quickened. How had the man got inside without her noticing or hearing the door? Perhaps when she'd fallen asleep, before Martin got back. But she had lit the stove and seen the entire room, and Martin had shone the torch around both rooms. There was nowhere to hide. She was almost certain she hadn't fallen asleep.

She breathed in deeply. A finger ran down her spine and sent a shiver right through her, but it was a pleasant sensation. She was shocked to find herself enjoying what was happening, despite not knowing who was touching her. She let out a sigh. It must be Martin, surely. She reached for him.

She found herself clutching at cold air. The pressure

against her spine and shoulder was gone, as if it had never been there. She grasped around herself, searching for whoever had been touching her but finding nothing. She let out a little sound, restrained but frightened. She leaned over and found the stove where she had left it, scrabbling around for the matches so she could light it.

She shone the light around the room but could see nothing. She stood up, shivering as she left the sleeping bags on the ground and walked around, examining all the corners. She opened the door that led into the adjoining room and checked that space too. This was even smaller than the main part and there were no hidden nooks; there was nobody there. She was shaking like crazy now. She climbed back into the sleeping bags and pulled them as tightly as she could around herself but found little relief.

It was only moments later when the door opened and Martin appeared, dripping wet. 'Satisfied now?' he said with a sneer. He pulled off his coat and threw it down. It was so wet that it sprayed water into the air and on to Susie's face. The cold shock of it was almost pleasurable. 'There's no one here,' he said. 'I've searched high and low, and nothing. You must have dreamed it, or seen a tree, just like I said.'

There was a chilly silence then. Martin undressed in the light of the stove. Susie considered whether she should tell him about what had just happened, about being touched by someone who had since disappeared. That the man she'd seen had been in the hut but must have moved with superhuman speed to get out again, or the only other explanation was even stranger. There was definitely someone here with them but she was no longer sure that this was a living, breathing person like herself and Martin. She knew, though, that he would either dismiss her as silly or tell her she had dreamed that too, made another mistake. She didn't want to hear him say those things. They'd had their discussions before when she'd tried to explain some of the stranger things that had happened to her in the past. Martin just wouldn't accept her experiences as anything other than an overactive imagination.

'I must have made a mistake,' she said, instead, although she was even more certain now that she hadn't. She trusted her own eyes because they had never let her down before, but she trusted her skin even more. It still tingled where she had felt the gentle pressure of someone's hand.

'No dry clothes left,' Martin said, pulling his sleeping bag from Susie's grasp and climbing into it, naked. 'God knows what I'll do tomorrow.'

'Well, at least we can go back to the hotel when the sun comes up,' Susie said, aiming for cheerful but hearing a strained voice as she spoke.

'I wouldn't bet on that,' Martin said. He didn't elaborate and, although Susie wondered what he meant, she also didn't want to know, didn't want to allow the possibility that they wouldn't get back to civilisation tomorrow, so she didn't ask. He lay down and turned his back on her, extinguishing the stove once more. The room went dark as death and chilled Susie to the bone. She could feel Martin's spine digging into her back and a mild heat from his skin, like a lukewarm bath. She knew she could turn towards him and grab on to get as much body heat as she needed; her husband was a human radiator in the right circumstances. But she didn't want to pull him close.

It was then that she felt tempted to tell him what she'd felt. About the hand that had touched her, and how she'd liked it and reached for the man. She wanted him to know that she hadn't cared whether it was him or not. It was all she could do to hold herself back. She let herself fall into the ground and remembered those feelings. Somehow they relaxed and warmed her. Soon, she was sleeping, dreaming of another man in the bothy, a man much gentler than Martin, more tender. A man who cared what she thought.

6

Shadows lingered in the corners of the room as Susie looked around, wishing her eyes hadn't adjusted and her night vision kicked in. It was better not to see. The bothy looked eerie; full of possibilities and hiding places. Martin still lay with his back to her, snoring. She'd found over the years with Martin that it was a myth about people only snoring while lying on their backs. It seemed Martin could snore for his country in just about any position. Susie couldn't sleep. She watched the back of Martin's head, moving, almost imperceptibly, to the rhythm of his heavy breathing.

It seemed that nothing ever stopped Martin

sleeping. Susie was always restless after a row or bad feelings between them, tired and with dry, sore eyes, but wakeful. She had spent too many nights listening to Martin snore, feeling jealous of the way he could enjoy oblivion, relaxed and content as a clean, well-fed baby. The things that had been said and done spun around her head but not his. He lost his temper easily and could sulk for hours, although she suspected that was more about punishing her than a true expression of what was going on inside. He couldn't really feel as strongly as he said he did if he could fall asleep like this so soon afterwards.

Bad feelings lingered for Susie. She might not show them in such an explosive way as Martin did, but she was sure she felt everything more keenly. What she felt now was a sense of injustice, of the unfairness of life. Too many times she had lain like this, wide, wide awake when she needed to sleep, the tension buzzing in her neck and making her feel sickened. It felt too much sometimes, the intensity of their reaction to one another. Sure, there was plenty of good stuff too, but when they rowed the badness between them was so powerful it made Susie feel physically sick. She had moments when she'd tell Martin it was all over, and she'd mean it as she said it. She'd always been glad, later, that she hadn't acted on it. She wondered again now, though. Did they have real problems, more than could be solved by reconnecting? Was expecting a second honeymoon to solve anything a little deluded?

When Susie really thought about it, their problems all came down to an incident she referred to as 'the weekend'. It had happened a few years into their marriage, the summer before their fourth anniversary, and it had all been her fault if you listened to what Martin had to say about it. They'd gone away for the weekend to the countryside; a cottage in the middle of nowhere. It had been idyllic at first, so far from other people, the quiet so complete at night that Susie woke up a couple of times gasping for breath and convinced she had died. It had been a heady couple of days, the sun beating down almost too hard, afternoons and evenings filled with wine and lovemaking. Everything was perfect until Sunday night. They had been drinking, of course, and Susie had again brought up the subject of having children.

It was the one thing she knew Martin didn't want to discuss any more but she couldn't help herself. It was the only thing she wanted to talk about; the only thing she could think about. At the time she was really convinced it was something she wanted and needed but, looking back, she wondered if hormones hadn't played a bigger part than she'd been aware of. Now she was just the other side of forty, the pull was all gone. She didn't think that was just to do with making the best of it. Intellectually, she had always seen Martin's point of view on the subject and even tended to agree. But back then she couldn't feel it. All she could feel was an empty, gaping wound, a hole inside her that needed fixing. In hindsight it was always a time bomb ticking away, waiting to ignite between the two of them.

Thinking about 'the weekend' made Susie feel the cold more keenly. She was shaking under the covers and tried to control it. She could remember the intensity of the argument they'd had that weekend, how she'd got hysterical and started kicking and hitting the wall so that Martin had felt the need to restrain her. She'd been so angry. One of Martin's unfortunate talents was that he knew where to aim for maximum collateral damage. It was perhaps his years of combat that lent him this edge, not real war but the one that played out every day in classrooms up and down the country. Apart from criminals, children are the only people we lock up all day so it should come as no surprise when they rebel. Not in Martin's classes, though. He taught in a tough, inner-city school but he had no problems with discipline. His colleagues talked to her about it in awed, whispery voices. They joked about whether he was as strict at home, making her want to say something although, of course, she didn't. They would raise a glass and ask him for his secret when they came around for dinner and he would blush and bat away the compliment. But Susie could see that they genuinely wanted to know. She could have told them. She lived with it, every day.

The things Martin had said that mellow Sunday evening would stay with Susie forever. She wished she could forget, and had tried to, but no amount of blanking out worked on these words, even though she'd half erased worse memories. She couldn't just remember what he'd said. She could conjure it up in her head, make it play as if she had it on tape. His voice, the sound of metal scraping against metal, the temperature of liquid nitrogen steaming in the air.

'If you wanted a baby so much why did you kill one when you had the chance?'

She remembered standing there, looking back at

him, incredulous. Her mouth actually fell open with the shock of his unkindness. She remembered how the anger had spread to every last blood vessel and all the cells inside her, filling them up like it was carried by her blood. She breathed. Even after all these years, remembering the way he'd spoken to her that night sent raw anger shocking through her body and smarting on her skin.

She sat up on the floor. Martin stirred, just a little, but he didn't wake properly. He rolled on to his back and was snoring again, louder than before. Susie was more wide awake than ever. She couldn't even imagine sleep, could hardly remember what it was like or how you did it. She thought about whether their relationship would have been different if she'd never told Martin about the abortion from her past. Perhaps. She was only glad that she'd stopped short of telling him the details around it. She wasn't sure why she had, what had stopped her, but something had made her close up and not want to share the rest of the story, about Jules and the things she'd lost before that baby. Perhaps it was her self-preservation instinct kicking in. On some level, she must have been aware of his talent for picking at old wounds and making them fresh, and this cut so deep she wasn't sure she'd be able to recover if it was opened up again.

She thought about the hands she had felt earlier. Could she have imagined it? Or was someone hiding in a corner somewhere, or in the other room? But she had not heard anyone come in and she'd looked everywhere. She hadn't heard anyone, full stop. She had just felt his touch. It had felt real at the time. Was she going insane? She knew Martin would think so, but then he tended to make that assumption about Susie just for believing in things science couldn't explain.

Anger at this idea infused her bones, warming her a little, making it feel like a more positive emotion than it was. She went with it. She pictured Martin, the way his face came right up to hers when he was in a temper, the spittle that filled the corners of his mouth occasionally heading to her face with the words he flung at her. They called it spitting mad for a reason. She wished she could have an outlet like that, a place for her anger to go. But she didn't dare. Feelings that strong led her deep into a big, black hole she might not manage to crawl from and, anyway, it would have been stupid to inflame him.

She lay back down and tried to make her body fall

into the ground, the meditation she'd been taught. It wasn't happening and she realised she was forcing it, which would never work. She turned on her side and saw Martin enjoying his blissful sleep. She wanted to hit him, hard, whack him away with the heel of her hand. She was shocked at the strength of this feeling, the violence of the images that flew through her head. Even during the weekend, how angry she'd become, she had not wanted to hurt Martin. She'd hit out at chairs and tables, inanimate things.

What was happening to her? She sat up again, suddenly sure it was something to do with the place they'd come to. Everything had been fine until they'd got to the bothy. This strange dwelling was poisoned somehow. She felt it keenly as she looked around her. In the dark, she could see nothing, but she still sensed a presence. Something outside of herself and Martin, outside of their marriage. She told herself she was being silly and lay back down.

Her violent impulses towards Martin had gone, thank God, as if she had thought them away. She pulled him towards her and curled herself into his body. He let out contented noises, sleepy but affectionate mumbling sounds. There was no affection in what Susie was doing, though. She needed his body heat if she was ever going to sleep. Sometimes, necessity is the mother of making up.

Susie jerked and her jaw snapped shut. It was a nasty way to wake up, one that had been happening to her the last few years and that the doctor had no explanation for. She pulled the sleeping bag up and around herself. Martin's body heat had warmed her mostly but her back had been a little exposed and the space between her shoulders felt frozen. Her sudden movement had not woken Martin, which was a blessing. This was something that had caused arguments between them. Martin was convinced she was doing it deliberately, had even mentioned the words 'attention seeking' in his analysis.

There was no light coming through the window and Susie wondered what time it was. Winter days took longer to start so it could be morning. She wished she hadn't taken off her watch the night before. She fumbled around for it now but couldn't find it. As her eyes adjusted to the dark she could make out the window. It wasn't pitch-black outside but a very dark indigo. This had to be the beginning of the sun coming up as the moonlight hadn't had this effect. The colour at the window was definitely different from that in the middle of the night. Susie should know; she had studied it for long enough when she couldn't sleep.

She lay there and thought about getting up. The idea of morning being around the corner made the events of the previous evening seem less frightening. She could easily believe she had imagined being touched. She had dreamed about it too and now it was hard to separate the two events. In her dream, the man had been as real and solid as she was. She had reached for him and he had materialised in front of her eyes. Not Martin, definitely not Martin. Tall and good-looking and ever so tender. As they lay down after making love he had asked her what she thought about things. She remembered this dream now and it warmed her enough to get out of bed.

She dressed, pulling on her trousers, fleece and then her coat again, which she'd worn all night and felt clammy to the touch and damp inside. She sat with her sleeping bag draped around her shoulders for a while, watching the indigo build at the window. It became the most beautiful deep, dark blue and she wanted to go outside and see dawn breaking.

Moving made her feel warmer. Every muscle in her body ached, though, especially her lower back; the hard floor was making its impact on her after so many hours lying there. She shook out her joints and made circles with her arms. It relieved the pain a little but, more importantly, it generated heat. She picked up the saucepan and came to the door of the bothy, pulling hard on the handle. This time, it opened easily.

The scene outside was like something out of a painting. Hills cut into the sky in the distance and the loch shone all the way out to the horizon. There wasn't a cloud for miles and Susie was hopeful that the new day would be better than the last one. The air felt crisp and clear but not too cold, not now that she was moving. She could hear the burn rushing behind the hut and, when she walked round with the pan, it came into view and she saw it was even bigger than she remembered from the day before. She recalled how it had rained. It must have swelled further after the downpour. It looked like it might burst its banks.

She walked to its edge and filled the saucepan with water; it sprayed on to her hands, chilling them. It was a pleasant feeling, though, and not like the freeze of the night. A cup of tea was just what she needed. Susie wasn't one of those people who believed a cup of tea cured all ills but she did like the taste. The feeling of a warm drink as it slid down inside you was a comfort; there was something to be said for that. She headed back with the full saucepan and began to feel optimistic about the day. Even the way she walked changed; there was a bounce in her step. It did cross her mind, mildly, briefly, that this was part of her problem. She got over things and couldn't be bothered with staying mad. She had no talent for sulking.

She opened the door and walked in. Martin was stirring, rubbing his eyes and making small moaning noises.

'What time is it?' he said, his voice breaking up with sleep.

'Morning?' suggested Susie, cheerfully. 'The sun's come up and that's about all I know about it.' She lit the stove and placed the pan on top of the light. 'Sleep okay?'

'Mmm,' Martin said.

Susie was unsure if this was an affirmative or denial but she wasn't interested enough to find out. Really, she was just being polite with the question and she had witnessed him sleeping well. When she thought about it, it was strange to be asking that question of someone she had been married to for ten years. Oddly formal. She didn't know why she had asked him that.

'You're making tea,' he said, stating the obvious.

'Uh huh,' she said.

He leaned back, stretching out his legs and chest. 'Why is it we all have to sound like Americans these days?' he said. He made it sound friendly enough, but it was definitely a criticism. 'It's the same with the kids at school with all their "gotten" and "dove" instead of "dived" and so on. I blame TV.'

'Well, I'm not one of your kids at school,' Susie said, grabbing their mugs from the floor where they'd left them the previous night and shoving a tea bag in each one. The water was beginning to buzz in the saucepan.

'What's that supposed to mean?' Martin's voice had taken on that hard edge again.

Looking up from the stove, Susie flicked blonde curls away from her eyes. 'It meant nothing. Just making conversation.' She managed to sound upbeat.

There was no answer to that other than Martin clearing his throat then pulling a sour-looking face. He coughed, a sound so familiar and so very Martin. Susie knew she would recognise it anywhere and from a distance of three hundred metres. It was strange, knowing someone that well and yet not being related to them. Well, legally, she supposed, she was related to Martin.

'Do we walk back today? Straight away?' Susie asked. 'Is there anything interesting to do or see all the way up here?'

Martin paused, and cleared his throat. The water began to boil and Susie grabbed the pan. 'What's the river looking like?' he asked her.

'Oh, very swollen. Like it might burst its banks,' she said.

'I'll go have a look soon.'

Susie poured. The sound of boiling water hitting cups held a comfort of its own and the scent of tea infusing filled the room with a metal smell. The air was warming up now, from the day but also from the small gas light. Susie added milk to both cups and then sugar to Martin's and passed it to him.

'The land around the other side of the hut was very boggy yesterday,' Martin told her. He nodded to his walking boots by the door. They were caked in mud. 'Not really passable.'

The muddy boots sat by the doorway, black as an

omen from the peat. Susie realised that Martin was trying to tell her something but she couldn't work out what. She looked from the shoes to her husband and then back again several times. She sipped tea. She tried not to think too hard about what he might be trying to say.

7

With her coat curled around her and a cup of tea warming her hands, Susie felt almost at home sitting to one side of the bothy. Martin was wandering around, holding a stick and looking into the distance. He was playing expert and she hated it. He'd been hiking barely more often than she had and was hardly an expert on the Scottish Highlands but that didn't stop him proclaiming himself as such with the way he acted. It was something that wouldn't have bothered her a few years ago but it had led to situations like this one, to them getting in a mess. Boggy land stretched away as far as Susie could see and Martin surveyed it as if it were his kingdom, hand to his chin and serious expression shadowing his brow. Then he turned on his heels and strode towards the river. His tea was sitting beside Susie's feet, misting the air around it and turning cold. Only Martin stood to lose from this but for some reason it annoyed her that he was letting the hot drink go to waste.

He headed back towards the hut, frowning. 'Like I thought, we aren't going anywhere today. The river's too swollen to cross and the land the other side is far too boggy to be passable. It's sodden.'

Susie looked around, following Martin's cue and looking towards first the river then the bog. Everywhere certainly looked damp and cold but, then, that was the Highlands for you. 'There must be a way through,' she said, convinced of his error. It was inconceivable that they should be trapped here.

Martin sucked his teeth like a plumber and shook his head. 'It's really not safe, Sue. I wouldn't lie to you about it.'

She wanted to ask what he knew, how he knew it, how he could possibly be so certain. Of course, she didn't. Besides anything else, she was stuck here with him. That thought made her feel a little sick and uneasy. The dark shadow of 'the weekend' played games in her stomach and she forced these stirring memories back down into the depths of her mind, where they belonged. She remembered she had a mobile phone with her. They could call for help, get rescued. She dug through her pockets, looking, and pulled the phone out. She had left it switched on overnight but the battery was still about half charged. No signal, though, of course. No masts for miles.

Martin pulled his phone out too. Much more organised and sensible, he had switched his off overnight. It played the greeting music as it came on. He stared at the screen, looking puzzled for a while. When he'd waited a few moments he waved it in the air, as though he was chasing a bee or a wasp. Susie smiled as she watched him. 'No signal,' he said, somewhat redundantly. 'We can keep trying.'

'Can't we have a go at walking back?' Susie said. 'I mean, what's the worst that could happen?'

Martin was still waving his phone around and didn't answer at first, showing no sign he'd even heard her speak.

'Can't we try?'

He turned his gaze towards her. 'I heard you the

first time,' he said. 'I was thinking about it. So, worst-case scenario, we get stuck in the bog and sink until we drown. Not that likely but there is the scenario where we get stuck, no signal to phone for help and we die of exposure overnight. That kind of thing. No, Sue, better to wait here, make the most of it.'

The tea was no longer hot in Susie's hands. She felt a chill go through her. She couldn't be trapped here with Martin all these miles from civilisation. She just couldn't. 'How long do you think we'll need to wait?' she asked. 'Till this afternoon? Tomorrow?'

He was shaking his head. 'Hard to say. It really depends on how the weather turns. If it stays dry we might get away in a few days but if the rain steps up it could be a while.' He paused, and looked up into the sky as if he might be able to tell by the forming clouds what would happen next. 'We have some food,' he said, 'and as much running water as we like. We won't die of thirst and we won't have to eat each other. In all prob-ability we'll get signals on our phones at some point. Coverage hops and changes all the time in remote places like this. That depends a bit on the weather, too.'

Phone coverage, hiking, cloud formations: Susie

wondered how many things Martin was an expert on. She supposed it came with the territory of being a teacher, setting yourself up as a fount of knowledge the way he had. If you weren't careful, you began to believe it yourself. She grabbed the saucepan and went to fill it from the river again. She needed more tea, if only for the warmth in her hands. She needed the comfort of it.

She bent towards the river to fill the pan. She heard a wolf whistle behind her. Turning, she saw Martin, standing innocently by the hut as if the sound had nothing to do with him. This wasn't his usual style but it made her smile. In the wrong context, she might have found the gesture offensive or irritating but this felt playful, ironic. She walked back towards him with the pan, grinning.

'What's amusing you?' he said.

She just shook her head as if he were mad. He looked confused. He moved aside for her to put the pan down on the lit stove.

'We must start putting that out between using it,' he said. 'We definitely need to conserve the gas now.'

She looked up and flicked the hair from her eyes. Martin stared down at her, his face impenetrable. She suddenly felt quite strongly that it couldn't have been her husband who had whistled. She looked around nervously, remembering the events of the previous night and the feeling of longing as she had reached for a body that hadn't been there. She shook herself. She must have been imagining it. But she probed the landscape around her for another face, for a place where someone might hide if they had the will. She saw nothing. They were on a plateau beside the loch where the land was flat for a good mile in every direction before it faded behind the dramatic landscape in the distance. There was nowhere for anyone to hide.

Morning turned to afternoon. The air was full of the false cheer of birdsong and the sun was high in the sky. There were very few clouds and the brightness of it all made Susie want to get up and go. She felt trapped by the strength of Martin's will and she couldn't believe for one moment that the land around was truly impassable.

Martin had gone off for the toilet and he came back in an upbeat mood. 'We need to think carefully about resources now,' he said. 'Have you switched off your phone? We should conserve the charge and keep trying for a signal once or twice a day.'

'Yes,' she said, scrambling inside her pockets for the phone. She turned it off but with a slightly resentful feeling. He was ordering her around, taking charge. It was only his nature, she supposed, the person he couldn't help but become in his line of work if he were to be at all successful. That didn't make it any easier to put up with, though. 'Are you sure we can't head back?' she said. 'It almost seems silly we wouldn't be able to. We're in Scotland. Not somewhere really remote or anything.'

'I know, I know. It does feel like you should just be able to walk home,' he said, waving a hand across his face, 'but, actually, we're rather remote out here. Don't sweat it, Sue. Just relax and enjoy the view.' He shook out his arms and legs. 'My clothes are almost dry now. Merely damp.' Despite the false cheer in his voice there was a hint of criticism, and she noted it.

'Well, that's good, then,' she said, holding back emotion as best she could. She looked out into the landscape, its huge contours and dramatic sweep across the sky. She wondered if anyone had ever felt so trapped in such an open space before. She picked up the pan and headed towards the river again. She didn't really want a drink but it was something to do.

The river rushed past; a force of nature. Susie

pushed the pan into its swell and felt its force pulling her arm, separating ball and socket in her shoulder. She pulled back and removed it from the water but it took some effort. The burn in full flow was a terrifying thing; it looked wild and angry. She knew that Martin was right and that she could never walk across the river safely as flooded as it was. A sudden urge took her, the feeling she should climb into the river and let the water take her. She could escape that way. She shook herself. What was she thinking? It was this place again, sending her slightly insane.

Back at the hut her husband was smugly looking off into the distance. 'Amazing, isn't it?' he said, with a smile. 'I can almost picture the glaciers that flowed through this valley. It must have been magnificent.'

Susie didn't respond. She remembered his comments about the drying clothes and looked at the freezing water she held in the saucepan in front of her. It would be so easy, just the turn of a wrist, the tip of a hand, to drench him again. The shock of this thought sent her cold and she placed the pan on to the stove as carefully as she could. It was hard to trust her body to do as it was told with some of the ideas going through her head.

'We maybe need to lay off on the tea for a bit after this, preserve the milk and gas,' Martin said, his voice full of expertise again.

'How long do you think we'll be stuck here?' she asked him.

He looked up at her, a smile on his face, amiable. 'Stuck here? You make it sound like your worst nightmare. Look at it, though.' He gestured at the panorama. 'Stuck here, with your husband, the love of your life. What a nightmare!'

A curl of hair slipped across Susie's face and her skin itched. She blew it out of the way and tried to smile. 'Of course not. I'd just kill for a shower and proper meal right now.' She was worried, though. Why did she feel uneasy about staying there with Martin? Was her intuition trying to tell her something?

'Well, we can maybe do something about the hot meal. Of a fashion.' He nodded at the small pile of tins she'd removed from her rucksack.

'Hmmm . . . Beans and sausages wasn't exactly what I'd had in mind,' Susie said.

Martin was perhaps trying to smile but it looked more like a grimace as he turned into the wind. 'You might consider that a feast in a few days' time,' he said.

'You think we might still be here in a few days?' She held her breath. Surely not days? Surely they'd be on their way tomorrow at the latest?

'Who knows? It depends if we get a signal on the phone sometime but that's not looking likely. It could take days to dry out enough for that land or river to be passable.'

Susie shook her head, grinning, but not in a good way. 'You make it sound so hopeless. Jesus, Martin, we just came on a little walk. Surely we can just walk back.'

Martin's expression turned hard; his opinion was being questioned. 'By all means try to walk back, love, and see how you get on with that,' he said. He called her 'love' but his voice was steel.

'I think I will.' Susie was surprised to hear herself say it.

Martin glanced up, sharp, grimacing again. He shrugged. A gust of wind took Susie's hair up into her eyes. She brushed away the curls and picked herself up. She was shocked at how clear she felt about the situation, and how rebellious towards her husband. She didn't care what Martin had said or what he thought. She wasn't staying here, trapped like this.

She didn't like it one bit and she found she didn't believe him either. Why was he trying to keep them both here?

Susie went inside. She gathered up her rucksack and repacked it with the things she'd brought along. She left the tins of food. Even if Martin didn't stay long enough to use them, the next people could have them. It might offend his economic sensibilities not to use what they had bought but it wasn't a waste; there would always be people coming to and from the bothy, people maybe needy of the little bit extra, too. As she pulled her bag finally on to her shoulder, Martin's face appeared around the corner of the door, looking suddenly kind and conciliatory.

'Are you sure about this?' he said.

Susie nodded, not looking up as she reached for her hat and gloves. 'I'll see you at base camp,' she said, still without eye contact.

'This is madness, Sue, especially on your own.'

'You think I can't do anything without you? That I'm not capable?'

'That's not what I said and it's not what I meant.' Martin's voice was raised but not shouting; a classroom voice. The parental voice he had never needed.

Susie stood up straight and looked him right in the eyes this time.

'Be careful,' he said, grabbing her arm.

She shook him away and stormed out of the hut. But the touch of tenderness had choked her up. Tears leaked from her eyes as she walked away.

The flooded river cut Susie's world in half and limited her options. There was no way in hell she was about to attempt to cross the rage of its flow alone. A back route across the bog was the only option. She had taken the spare map and the only compass. Martin was better at navigating than she was and wouldn't need the compass so much, she decided, although she felt a little guilty about it. The route back looked less severe than the one they'd followed to get here, all gentle slopes and even a path once she'd negotiated the stretch of mud. She strode out, feeling confident. The ground was solid enough under her feet, just a little spongy in places, nothing more. She was more certain than ever that Martin had been wrong.

It was a bright, clear winter's afternoon and the sun hung low in the sky, sharp and glaring. She shielded her eyes as she walked, and wished she had sunglasses with her; she hadn't brought any with her on the trip, hadn't imagined for a moment she'd need them. She marched onward and her body warmed with the exercise. Her legs and back felt good for the activity after the two nights lying on the cold floor. She felt free, freer than she had in years. It made her feet lighter as she trod onward and she had a sudden sense of empathy with Martin. She wondered if this was how he felt, those times he stormed off in a temper. Perhaps this was why he needed to do it, to feel the freedom under his feet. To feel the physical, the pure sensation of being an animal and using his muscles, the rhythm of one foot after another. She thought she might take more chances for a stomp after this now she knew how good it was.

Doubts crept into her head as she walked and the ground grew soggier. She could see the gleam of liquid resting on the surface of the bog ahead of her; a flooded vista. She didn't sink too far into the ground where she was walking so she stepped onward. How bad could it really be? She didn't believe you could actually drown in mud or sinking sand; at least, not in Scotland. The whole idea was the stuff of childhood nonsense, night-mares told by friends to see if you would scare; it had no basis in reality, not here.

As she made her way across the flat stretch of mud, though, she began to wonder. Her boots were light-weight, not designed for heavy-duty walking. They were sinking deeper and making increasingly long, wet squelches as she pulled up her feet to step forward. Her legs up above the ankle were jet-black with peat and occasionally it was a real effort to pull her foot from where the mud gripped and held on. She considered then whether she ought to turn back. But the idea of going back to the bothy filled her with dread. There was something bad there, a presence that lurked. It was that which had touched her, and the same evil was sending the vivid, violent thoughts that she kept having. God knows what it was doing to Martin but he wasn't himself either. She felt strongly that going back would be the end of everything. This drove her forward.

The path and safety were just in sight when she got stuck. Her foot was held fast and her leg sunk up to the knee. She struggled, trying to pull it out by using the rest of her body as a lever but she just sunk further. She tried again. And then again. But it was no good; she was stuck fast and going nowhere. Water seeped into the space around her feet, making her toes throb with the chill. She held fast with her boot on the firmer land behind at least but that was sinking too, ever so slowly, the whole situation a leisurely death trap like something out of a cowboy film. She pulled her mobile phone from her pocket and switched it on. The time it took to come alive felt like an eternity, and then, no signal.

Susie's legs were sore from the walk and from fighting against the sink of the ground. She could feel the earth pulling her in, piecemeal, eating her slowly. She breathed in deeply, trying not to panic. Then she yelled; for Martin, for anyone. She couldn't imagine there was a soul close enough to hear her shouts but she had to try. She couldn't accept that she wouldn't be heard, wouldn't be helped. But who goes hiking right up in the hills in November? Herself and Martin, that's who. She hoped there were other people as foolhardy around.

She tried again to drag herself from the vice grip of the land. She was going nowhere except deeper into the mud.

8

The wind blew and whistled over the flat ground around Susie. She had stopped struggling against the mud and trying to free her foot. She was no longer sinking; just stuck fast. Around her the land shone under the bright sunshine, which made the water on its surface glisten like a precious metal. In different circumstances, she would have enjoyed this view, admired it or even tried to paint it, struggling to capture the exact nature of the light or texture of the sodden earth. Even in her current predicament, she found herself wishing she had brought her paints along with her on the holiday. It was comforting that such ordinary thoughts could still come into her head.

She wanted to sit down more than she could say but was almost sure if she did that she would begin sinking again. She supposed that drowning in the mud might be terrible, but that it might actually be better than dying of exposure in the night. Quicker, if nothing else. She tried not to imagine what that would be like, dying of the cold and wind in the dark; freezing to death as the frost came down like a spell, turning her to stone. She had stopped being scared, though, given up on it not long after she had given up shouting for help.

She was ready to flop on to her back and let the soil take her when there was a familiar cough in the distance. She turned to look and saw Martin getting nearer, walking carefully through the mud to avoid the worst patches; her knight in corduroy armour. He wasn't exactly the tall dark stranger on the powerful steed she'd envisaged when she was younger, but he was what she'd got, and he was going to save her now. She had never been so glad to see anyone in her entire life. She didn't even care if he said 'I told you so' because, to be fair, he had.

'You look a bit stuck,' he said, instead, making her smile despite everything. He sounded cheerful, as if he had found her outside the house, struggling to open the door with a load of heavy shopping. She loved him for being this way, for not making a fuss or blaming her or being haughty about the situation. She knew now that she should have taken his advice about their predicament at face value instead of listening to the mad voice of her paranoia. Martin had a temper, but that didn't make him the bogeyman. She wondered what strange phenomenon was making her see her husband as some screaming psycho. Two words came into her head as she considered this: *the bothy*. But that wasn't possible. Even Susie, with all her special sensitivities and experiences, found the idea of a malevolent building a bit ridiculous.

'How did you know I needed your help?' she said. 'How did you know I was stuck and you should come?'

'I kept an eye on you,' he said. 'I was concerned about you getting across so I watched from the bothy and kept track of your movements. I was doing other stuff between but I kept checking and when I saw you hadn't moved in a while, I knew I had to come.' He knelt down as he spoke, spreading his weight over the mud towards her. 'Lean over here, where it's drier,' he said. She wasn't sure how he knew what to do but he seemed very capable in this situation all of sudden.

'Grab me here.' She took hold of his arm as instructed, and he gripped her by the waist and under an armpit. He pulled. There was a wet, sucking sound and she moved, but not right out of the mud yet. He tugged again, then she was crawling towards him on her hands and knees.

Martin held out his arms and Susie came to him like a child. He grabbed her and they held each other, knees and feet dug into the mud but not sinking. Martin squeezed her hard and she felt it, folding into him and letting him envelope her. She held on tight. It struck her hard then: she could have died. He had saved her life. She felt a euphoria rising from her stomach.

'Don't ever scare me like that again,' he chided.

'I'll listen next time,' she told him.

Martin laughed. 'I can't imagine for a moment you will. You'll always be your own person, Sue. It's one of the things I love about you.'

She was taken aback by this, and found herself moving from his grip to look at his face and find out if he was serious. If she had ever stopped to think of reasons Martin might love her, this certainly wouldn't have been on the list. She couldn't imagine for a moment that it was true, although she guessed he could have meant it. It was the kind of thing people said in situations like this, when they thought their loved one had been in danger, she supposed. That, and something you might say when you were wooing a partner. But it wasn't something men usually meant, or lived by, in her experience, and certainly not men like Martin. Still, she enjoyed the feeling now of his arms around her, and liked it that he had said this even if it wasn't true. His strong body beside her was a comfort and made her feel secure, and that everything would be all right. She was glad that she had married him, that he had been the one.

Words came to her then, like a haunting. Words she hadn't allowed to run amok around her head for a long time.

I wish I'd never met you, Sue.

They came like a recording in her brain and she could hear them echo across the flat land then fly off towards the hills with the wind. It was Martin's voice. She shivered all over. Pictures followed, Martin looming over her, her hands pinned down tight; events she hardly dared to remember from that dreadful weekend away. She shuddered now. There were reasons she didn't let herself remember that.

Susie shook away from Martin's grip, which pulled her back almost as insistently as the mud had. She felt trapped in his arms, suffocating. She wriggled and bucked from under him. She stood up and shook herself down. He was left holding out his arms as if incredulous at her not being wrapped around him any more. Then he recovered himself and stood up.

'Let's get back,' he said. 'We'll make tea and beans with sausages.'

Susie nodded and tried not to flinch when he reached for her hand.

The sky was overcast when they got back; the gunmetal grey of winter in the British Isles.

'Do you think it'll rain again?' Susie asked Martin.

He scowled up at the clouds, examining them at length, as if an expert on these matters. 'I don't think so,' he said, 'and I bloody hope not.'

'Yeah, you and me both,' Susie said. She was cold again, her jeans and boots caked black from her recent misadventure. Martin also looked as though he had been dipped in oil up to the knees.

'We should make a fire,' he said. 'One thing we can have for free. I quite fancy a night curled up there telling ghost stories or something. It'll be like scout camp.'

Susie tried to smile but the mention of ghost stories snagged her face so that she couldn't. It was easy to talk about these things, joke about them or try to scare other people if you didn't believe in any of it yourself, like Martin. But Susie's experience of life was different. She'd seen and heard things, sensed them, like someone's touch the previous night. These things appeared to seek her out. She thought about being touched. It had felt good at the time but now it seemed calculated. What an easy way to put distance between a husband and wife, when you thought about it. A cold feeling washed over her as she considered this. She didn't want to sleep at the bothy even one more night. The idea of lying on its floor and letting sleep take her was terrifying. She hadn't been this scared of bedtime since she was a teenager.

Back in those days, she'd gone through a stage of waking up from deep sleep to find a dark presence pressing down on her body and pinning her to the bed. She had thought at first that it would rape her but that had never happened. It had just held her tight, trapped on her bed, and finally let go its vice-like grip after a few minutes. In a weird way, though, she had welcomed this presence, the feeling of being wanted this way. It was the closest she'd come to sex at the time. She'd heard a load of rational explanations for what had happened to her since: lucid dreaming, sleep paralysis, things like that. That was the problem with rational explanations; they never really explained anything.

The sun was beginning to set, leaking blood-red around the clouds in the vast Scottish sky. 'Red sky at night,' Martin said, leaving the implication of a good day to come between them in the air. 'We'll be out of here before you know it.'

Hope at this idea warmed Susie inside and she smiled slightly. 'Yes,' she said.

'Come on,' Martin said. 'Let's go fetch some peat to dry out for the fire. The wood won't last much longer and there's no more anywhere around here, not this side of the river anyway. We shouldn't really get into stripping the land bare but since we're here just a couple of nights it's hardly too much of a worry.' He walked off in the direction of the bog. The light was fading as Susie followed him and she recalled the journey here; how the light had dropped so quickly it had seemed like a lamp switching off. At least, that was how she remembered it although, in hindsight, she saw it couldn't have been that way. There must have been a gradual fading out, even if this took place over a relatively short space of time. The sun didn't just switch off like that, black out, not unless there was an eclipse and, even then, it was just for a moment. Its influence could only slowly fade away, like the pull of a lost lover. Susie knew enough about that to feel the comparison. A name came into her head then, flashed there just for a moment. *Jules*. She shivered. She would not think about him. Her head was all over the place at the moment and that was the last thing she needed.

The peat was cool and clammy to the touch but not unpleasant. Martin had brought carrier bags with him to transport it back and they filled them with the sticky earth. They worked quickly, not needing to talk to know where the other would go next, what they would do. It was a symbiotic relationship they shared, Susie thought. Barnacles on a whale's skin, pilot fish. They worked well together, always. That must mean their marriage had been right, no matter what rows had come since, Susie told herself. She knew these practical things were important for a life together, more real than passion or being held so tight you couldn't help but feel loved. Soon they would have a fire blazing in the hut. That was something to look forward to, a different kind of sensual pleasure. It had not taken long for her to forget completely the words that had haunted her in the bog. Now all she remembered was that Martin had rescued her from the peat and held her in his arms.

The red glow from the fire was comforting and the small room had warmed considerably, but the flames lit the place in strange patterns, making the shadows dance. The peat they had collected was spread in a layer in front of the fire, where Martin said it would dry out nicely. He stood up again and poked at the hearth. Susie wasn't sure why. It seemed her husband was armed with a plethora of practical knowledge she had never guessed at. Where had he learnt this? Had it happened in those mysterious sessions where they split boys from girls and her group had watched a video of a woman giving birth? She had always assumed the boys had learnt similar facts of life but perhaps she had been wrong.

Sparks and crackles settled as Martin moved back from the grate. He smiled and sat back down beside her. They had arranged the sleeping bags and rucksacks against the back wall as a makeshift settee. It wasn't exactly the epitome of comfort but in relative terms it was pleasant enough. Martin put an arm around her and sat back. A draught blew across Susie's face, and then the hearth, making the fire sputter. Susie shuddered and remembered the events of the previous evening again, then the cold empty space where a man should have been. Her eyes darted around the room, where the shadows played. Could there really be someone hiding in the countryside nearby, a man who knew the land well and was quick on his feet? How could anyone be fast enough? Could it be something more ethereal she had felt, like the presence that had followed her around at fourteen?

'You want to hear a ghost story?' Martin asked her then, as if he had been reading her mind. The comment that seemed offhand earlier had had serious intention behind it, Susie realised.

'You don't believe in ghosts,' she said. 'What's the point?'

'You do.'

Susie cleared her throat. 'That's not really true. I'm just not as certain as you about it. Like that quote from Shakespeare about more things in heaven and earth.'

'How beautifully paraphrased.' His voice held the edge of the teacher inside but not in such a bad way. He was teasing her. 'It's Hamlet saying that,' he told her, as if he imagined she didn't know, 'and he was a crazy kind of guy.'

'You can't know that! Shakespeare leaves it open.' Her voice was full of pleasure at the interaction. 'How are you always so sure of everything?'

He laughed, then leaned over to kiss her. 'Complete mentalist, Hamlet. Everyone knows. Look how he turned down that fox Ophelia.' His lips met hers again, soft and wet. He had always been a good kisser. 'Sometimes things are just true or not true.'

'I think it's more complicated than that,' she said. 'Anyway, go on, then, tell me this ghost story.' The draught hit her face and moved her curls again, brushing them against her neck and sending tremors through her.

'It was a dark and stormy night in rural England somewhere . . .' he began.

'What a bloody cliché,' she said.

'Shh and listen,' he chided. He continued. 'The mist had settled over the moors and at a boarding school in North Yorkshire girls were getting ready for bed. They ran around the dorm in long nighties, brushing their hair a hundred times—'

'Girls don't actually do that except in books.'

He spoke louder to drown her out and held up a hand as if that would block her words. 'Brushing their hair a hundred times and talking about what it might be like to kiss a boy, what might happen when they lose their virginity. They were girls at that stage, the kind who conjure up spirits.'

Susie didn't interrupt again, but couldn't help feeling Martin had read too much classic fiction as he continued to describe the moors and their haunting winds with shades of *Wuthering Heights*, the girls like something out of Enid Blyton, though years out of date. How many fifteen-year-olds these days don't know first-hand about the art of losing their virginity?

'One girl spotted lights in the distance.' Martin waved his hands around in circles to indicate the lights she had seen; he was hamming it up now. 'Two lights there were, dancing together, moving in harmony and always the same distance apart, like car headlights. Except that the way they moved, side to side, up and down, they couldn't be headlights. It would be impossible for a car to move like that.

'This girl pointed out the lights to her dorm mates, who came to watch. The girls crowded the window, misting up the glass with their breath as they watched the lights, hypnotised. They giggled and pointed and then . . .' He paused, then let out a huge scream, holding on to his own face and making Susie start and sit up, thinking at first something was wrong with him. Then she turned to look at him and realised this was still part of the act.

'The girl who had screamed backed away towards the door, deathly pale. "They're not lights, not in the distance," she said. The other girls looked closer now, and they all saw it at once. Like she'd said, not lights in the distance.' He brought his face close to Susie's and whispered in a fast, frightened voice. 'Bright white eyes, glowing, just the other side of the window.'

Susie felt a chill come over her body very briefly, but she didn't think it was the story. She hadn't seen the twist coming but it wasn't scary. It wasn't real enough to set her properly on edge.

'I'll tell you a ghost story,' she said. 'A real one, though.'

'What makes you think my story wasn't true?' he said, feigning incredulity.

Susie didn't elaborate but playfully tapped him on the arm and continued to talk. 'This is something that actually happened to my mother, weeks after her dad died. There were witnesses too, my gran was there and swore it was all true exactly the way my mum told it.'

'Your mother's a mentalist, though. Your gran as well, probably. Even though I never met her I think I can make that assumption given what I know about the female line in this particular family.'

Susie frowned. She was annoyed at where Martin was going and wondered if he was trying to upset her. She looked at him but there were no signs in the expression on his face. She decided to leave it and carried on with her story. 'She was hanging out the washing with her mum, my gran, when she heard her dad's voice calling her clear as day. She turned to go inside and see what he wanted, then remembered she wouldn't find him in the house any more and stopped short. "That was odd," she told my gran. "I could have sworn I heard Dad shouting for me. Mind playing tricks on me." My gran nodded and told her that things like that happen when you lose someone close. Mum was a bit shaken up, though, and she went into the house. That was when the doorbell went. She went to answer it and, as if she had an instinct something strange was going on, my gran followed so that they were both there to open the door. It was a couple of police officers. They'd come for Granddad because he'd missed a court appearance, something to do with his car tax. Apparently my gran went and got the shovel and told them to go dig him up. I wish I'd been there to see the looks on their faces.'

Martin laughed. Then he said, 'Told you your mum was a mentalist, Sue.'

Now she was properly offended. She'd taken the high ground and ignored his goading but he couldn't stop. Her irritation must have shown in her face because he nudged her with an elbow and said, 'I'm just joshing, silly girl.' But she couldn't laugh. 'I admit that is a compelling ghost story, if you like that kind of thing,' he said. 'But it could just be an unusual and bizarre coincidence. I mean, your gran was dead right about the newly bereaved conjuring up voices of their loved ones. It's very common. Your brain can make a sound feel very real without you even knowing.'

Susie was well aware of this. She had experienced it, earlier, out on the bog: Martin's voice clear, as if he'd been speaking in her head. Other things, too: the wolf whistle she'd been sure she'd heard outside the hut. Remembering this combined with her own ghost story made an unease settle over her. She pulled one of the sleeping bags tight around her shoulders.

'Cold?' Martin said. He got up to play with the fire again, adding more wood and shoving it around the grate.

But Susie wasn't cold. Her back felt insecure and vulnerable. She could imagine fingers brushing over her skin, making her want more. She could almost conjure up the feeling of the same hands around her neck, tightening like a noose, cutting off her air supply and crushing her throat.

'That wasn't the only time she heard his voice,' she said then, her words quiet and precise.

'Oh yeah?' Martin turned and smiled from the grate.

'Yeah. She heard him again – it woke her from a dream. That was the night her mother died.'

Martin walked back to their makeshift seating arrangement. 'Compelling stuff. I could almost believe in it all if I heard enough stories like that. Well, if I was happy to leave my common sense sat on the sideboard at home.' This was one of his favourite sayings, and one that made him sound more like a Yorkshireman than almost anything else could.

Stories like that; Susie had heard a hundred more. Some about her own family like this one; others she'd collected over the years, swapped for her story at late-night parties and in hotel bars. Then there were her own bizarre experiences. The presence that had crushed her to her bed as an emerging woman, happy, it seemed, to rest on top of her and pin her down. The caress of a lover in a dark room and a man, clear as day, smoking outside the window. She looked for that man now, and for anything in the window that she could have mistaken for a man or a trail of smoke. The shadow of a tree like Martin had suggested.

There was nothing there, though, only blackness. The skin on her arms and back tingled with the thought of being touched. She ached for it, then, a hand on her arm or across her waist. Even the sweet pressing down, the way it had felt when she was just fourteen and knew nothing about real men and how they poisoned you. She should have stuck with that phantom lover, whatever it was, the thing that had wanted nothing more than to be as close as it could to her skin.

Martin moved his hand to rest on the back of

Susie's neck, making her body jump away from him with shock. He turned and looked down at her, amused, and then he laughed. His laugh looked weird: manic and wrong and out of place. How had she ended up here, in the middle of nowhere with this man who, as she looked at him now, felt like a stranger?

9

Dust motes swam and shifted in the beam of light coming through the window, and the rising day woke Susie but not Martin. She stirred, feeling cold to the core and wishing she could shower and heat through her bones in the steam. She hoped above hope that the river's flow might have ebbed by now and that they would be able to go home.

There was still water in the pot from the night before. She made tea outside the hut and watched the sun come up. The sky grew bluer as dawn cracked it open, although parts were as red as they had been at sunset the evening before, like someone had bled all over the clouds, and she wondered which part of the old shepherds' rhyme she should believe. She hoped it would not rain again and put their return to civilisation back even longer. It had been a good thirty-six hours since the last downpour. She cupped her mug and let it warm her hands, stepping from one foot to the other and staring out towards the burn. It still looked rather serious from where she was standing but her heart leapt with the idea that today could be the day they set off back.

When she had finished her drink, she headed for the river. She was no expert but the burn in spate like this looked frightening and powerful to her and she still didn't think they could cross it. It had ebbed a little, she could see that, its rush being slightly less loud and its borders lower, a damp patch of mud left where it had claimed the land around it before. Still, it was flowing hard past her, and she could not imagine trudging through. She had struggled crossing the river when they had first arrived and she was certain it had been calmer than it was now. There was no sign of any stepping stones as the water rushed by, no easy route across. She sighed, and prayed that when Martin woke up he would see something different and find them a way across the furious water.

The chill was making her shake now, and she decided to walk. It was the only way she could think to keep warm. When Martin woke up she could set the fire going again but she didn't want to disturb him and she was still clinging to the hope they might be able to set off back to the hotel instead. She strode away from the hut, taking care not to go too far and to avoid the places where the land glimmered. It struck her that her attempt to cross the bog could have acquired her a certain immortality and a place in the British Museum next to Lindow Man. She couldn't imagine drowning in mud any more than she could envisage dying of exposure. In fact, the truth was, she couldn't imagine dying at all. Of course, she knew it would happen, one way or another, but she found it hard to believe. A bit like Martin with his ghosts, she supposed, although, for her, the idea of life continuing somehow made much more sense.

She had seen a man die once. It had been an accident; he'd been run over by a car on the Mile End Road, near where she worked in East London. She had tried to help him, put pressure on his leg where the blood was pouring out, making sure no one moved him and covering him with her coat until the ambulance came. He was talking at first but then began slipping in and out of consciousness. She tried to keep him awake, urging him to talk. The bleeding in his leg stopped and she put him in the recovery position. But she could feel him slipping away, so she put her arms around him and held him close, saying all the soothing things she could think of. When he passed it was gentle but perceptible to her. She held him longer. She was sobbing by the time the first paramedic arrived on the scene and pulled her away. A second, younger paramedic had grabbed her by the arm and told her she'd done all she could. Internal bleeding, he reckoned. He gave her back her coat; it was caked in blood. When she got home she couldn't bring herself to get it cleaned. A week later, she had a sudden sense that Martin would have a problem with what she'd done, tell her she shouldn't have interfered or got suspicious about her involvement with the man. She hid the coat at the back of a cupboard under a load of boxes. In the end, she threw it out with the rubbish.

She had never found out who the man was. In fact, she'd deliberately avoided the news for a while afterwards. Knowing the details would have made it too real. If she knew his name, stuff about his family, she wasn't at all sure she could cope. So she had switched off the TV when the local news came on, and kept the radio off. She had almost forgotten the man until now and wasn't sure why he suddenly came to mind. It was the bothy, she decided. Something about being there brought death to mind. That thought sent a shiver through her. She walked faster, round and round the hut, increasing the scope of her circles as much as she dared. She wondered what there was here, haunting her. Someone who had drowned in the river or stuck in the mud? Someone who was going to? She believed that if ghosts existed they could come from the future as well as the past. Why not? If they existed at all there was no reason to suspect their existence obeyed our rules of time and space; in fact, quite the opposite was more logical.

She marched round in a circle one more time. She wanted to wake Martin up, find out if there was any chance of attempting the trip home today, but she knew that could be a mistake. She considered her options. She could make a pot of coffee or bring him breakfast. There wasn't exactly a lot of food left but then they couldn't, surely, be here that much longer. It would be fine, and it would be a nice, romantic moment between them. She headed back in.

In fact, there wasn't much food left at all: two bananas, a bar of dark chocolate, an apple and three cans of beans and sausages. She dug in her bag for the coffee tin, and the small plastic cafetière she had brought along. The pan still had a bit of water in it and she heated this first. Still warm from when she had made tea earlier, it boiled quickly, and she filled the coffee pot and left it to brew, emptying what was left of the water on to the ground. She opened a can of the beans and poured it into the saucepan.

It was okay, standing by the stove. She felt useful; part of nature, an animal providing. There was a very primal pleasure in it. She heated the food until it bubbled and spat, stirring all the time, then emptied it into the two tin bowls. She dropped a spoon into each, then scooped up the coffee and milk. She went inside and placed them on the floor beside the door. Then she came back for the bowls.

The smell of food and coffee woke Martin from his slumber. 'Hey, baby,' she said, as she saw him move around and became sure he was awake.

'Hey,' he said, his voice cracked with sleep.

She poured coffee into mugs, adding milk and sugar to Martin's.

'Wow, that's coffee I can smell,' he said. 'What a treat.'

Susie smiled and passed the cup to Martin. He sat up and took it from her.

'What else?' he said.

'Breakfast.' Susie spun on her heels and passed him the bowl with a flourish.

At first Martin accepted it with a smile, spooning food into his mouth. Then he appeared to rouse a little better from sleep, looking at what she'd given him a bit more closely. 'How much did you use?' he said.

'Just one tin. There's another couple, and some fruit. I figured we'd be gone soon. Today, hopefully.' She was chewing away.

'For God's sake, Sue.' Martin put down the bowl. 'What makes you think a few hours without rain are going to undo what's happened on the weeks and weeks it's been pouring down for?' He ran his fingers through his hair.

Susie's spoon was poised halfway to her mouth. She put it down. 'How long are we going to be here, Martin?'

He shrugged. 'Who knows? Anyway, we might as well eat it now. It's been heated and won't keep, so eat it while it's hot. But we have to conserve resources after this.'

A lead weight plummeted in Susie's stomach. *Undo weeks of rain.* Did that mean Martin thought they'd be here for weeks? Because it just wasn't possible. She was due back at work a week on Wednesday. This was supposed to be a holiday, not an emigration. Why had she ever let him persuade her to come out on this godforsaken trip to the middle of nowhere? Her instincts had been right; she should have followed them.

The food was cloying now, thick and heavy with the recent knowledge. She kept shovelling it into her mouth but found it hard to swallow the chunks of sausage and the beans. She stopped eating.

'You want to get that down you. Who knows when we'll be eating next?' Martin said.

Susie didn't want to admit it, but he was right. *Martin might be less bloody annoying*, she thought, *if he didn't have a point quite so often.* He was too bloody logical, that was his problem. She force-fed herself, chewed and swallowed, went through the motions. She watched Martin as he ate. He sat up straighter and grabbed for the coffee.

'It really was a sweet gesture,' he said. 'I'm sorry if I spoilt it.'

He didn't sound very sorry and Susie wasn't at all sure he meant a word of it. 'It's okay,' she said anyway. She chewed on a piece of sausage, which felt like a foreign body in her mouth. 'Will you come and check out the river soon, see if we can cross?'

He had a mouthful of food and paused before swallowing. 'Of course,' he said when he had done so.

Soon the food was gone. Susie's belly felt full enough, even if it had been an effort to get down. She drank the rest of her coffee. There were too many grounds at the bottom; the plastic cafetière was not a perfect creation. She gagged on these a little, then stepped outside to spit them out. Martin came past her and was walking away. She followed him, thinking he was heading for the river.

'Getting a piss first,' he said, nodding back in her direction.

Susie turned back towards the hut, feeling a slight flush across her cheeks at the thought she hadn't twigged that.

Moments later, Martin was back. 'Let's go and find this raging torrent, then.'

She smiled and nodded and they headed to the river together. She took every step with a heavy heart, pretty sure of what the answer was going to be once they got there. Moments later, they were standing on its banks and Martin was walking up and down the near shore, his hand on his chin as if trying to work something out. After some deliberation, he turned to Susie, his head cocked to one side.

'What do you think, Sue?'

She snorted. 'Like I'd have a clue. I suspect you're going to say no, though.'

'There you go, then, you do have some idea.' He gestured flippantly as he turned to head back. 'No chance, I'm afraid. Not sure why you even wasted my time dragging me down here to be honest.'

She had no answer to that. *Hope*, she supposed. *Constant optimism*. But she couldn't say anything like this to Martin. He would never understand. It didn't work that way for him. He was all about the truth and logic. His mind worked in a straight line and no other evidence was admissible. She rushed after him, though, caught up and half skipped to stay level with his brisk walking pace.

'What about the bog route? Can we try that way?'

Martin stopped in his tracks, turning towards her with a sardonic curl to his lips. 'You really want to try that again?'

She stared at him, the way he looked down from his six-foot-odd height, the curve of his mouth, everything about his demeanour. 'Why do you think you're so much better than everyone else?' she said. It came out in rush, before she'd really thought about it.

He laughed then. 'Is that what you think of me?' He shook his head and walked off from her, laughing as he went but in a distraught, can't-believe-this, end-of-his-tether kind of way.

Susie walked back to the bothy, too, but more slowly. She felt so helpless, stuck out here with Martin. She didn't know enough about the land or river to make her own call but didn't really trust his. She had learnt enough she hadn't known before about Martin on this trip to understand he knew what he was doing, but that wasn't her worry. It was his motives that she questioned. Something inside her was sending out warning signals, telling her that having her trapped in a hut at his mercy for several days was exactly what he wanted and not for any good reasons. She remembered 'the weekend' and the things he had done that she'd been trying to forget for so long. She'd had to forget them or she could never have stayed in her marriage.

She reminded herself that Martin was not out to scare her. He was her husband, and he loved her. She repeated it over and over and over like a mantra.

When Susie got back to the hut, Martin had turned off the stove and was filling the fire with the dried-out peat. She had walked the last stretch towards the hut quickly and was out of breath. She came inside the door then stood leaning over, hands on knees and bent double. Martin threw sods of the earthy mixture into the grate and prodded it around with the big wooden stick he'd found outside the bothy. All that was left of last night's fire was ashes.

'We can cook on the fire,' he said. 'We need to save the gas.'

Susie nodded. She was still breathing heavily. She couldn't catch her breath and, as she stood waiting to, watching her husband, it struck her it might not happen. She began to panic and her breath came in faster and sharper with each moment she thought about it. It took Martin a while to realise what was happening.

He turned to her, frowning, then caught sight of her pale face. He moved fast towards her.

'Sit down, Sue,' he said, an arm on her shoulder. She did as she was told and parked herself on the hard floor. He placed his hands one each on her shoulders and held firm. 'Look at me, Sue. Breathe with me.' He sucked in air and breathed out in an exaggerated fashion. 'Come on, Sue. Breathe.'

In, out, she followed his instructions and breathed. All she managed was to do as he said; anything else was too damn terrifying. Time passed and her breathing and heartbeat slowed. She settled. Finally, she could talk again. 'Thanks,' she said.

'You okay?' He was still holding fast to her shoulders, pinning her in the seated position, and it was a little uncomfortable.

Susie nodded, and looked up at him. Not for the first time since they'd been here, she felt like a child. He was doing his father-figure act again. Not that she could really complain; what kind of mess would she be in now had he not been around to calm her down? More proof that their marriage was right, surely? Her lungs were working normally now; the panic was over. 'Sorry,' she said.

Martin shook his head vigorously. 'No need to be,' he told her.

'I'm just scared,' she said. 'It feels like we'll be here for ever. I feel like I'm trapped.'

Martin smiled. Susie wondered if the smile was meant to reassure her but it looked malevolent. 'But you're with *me*,' he told her.

Susie couldn't explain that this was part of the problem, that his intentions concerned her. She nodded as if she understood him and tried to stand up.

'Perhaps we should have a go with the mobiles again,' he said.

She nodded, and walked to the part of the hut where her things were piled. Her rucksack lay beside them, open and leaking items on to the bothy floor. She had not properly unpacked since her bid for freedom but had left the bag in the hut, pulling the things she needed from it one at time, letting the rest litter the floor where they fell. She found her phone sitting to the side of all this.

They hadn't tried their mobile phones for a while. Susie didn't imagine for a moment that there would be a signal this time. Why would it suddenly change after all the times before when they'd got nothing? Despite

Martin's theories about coverage switching between zones, it did not seem likely. She tried anyway, turning on the phone and waiting for the welcome signal, then the pip that indicated a search for network.

The welcome message from Martin's phone echoed around the hut shortly after hers. They sat looking at the phones, at each other, as they searched for any connection to the outside world. Susie stared at the display on her mobile, then Martin's. No bars. She stared and stared at hers, hoping something would suddenly manifest there.

Ten minutes later, still nothing. Then Susie's phone began making the battery-low noise. She swore and turned it off. She knew from experience that it wouldn't last much longer, especially if she was turning it on and off. It wasn't much of a warning on her phone and the beeping pretty much indicated that the battery was at the end of its life. She threw the phone on to the pile of her stuff.

Everything felt suddenly so hopeless. She let out a small yelp and swore several times. 'I can't believe this is happening to me,' she said, her voice raised and tense. 'I can't believe the mess we're in. It's cold and the floor's hard and we're going to run out of food and

I'm hungry as it is and I just want to get back to the hotel and see other people . . .' She carried on gabbling like this, going on about the predicament they were in, what a nightmare it all was. She couldn't stop herself.

A hard, sharp shock across her face. Susie looked up, her mouth open, to see Martin standing right in front of her. He was looking at his own hand as if he wasn't in control of it. He had slapped her. She looked from his hand to the wall and then back again. Involuntary, her own hand came up to her face, touching the skin as if nursing the impact.

'Oh, don't be such a baby,' he said. 'You were panicking. It was the right thing to do.'

The heat of the slap seemed to grow and glow across her skin. She hadn't been hyperventilating and she hadn't been shouting. She had gabbled a bit but, seriously, maybe a mark four on the panic scale, nothing compared to how she had got earlier when she couldn't breathe, or on the scramble on the journey here. The slap had been totally unnecessary.

Martin looked away and wouldn't meet her eyes. *He knew*, Susie thought. *He bloody knew*. He had slapped her. Not because it was the right thing to do and not because she was panicking. He had slapped her because he had wanted to. The impact flamed her face still but he was acting like nothing had happened, and finished filling the grate and lighting the fire. She let herself fall to the ground and sit back against the wall. She grabbed for her sleeping bag. She held on to it like it was a stuffed toy; a child's blankie. She pulled it towards her and hugged it tight and tried not to think about what had just happened, or how much danger she might be in, trapped here so far away from help.

10

Susie didn't speak much for the rest of the day. The slap hung over her like the darkest black cloud, and she wanted to tackle Martin about what he'd done but she was too scared. This fear was fed in part by the things that might happen to their marriage if she forced the issue, but also by something else. It was very frightening for her to realise she was wary of Martin, hesitant about upsetting him. For some reason, the hunting knife he'd brought with him kept coming into her head when she thought about arguing with him. She told herself she was being ridiculous; her husband would never hurt her. Sure, things had got a little crazy on that long ago weekend in that cottage in the middle of nowhere but Martin wasn't an abusive man; theirs wasn't that kind of marriage. Yet something told her he was capable of anything, here in this strange and haunting place.

Susie went to bed early, feeling hungry, and she dreamed of food. Rich meats and stodgy puddings, carvery roasts and buttered potatoes. She dreamed of chocolate, of sickly Turkish Delight on paper plates, of huge piles of greasy chips, hot and sticky on her fingers and lips. She woke up, her mouth watering and stomach growling angrily at her, the build-up of acids burning against soft tissue. She had to sit up in her sleeping bag and bend herself double. This took the pain away but woke Martin, who was not impressed.

'Sleep,' he said, an angry edge to his voice. She wished she could fall back into unconsciousness as readily as he could.

The first light woke Susie early again. She got up right away and went outside to make tea. Her stomach felt very empty and she ate one of the bananas that were left, recklessly, knowing Martin would chide her about it later. It was black from the cold but tasted really good. As she waited for the water to boil, she noticed the weight of her hair. She examined its length. It looked darker, and was beginning to hang in clumps. There was a little milk left and she drank some mouthfuls straight from the carton. It was all she could do not to tip the carton and glug it all down. But they should save it for tea, eke out its goodness, and she had enough self-control to do the right thing.

They had been at the bothy for just four days but already the supplies of food were looking seriously depleted. There was one more blackened banana, a couple of tins of beans with sausages and some squares of chocolate, about half a bar. Susie thought it was pretty frightening how inadequately prepared they'd been. All Martin's fault. He thought he was such an expert on this outward-bound stuff but he hadn't thought it through at all. He had the cheek to get all high and mighty about a forgotten torch, like that was a life-or-death thing, but he was happy to bring them both somewhere like this with a few cans of beans and a change of clothes. It was enough to make her want to slap him the way he had her. She could recall the feel of his hand so well that her face began to smart again.

She decided to go off and stomp the emotions out

before they got the better of her. Her feet were restless for it and she couldn't believe she had never found this outlet before. She walked away from the hut, out towards the bog where she'd got stuck. She'd rather get eaten by the mud than do anything nasty to her husband. The further she got from the bothy, the better she felt. Surely it wasn't the hut itself that was doing this to her? That was silly and yet . . . No, she figured, it was the walk doing its job. That was the whole point, after all. She carried on going, out further than she thought she would dare, right into the mud, where she stepped and squelched until her legs ached like they would break. She didn't get stuck and was almost tempted to strike out for the path on the other side of the bog. One thought stopped her; she wasn't at all sure Martin would come for her if she sunk into the mud again. He was asleep and wouldn't be looking out for her in the first place or tracking her progress across the flat land. But even if he saw her trapped by the peat like a fly in amber, she wasn't at all convinced he would come. Something had changed in him.

As she walked, Susie thought her way out of her marriage. She would leave Martin, buy one of the flats near town, the new build with the wood on the fronts of the apartment blocks and floor-to-ceiling windows. She would live there with plants and cats, nurturing life in the ways left open to her now, and find herself a sophisticated lover for dinner in good restaurants. Or perhaps a young man, a toy for nights of passion. Hell, she might even get pregnant. It wasn't beyond the realms of possibility. Otherwise, she would live an independent life with no one else to think of. She might even write that novel she'd often talked about. If she died alone, and was eaten by the cats, then there were worse things could happen. She could be eaten another way, from the inside out, by the rage she felt towards her husband. That was a more unpleasant thought, more terrible than any of the fears she had about old age and loneliness. She did fine on her own, drinking coffee with the paper in cafés at the weekend. She had even gone out to dinner alone before, on business trips and so on. It wasn't so bad; much worse in theory than in practice.

Deep down she knew it, though. She was as trapped in her life with Martin as she was in the bothy with him here and now. Everything they had was tied up together: the equity in the house, the fixtures and furnishings they had bought together, their mutual friends, the lifestyle they shared. Undoing years of building a life together was too much to expect; too hard to do. Even their childlessness was something they'd done together. If she met someone else her own age they would almost certainly have kids already. She didn't think she could deal with someone else's children in her life. It would make her too mindful of what she hadn't done, what she didn't have.

She thought about all these reasons. Excuses, her younger self would have called them. Was there a single valid justification among them for staying with Martin if she wasn't happy? Right here, right now, there was the river and the bog and neither was passable. Except that she didn't know that for sure, either. She only had Martin's word for it. She thought again about striking out alone for safety. Fear of getting stuck held her back.

So she kept walking because, while she was walking, she had her legs to focus on, the muscles, the movement, the push then pull of one foot in front of the other. After long enough walking in mud, she had the pain of her shins and thighs from the repeated effort. It was a good, sweet pain. It took her mind off the hunger, and off the man in the hut, off everything. Because that was by far the worst thing about being stranded here: there was far too much time to think.

Returning from her walk, Susie found Martin sprawled on his sleeping bag in front of the crackling fire. His eyes were closed but she could tell he was awake because his breathing was shallow. She wondered if he was meditating, if he still did that. She knew he used to but, then, he used to read Buddhist texts and talk a lot about the Dalai Lama and he didn't do any of that any more. She wondered what he might be thinking. She sat on the edge of the sleeping bags, lowering herself gently so as not to be accused of disturbing him. What was he doing? Why was he pretending to be asleep? She had never wished more that she could see inside his head. She watched his eyes. They didn't move under his closed lids. If he had violent intentions towards her, she wouldn't stand a chance.

Susie wondered what the staff were thinking at the hotel, and whether they'd been missed yet. The problem was that even if they had noticed their absence, how would they know where to look for them? They had left no details of their planned trek before they left.

Like so many things, that was Martin's fault. She felt a stab of anger towards him.

'Martin.' She spoke sharply.

His eyes snapped open. He didn't look as though he'd been woken up. In fact, he looked alert and wakeful. 'Yes, dear,' he said, his voice brimming with sarcasm.

'Have you checked the river today?'

'I went out earlier,' he said. 'Still a bit of a rage out there, I'm afraid.'

So he had been awake. And he'd been out. Yet everything about how he was lying there tried to give her the impression otherwise. 'Wow. I would have thought we'd be out of here by now,' Susie said. 'It can't be worse than on the day we arrived, can it, surely?'

Martin shrugged. 'Maybe we shouldn't have crossed it then. It was a nightmare if I remember it right. If I'd been able to see properly I might have turned us back then and there.'

'For sure we shouldn't have crossed then,' Susie snapped. 'Then we wouldn't have ended up in this mess, would we?' Emotion was flowing from these words like an electric charge; much more than she'd planned for.

'You blame me?' Martin said. His voice was as flat as the surface of the stepping stones she'd brushed with one hand as she crossed the river on the night they'd arrived. 'You think this is my fault?'

'You're the one who insisted we come here,' she blurted out. She swallowed as she spoke, trying to bite back the words almost as soon as she'd said them.

'I see,' Martin said. He closed his eyes again.

Susie looked at her sleeping bag lying next to his. She didn't want to be that close to him, not for now, although she knew she'd give up when she needed his body heat later that night, the way she always did. She sat partly on the hut's bare floor for now, though, rather than pull her sleeping bag from under Martin, where it was trapped slightly, snagged with his. The surface of the floor was rough and chilled, despite the heat from the fire.

'It was supposed to be an adventure, for a change,' Martin said, without opening his eyes. 'Something to take us out of the daily grind. I couldn't have predicted this but, had I been able to, I would have done the same thing. If life is all experience then we haven't been living it for years, Sue.'

Martin spoke quietly but his words were clear as day to her. He was dissatisfied with their marriage too.

Despite her visions earlier, of the apartment and the cats, she knew as soon as she felt it might be a real possibility that it wasn't what she wanted. She tried to tell herself it was good that he'd said it. They could shake things up together, both become happier. Her emotions didn't catch up with her brain, though. Perhaps it was the grind of hunger. Maybe it was something more sinister. Whatever the reason, his comment scratched at her bad mood, making it explode like the head of a match.

'You make it sound like that's my fault,' she said. Her voice was firm and cold; hard. It was uncharacteristic for her and it made Martin sit up and stare. The expression that came over his face made him look like a stranger. His eyes flashed, and his mouth made a cruel gash across his features. It reminded her of one thing, one time between them, and she knew she should back down for her own sake except that she couldn't. Why should she not say what she thought? Just because he was prepared to go so far with the things he did and said? Because he could do her damage; because of 'the weekend'? None of these reasons were enough and she would rather die than be bullied a moment longer.

'You slapped me, you arsehole,' she said with venom.

'Ah, so this is what it's all about then, Sue.' He cleared his throat and let out an angry sound.

'No, that's not what it's all about. It's about so much more. It's about . . .' She trailed off. There were a thousand things she wanted to say but she realised saying them would mark the beginning of the end, the start of that path to the apartment with the cats and plants. She wasn't ready to go there yet.

'You were getting hysterical, Sue. I wanted to calm you down.' Martin spoke calmly and with little emotion. 'I didn't want a repeat of the nightmare scenario of you sinking to your death in the bog when maybe I might not notice and come after you.'

Susie looked at him. His eyes were open and clear, his hands held out slightly to his sides. He seemed genuine and made her feel like she was getting it all wrong. But the thing was, she could remember the incident and she hadn't been hysterical at all. Upset, yes, rightly so, and she had been expressing that emotion without too much restraint, listing the things that were wrong with this situation, but her behaviour hadn't been out of proportion to what was happening. There had been no fast breathing, no panic. No reason to slap her.

'I wasn't hysterical,' she said at last. 'I'd just taken in what was really happening here and it bothered me but I was just talking. You didn't need to slap me.'

Martin was picking his teeth with a piece of paper he'd ripped off one of the chocolate wrappers. 'You sure looked hysterical from where I was standing.'

She stared back at him, her arms crossed. She didn't bother arguing any more. There was no point. It would only go back and forth now, like children in the playground, *'tis, 'tisn't, 'tis, not,* and so on. Her stomach growled, loudly.

'It is about dinnertime,' Martin said.

Susie laughed, but not in a good way. 'Dinner!' She made the word sound ridiculous.

'Enjoy it while you can.' Martin sat up and grabbed the stick he used to poke the fire.

Susie turned sharply and walked out of the door to bring the food in, and the stove. She stared at the pile of their provisions. She was almost certain there was less there than there had been before; just one tin of the beans and sausages left. Had Martin had the other to himself? That would have been incredibly selfish under the circumstances but what could she really say about it? She'd scoffed a banana and hadn't thought about Martin for a moment. Now she considered it, that had been selfish, too. But she'd been so hungry she felt sick and hardly able to help herself. She'd held back from drinking the milk, hadn't she?

Inside the hut, Susie handed the last tin of beans to Martin. She wondered if she should mention that it was the last one. But he should know that, right? It was just the two of them here so it must have been Martin who'd eaten the other one. The thought of less than a half a can of food was too much to bear, anyway, and so she didn't say anything in case he made them eke it out. Martin emptied the can into their cooking pot and held it over the fire. Susie divvied up the chocolate. She wouldn't eat hers now; she would save it for later. She handed Martin his, though, and he shoved the whole lot into his mouth.

She couldn't believe it had come to this; trapped in this place with next to nothing to eat. She stared at the cooking pot, and at Martin. She could have cried but she didn't have the heart or energy for it.

'We can live for weeks without eating,' Martin said, as if reading her thoughts. 'We could even try to fish, or hunt, or whatever.'

She listened to his words and to the buzz of the fire.

They could live for weeks without food, she was sure he was right. Sooner or later her stomach would stop trying to eat itself and her metabolism would slow right down. She couldn't imagine for a moment they would be trapped out here long enough that they would starve to death, and the river was a constant supply of fresh water nearby.

She knew all of these things but it made no difference. Something about the situation felt desperate. It felt like the end of the world.

11

Susie woke up with a gasp. The fire had gone out and the hut was so dark it was like being blind. She could feel a hand, lightly brushing against her face, then down over her breasts to her waist. It touched her lightly, expertly, and she knew right away it wasn't Martin. She could hear him snoring on the sleeping bag next to her, anyway, but this was only confirmation of what was clear to her already. Her night vision was not kicking in and she couldn't see a thing in the hut. Lips brushed her cheek. She felt a presence beside her, someone on the opposite side of her body from Martin.

The lips moved over her face, placing gentle kisses on her skin, and fingers made small circles on the top of her arms. She shivered with pleasure. Without missing a beat, another hand slid the sleeping bag from her body and ran over her clothes. She was strangely warm even out of the covers, even though she could feel the cold air against her bare skin. Her breathing came in short bursts. She was suddenly afraid. There was someone in the hut, touching her. A man. But at the same time as being afraid, she was aroused, terribly and intensely so. What was it Martin had said? About life being experience and how they weren't living at all. She felt the truth of his words as she moved her lips to meet the lover she couldn't see. It was a cold, hard kiss.

He kissed her harder, further, more. Thoughts flitted in and out of her head, about how strange this was, how wrong; Martin lying next to her and a man she couldn't see. She didn't care as she kissed and was kissed back. His hands wandered over her back and waist, down to her legs. She moaned and arched her spine as he touched a thigh. She hadn't been so turned on in a very long time.

Then she felt his weight on top of her, the real,

heavy haul of him pressing down. He wrapped right round her and squeezed tight. She could hardly breathe. She was frightened; until now she had thought she might be imagining everything. But there was someone or something here, in the bothy; it was a man's hands she could feel on her body. He might do anything. She could hardly move under the weight of him and her lungs were so restricted she didn't think she'd be able to call for Martin if this man continued to squeeze the air from inside her.

The force pressing down felt stronger and stronger. It thrilled and appalled her at the same time. His hands were under her T-shirt now. She wasn't sure how far she'd let him go, but she knew she didn't want him to stop. She let out a loud moan and Martin stirred, but he didn't wake up. The weight on top of her pressed down, harder and harder, the kissing was rougher and more vicious so that she thought his passion might kill her. She began to struggle against him but she couldn't move at all. She tried to buck and kick but it was like she'd been tied down. She tried to scream; no sound came out.

She woke with a start, in the same room and position, but it was daytime now, with bright light making a white rectangle on the floor near the sleeping bags. She sat up and gasped for breath. She had been dreaming, that was all. Her heart was beating like crazy and she was breathing fast. She tried to slow this down, taking long draughts of air and telling herself it was all a dream. She looked around the room, glad it was light and that she could see every possible hidey hole. She wasn't sure what the most disturbing part was: the sensation of being held so very still by whatever force it had been, or that of enjoying it. She leaned on her elbows and looked at Martin in the sleeping bag next to her. Whatever had gone on, he had been completely oblivious to it all, that much was clear.

As she lay there waiting for her breathing to return to normal, Jules came creeping into her head, the way he sometimes did first thing in the morning, when her defences were down. He had been her lover at university and things had ended about as badly as possible. It was a time in her life that she tried to not dwell on because it made her too sad. Except now, when she thought about him, she felt a happy nostalgia. It was almost as if he were still around and in her life somehow. She waited for the usual maudlin feelings that overtook her whenever she let herself think about Jules but they didn't come.

Susie watched her husband sleep yet again; his deep breathing moving his chest like it was a machine. Not for the first time, she envied his easy peace. It seemed that nothing disturbed Martin's dreams and he slept the sleep of complete certainty. Whatever else she could say about Martin, he believed in himself, in his own actions. He might be wrong and he might be unreasonable quite a lot of the time, but he was completely convinced of his own righteousness. She imagined this was where he got his inner peace. She knew she would never have that much certainty about anything. As Martin liked to point out, nothing was set in concrete with Susie, everything was fluid. She could always see the grey in any issue or person. They say opposites attract and this certainly made sense when it came to this particular marriage, but should opposites stay together, or should they spend a hedonistic few weeks in bed before going their separate ways?

She was wakeful now. Strangely, all sense of hunger had left her. She still had the pieces of chocolate from the previous day and the banana but she decided she would save those for when she really felt the need. She wondered if she had somehow blocked out the hunger, some complex psychological connection which meant that her body as well as her mind accepted the end of food. She somehow doubted her peace with that particular situation would last.

Her T-shirt had ridden up her back and belly, almost as if the dream had been real, and she pulled it down and wrapped herself in the sleeping bag. She was cold and wanted to light the fire, but Martin didn't look like waking up anytime soon. She put on her fleece, then her coat. She would warm up by going for a walk. She stood up a little too fast, blood rushing from her head and making her dizzy. She leaned against the wall and stood still, dropping her head until she no longer felt light-headed.

She opened the door and stepped out. Frost had carved its white patterns on the ground around about, over the bog. She wondered for a moment if the peat might be passable in the frost, if it would make the ground hard enough for her to walk right across. She could just go, now, before Martin even woke up, and be at the hotel before bedtime. The idea of the crisp, warm sheets against clean skin after a hot shower was almost too much to think about.

Then she realised that, if she did that, she would be sleeping on her own. Still unnerved by her strange dream, she didn't like that thought at all and she decided to wait for Martin after all. She headed away from the bothy, though, and down towards the river for a look. Over the river was the shorter route back and she lived in hope that its flow would have waned today and they would be able to cross. It felt possible; the weather had stayed damp but there'd not been another proper downfall.

Before she got as far as the river, Susie was already feeling warmed. The sun was beginning to make its presence known. Like the frost, the cold in her bones was fading. She could no longer believe that she used not to walk all the time, the way she had since she'd been here. She would take that one good thing away from this holiday at least. When she had turned thirty, over a decade ago now, she'd been under the mistaken impression she knew everything there was to know about herself and yet she kept learning. Perhaps she needed a longer trip, to go away to find herself the way people did. She used to think that was nonsense but now she knew what that was all about. It was like you lost yourself in other people –

husbands, wives, brothers, sisters. You had to be away from them, estranged, to get that person back. God knows how much of herself she would have lost if she'd had kids.

The river spread across the land in front of her, a natural barrier between the world she found herself in and the one where she belonged. She looked at it with a sigh. She knew instinctively that it was still flowing too fast. Watching it now, she couldn't understand how she didn't get this the first few days she was here, meaning she'd had to defer to Martin. Now she found it obvious. Warmed by her walk, though, she stopped for a rest. There was a large stone set by the river, almost as if it had been put there for someone to sit and watch the natural beauty on show. She sat down and stared as the river rushed by, trapping her there with the husband she wasn't sure she loved any more and with something else, too. Someone else? Whatever she was feeling and experiencing in the hut, she didn't think it was a person, not in the usual sense of a living, breathing human, and she didn't think it was really a dream either. It was stranger than that, more important.

She sat in the fresh air looking at the nature all

around her and tried to shake off the feeling that she'd been with a ghost.

When Susie got back to the hut, Martin was up and about. He had been out for the toilet and was on his way back, whistling.

'You sound cheerful,' she said. It was the first unnecessary thing she'd said to him for days, aside from when they rowed. Something about the way he whistled, the good old normality of the sound, made her want to build bridges.

He smiled. 'I guess I feel pretty damn good considering,' he said. 'I wanted an adventure and it looks like we're getting one. And, besides, I don't feel hungry this morning, which is something to celebrate.'

'I know. I'm the same.' She wondered how that worked, what mechanism it was that had switched on for both of them. It crossed her mind for a moment that her dream might have seemed as real as it did because it had some basis in reality. Like those experiments where they showered water on to people's faces and it made them dream of rain. Had Martin made love to her while she was sleeping? Is that what had caused her dream and woken her up? She had been able to hear him snoring, but that could have been part of the dream she was having. She stood there, staring at him for a moment. He certainly seemed rather happy all of a sudden.

'What?' Martin asked her, looking bemused.

Susie realised she'd been staring for just a little too long. 'Nothing,' she said, lowering her eyes. 'Let me help you with the fire.'

After Susie's walk in the bright morning, the hut inside felt dark and grey. She piled the driest bits of peat she could find on to the grate and lit matches. She poked the hearth with a stick the way she'd seen Martin do. It wasn't working. She turned to see him watching her, smiling.

'You use the kindling,' he said, pointing her to a pile of twigs and straw near the wall.

She knew that the day before she would have found this action irritating, his attitude smug, but right now she didn't care. She was no longer hungry and that helped her mood. She wondered too if the tender caresses she had felt made a difference. It was easier to be forgiving when you felt loved and cherished. She turned; Martin grasped her hand on the stick and helped her tease the fire awake. She lifted her head, holding it steady for a kiss.

At first, she thought he was going to miss her cue. But he looked down and saw it. He moved towards her, planting a kiss on her lips but it was all wrong. Perfunctory; like she was a habit, not a lover. She remembered again the sense she had had earlier, the moment she had been reached for, that it wasn't Martin kissing and touching her. She reminded herself she had woken up, that it had all been a dream. Yet something about it felt real, and it lingered. And she had felt a man's touch before, at a time when she was certain she had been awake. She struggled now; she had never had so much difficulty with reality. She put it down to the lack of food and the strained circumstances. That must be what had been sending her into this negative spiral about Martin too, about their marriage, when there was nothing going wrong, not when she really thought about it. They had plenty that was good together.

She turned and looked at Martin. 'I'm sorry if I've been a bitch,' she said.

'I'm used to it,' he said, with a bitter laugh. Then his face melted a little, as if he had thought better of the first comment. 'Difficult situation,' he said.

'I walked down to the river. I don't think we're getting across today.'

'Well, then, the adventure continues,' he said.

'Yes, I suppose it does. Do you think there's any point in checking the phones again?' She perked up as she remembered that Martin had said the signals flashed and changed with the weather, thinking how it had been less cloudy for a couple of days now. The fire sent Martin's face orange and it suited him.

'We've not had a signal so far; I don't see why it would change.'

She didn't understand his change of heart; he had explained to her before why it might change. She sighed. 'We could try, though.'

He smiled then, as if indulging her. 'Of course. You can do what you want anyway,' he said.

Susie felt a bit stupid then, asking for his approval to do this when he was quite right: she could have just got on with it. She walked to the rucksacks, which were piled in a corner now, and hunted through pockets for the phones. She found her own quickly, then Martin's, and pressed hard against the buttons that turned them on. Her mobile didn't respond at all; it was completely dead. She had more joy with Martin's, which bleeped on and looked for a signal but, with dreary inevitability, didn't find anything. It had only been on a minute when it started to beep loudly and display 'battery low'. She switched it off quickly in the hope she would preserve enough to make a call if they ever did get a signal.

She flung herself down on to her sleeping bag, feeling hopeless. They would be here for ever. They would die here, and rot, for all anyone would know or care about their whereabouts. Martin turned from the fire and saw her there, and his eyes filled with compassion.

'No luck, I take it,' he said, walking towards her. He sat beside her and took her hand in his, gentle, caressing. And the way he touched her, it was the way she'd been touched the night before, and suddenly she felt it could have been Martin after all.

'Did we make love?' she asked him. 'Last night, after we went to bed?'

He let out a small, sharp laugh. 'I'd like to hope you would have remembered if we did.' He stood up and was all business again for a moment, looking through the pile of things around the rucksacks. 'Sometimes I wonder if you're all there,' he told the wall.

She watched as he continued to busy himself with their stuff. She wondered what he was doing, why he was pretending. She knew that now he'd lit the fire there was nothing to do. She remembered the chocolate in her pocket. A slight pang of hunger hit her with the memory and she pulled it from her pocket. Martin turned at just that moment.

'I hope you're going to share that,' he said.

It had been the last thing on her mind. 'It's mine!' The words came out quick and sharp. 'From before. You ate yours but I saved mine for later.'

'I see,' he said. 'That's nice for you.' His voice was as sharp and shocking as the slap he had given her. She almost wished he would slap her again, rather than act this way towards her. Your body recovered quickly from a physical hit, a smack in the face and, before you knew it, it was like it had never happened. But she carried with her every time he had spoken to her like this, every time he had turned away or stormed off into the night, leaving her bed cold and empty.

Still, she felt guilty, and she broke the section of the chocolate bar she'd saved into two, offering one to him. He didn't even acknowledge the gesture and she stood like a beggar with her arms out into the room. She wanted to cry then. It had been desperate, day after day going to the burn to be told by Martin they couldn't get across. Losing the charge on the phone had seemed the last straw. But standing there, holding out a piece of chocolate to her husband and him not taking it, seemed utterly sad. Like the end of their marriage. She wished that her dream had been true, that there was someone here to love her, whether they were a living person or some other kind of entity.

Without turning to look at her, Martin began to speak. 'There's something I've wanted to know for a while,' he said, ice-cold. 'Sue, I think there's someone else. Are you seeing someone else?'

The randomness of this question shook her inside out and she laughed loudly. 'Excuse me?'

'You heard me.'

She laughed again. She couldn't help it. She wanted to throw her hands up in the air and say she wished there was someone else. That someone else would make this whole matter so much easier. That she was even dreaming about someone else, so vividly she had felt hands all over her body. She wondered if this was what he meant, if somehow he was sensing it.

'You were calling someone's name in your sleep last night.' He spoke quietly.

Her eyes widened as she stared at him in disbelief. She shook herself. She didn't understand but realised she might give him the wrong impression with her shocked behaviour.

'There is someone, isn't there?'

'No, Martin, of course there isn't. It must have been a dream.'

He shook his head, hard, from side to side. 'The way you said his name, like you were being kissed and held. You were all breathless and lovely and I almost grabbed you but then you said his name.'

She breathed. 'It was definitely a dream. There isn't another man in my life. No one I'm interested in, even. Nothing.'

Martin's eyes flicked away from her gaze, then down to the floor.

'What was it?' she said.

'What do you mean?' He looked genuinely confused.

'The name?' she said.

The confusion danced on his face, etching itself further into his features. 'You really don't know?'

She shook her head.

'You called out Jules, over and over.'

She gasped and put a hand to her mouth.

had been diff

12

Jules. Of course. He had been on her mind and this had slipped until he came out whispered from her lips. She had to stifle laughter at the misunderstanding. If only Martin knew just how over it was with Jules, exactly how unattainable her former lover was.

Not that she hadn't loved Jules at the time. More than she loved Martin? She wasn't sure about that. It had been different, she could say that. It had been beautiful in a way love can only be when you're young. Later it's just too measured and cautious, no matter how well it lasts. A precious creature, he had called her, with her hair down to her waist and willowy figure. But he'd been beautiful too; the archetypal tall, dark and handsome.

The way she had felt about Jules had consumed her. She had been unable to think about another thing for months. It was the first year at university and she had fallen behind in her studies thanks to days and nights and more days spent in his bed, kissing, making love, eating nothing but chocolate, and drinking tea and red wine. Lectures just didn't have the same allure as days spent this way. She was drunk on his love, completely taken over.

'Of course there isn't anyone else. I can't believe you can even ask that. I had a weird dream, that's all,' she told Martin. Thinking about it, she had to sit down to compose herself. In a way, she thought, there had always been someone else and Martin was absolutely right to be suspicious. It wasn't anything like the conclusions he was drawing, that was all. Jules had stayed with her, though, the promise of what they could have been, what they might have had together. The back of her mind had always been haunted by the thought of something unfulfilled that could have meant a different life. Better? She was a realist and knew it might have mapped out totally differently to her dream of it. Her thoughts and feelings about what could have been were based on promises written on sugared paper, the kind that melts away to nothing in your mouth. They might have lived happily ever after, that was true. They might also have grown to hate each other and act in ways that tore them both apart.

She thought about Jules now. His strong, gentle hands and brown eyes. She had never felt such tenderness for another human being, before or since. What she had with Martin was different; even when they were first together it did not compare. It was enough for a marriage, she'd decided, being a practical kind of person. Really, the only surprise to her now she thought about it was that she didn't wail *Jules* in her sleep every night. She did wonder why it was happening now, here in the bothy. And hope crept in the back door, with a feeling about Jules, that he had somehow found a way to come to her at last, after all these years. She had expected this at first, for him to wake her in the night by sheer strength of will, returning to her side against all the odds. She had seen people in the street and thought that they were Jules. She'd even walked up to men, more than once, and tapped them on the shoulder she was so convinced, her heart beating so fast she thought it might escape her chest, shatter her breastbone and have a life of its own. And then the letdown, the bitter sting that it wasn't him and he was still gone.

It had taken Susie a long time to accept that her Jules had gone for ever. She was the only person allowed to call him that: Jules. To the rest of the world he was Julian, and he was very strict about that. But he said he liked the way Susie said Jules, the way her voice lifted towards the end of the word and sucked it up. He said it made the name special because it was only her who used it, that it made him a different person with her from the one he was for the rest of the world; a better person. He treated her like she was a precious thing; a jewel to be treasured, a delicate piece of porcelain to be handled with care. It was the opposite of Martin's down-to-earth, practical kind of loving. She used to think this marked difference was why she had gone for Martin. He could never remind her of Jules and her shattered heart.

It had been years since Susie had really thought about those moments, properly brought them to mind. It surprised her, the intensity of what she felt now that she did. As she looked up at Martin, she was crying.

'Shit. There is someone else, isn't there?' he said. He

folded his arms across his chest and looked severe. He looked like one wrong word would send him storming out of the room.

She stared back at him, a slight nausea coming along with the intensity of the feelings she was having. 'It really isn't like that.'

'Then what is it like?'

She almost told Martin to shove it all. The way he was standing, the self-righteousness. She didn't want to explain Jules to him. She wasn't sure why she felt this way, but she did. She knew, though, that this was another of those marriage-breaking moments and that she had to tell him the story. 'It was Jules who got me pregnant,' she said. She saw relief spread over his face as he realised this was a man from her deep past; they had talked about the abortion before, how it had made her feel ill for months and she felt she had never completely left it in the past. She just hadn't told him the other details.

Then he looked confused, his face screwing up as he thought about it. 'You still dream about him?'

'Yes,' she told him. 'No. I don't know. I don't remember dreaming about him but what happened with Jules was complicated.'

Martin raised an eyebrow, giving her a look that said to carry on.

'Jules died, Martin.'

Her husband was struck silent for a moment. It was strange the way surprise pulled his face long. It wasn't an emotion she was used to seeing him wear. 'Oh my God,' he said. 'Jesus. Why did you never tell me this before?'

Susie shrugged. She was still crying silently, salty trails running down her cheeks.

It had been the coldest morning of her life. They'd been to a restaurant the night before; Valentine's Day. She'd thought it was a bit of a waste of money at the time but, in hindsight, she was glad she'd relented. It had been an almost perfect evening. Italian food, red wine, putting the world to rights the way you do a few glasses in. They'd come back to his college room and made love viciously, like they meant it, and fallen asleep wrapped up in one another. She told Martin about what happened but missed some of these intimate details. She was careful not to let on how different love had been back then. She made sure not to make a comparison of any kind.

'I woke up feeling chilled,' she said. 'I moved closer

to Jules, hoping to get warm, and that was when I realised.' She paused to swallow a sob. 'It was Jules who was making me cold. Stone-cold.'

Martin stared into her eyes as he listened. His expression said it all: do I know anything about this woman? There were few surprises this far into a marriage and, considering, he was taking it pretty well.

'I don't know what noises I was making but they brought me help. Before I knew it there was someone knocking so hard I thought they might break down the door. It took all I had in me to get up and answer it.'

She was rocking now, forward and back as she told the story and let herself cry. It was years since she'd thought about any of this but as she told the story out loud everything felt incredibly raw.

'His name was John,' she said, through her grief.

Martin looked confused. 'But you said Jules.' He slipped a fatherly arm around her.

'No, I mean the boy at the door. His next-door neighbour. His name was John. I found that out later. I don't think he ever got over finding us there.'

Martin pulled her close and then squeezed. She pulled away, making an excuse about needing some tissues.

'When did you find out you were pregnant?' he asked her.

'Two weeks after he died. I was terrified. Part of me couldn't countenance doing anything except having the baby but I was in such a state. In the end, my mum took over and "dealt" with it. She wasn't having my life ruined by this, she told me.' Susie laughed then, lightly, ironically. In many ways she felt this moment was exactly when her life went wrong. If she had kept the baby she would have always had something of Jules, to have and to hold, to love and to cherish, even if she couldn't have him. Looking back, she felt that falling pregnant could have been fate, trying to keep Jules in this world. With the help of her mother, though, she had spat in the face of fate. Well, fate didn't let you get away with things like that. It always hit back, violently and in ways you couldn't imagine. Of that much she was completely sure.

Arms wrapped her up then, pulling her close again. She felt Martin's body heat as he curled around her. She surrendered to it this time and tried not to panic. 'I can't believe you've been carrying that around with you all this time and you've only just told me,' he said. He squeezed her tight then, too tight. The way he was holding her was oppressive. She was scared, suddenly, that his intentions were not good towards her. She could hardly breathe. 'What's wrong?' he said. He looked more annoyed than concerned.

'I don't know.' She tried to breathe. 'It's this place. I don't feel like we're alone. It feels like something's haunting us.'

Martin laughed, a sound of genuine amusement. 'Haunted!' he said. 'You have a very vivid imagination, Sue.'

He acted like he knew everything in the world, but he didn't know everything. He didn't know why Susie had been moaning in her sleep, what had made her call out that name after all these years. He knew nothing about that and nothing about this bothy. He had all his superior ways but his mind was closed to anything he couldn't explain with logic and that was a weakness, not a strength the way he saw it. She wondered again if her Jules had come to find her after all this time. She didn't dare hope it could really be him but she found she wanted it to be. She desired it. Feelings this strong must be powerful too. She'd bet they could make anything happen.

She managed a weak smile. 'You're right,' she said.

'I'm being silly. I guess all this stuff to do with Jules has freaked me out a bit. I wonder why I was calling for him last night, of all nights.'

Martin shrugged. He looked at her as if he'd like to peel back her head and examine the thoughts there for himself. She could tell he knew there was something not quite right about the words that had just come from her mouth but he didn't know what.

There was a banging coming from the corner of the hut, by the place where they kept their belongings in a large, unruly pile. Susie had been lying down for several hours, recovering from conjuring up Julian. She had just about begun to breathe normally again. She sat up now, and looked across the room. It was only about lunchtime but the light wasn't good outside, and the main glow in the hut was coming from the orange of the fire. She was completely drained; her legs and arms ached from walking and from the shock. She found it hard to believe she still felt it all that deeply. She couldn't imagine being this way years after Martin had died. Admittedly, they'd been through more of the average, real-life issues together, lived their lives in the realms of the concrete. It wasn't fair to compare it with a magical few months when she had first tasted freedom, first tasted sex. She watched now as Martin rooted through their belongings. She hardly had the energy to question it, but his actions didn't look right.

'What's wrong?' she asked him. Her voice was weak and low.

'I can't find the gas stove or the mobile phones.' He didn't look up from his task.

'The stove's out of fuel so what's the point? The phones are there. I had them, like, an hour ago,' she told him.

'Well, they're not here now. Are you sure you put them back?' He turned towards her.

'Certain.'

'Hmm. Well, you must be mistaken about it,' he said.

She tried not to feel irritated. He was obviously stressed about not being able to find these particular items and it wasn't personal. She realised she said this to herself a lot in Martin's company. *It's not personal.* At some point it surely was. She stood up and walked over to the bags. 'The gas stove's run out and I checked the phones for a signal just a couple of hours ago. I'm not quite sure what you're trying to achieve, Martin.'

He turned his head up towards her, his face held in a tight, angry ball. 'What I'm trying to achieve is to locate our stuff. Hopefully, we'll be on the move soon, and I want to make sure we have everything.'

'Where else could it be?' Susie couldn't help letting the amusement out in her voice.

'You tell me,' he said. He pulled his arm out from her rucksack and flung the bag down on to the floor in a temper.

'Jesus, Martin.' She pushed past him to where the bags were leaning against the wall. She went into the pocket where she'd put the mobile phones but there was no sign of them. She was confused; she could have sworn she'd put them back in the exact place where she'd found them. She dug inside the rucksack, searching and probing. All the time Martin watched, his hands folded across his chest and a mean, knowing look on his face. There was no sign of the phones inside the rucksack. She searched Martin's bag: still nothing. She rummaged through the pile of cooking equipment next to the bags and could see he was right about the stove not being there. 'This doesn't make any sense,' she said, retracing her steps and trying again in the front pocket of her own rucksack. 'I put them back in there!' She gestured at the outside pocket in disbelief.

'I know. It doesn't make any sense at all.' Martin was standing still, looming over her, staring at her like she had just spat in his face.

'Well, it's not me,' she said. 'Honestly, I switched them on, well, yours on; mine was out of charge and wouldn't come on at all. I checked if there was a signal and there wasn't so I switched it off again and I put them both back. I can't have made a mistake.' She gestured at the small space around them. 'There's nowhere to lose anything,' she said. 'And I haven't been out of the hut.'

'God knows what you've done with them.'

She wanted to argue, say that she'd done nothing with their belongings, that he must have moved them. That somehow they must be missing them in their search. But Martin's mood had darkened. His brow contracted over his face, putting his features into shadow. She knew this was not a good time to row with him and so she stopped short of saying anything. She continued to rifle through their things, looking for any of the missing items, but nothing. She tried to remember, step by step, move by move, what she'd done when she'd finished with the phones. She could clearly see a picture in her head of putting them back into the front pocket of her bag. Was that today? Was there any chance she was remembering that from another day?

It was looking around the rest of the hut that confused her, though. There was nowhere for anything to be lost. It wasn't a big space and it wasn't cluttered. They had piled up the items they'd brought with them in that corner and nowhere else. Neither of them had been into the other room, the one without the lit fire, because it was just too cold and, anyway, it was flat empty when she'd checked there. The bothy wasn't a place that had nooks and crannies. Every wall and piece of floor in the building was clear, empty space.

It made no sense. Martin was looking for the phones so he surely hadn't moved them elsewhere. He would remember. Martin had his faults and Susie could write a thesis on what they were and how they affected her life. Lack of organisation was not one of them, though. He didn't forget things. He didn't move them without noting it. If Martin had moved them then it was deliberate, some game so that he could lose his temper, bang things around and unsettle her. But he wouldn't want to do that, would he? The problem was that the more she thought about it, the more she tried to work out how the phones or stove could have ended up elsewhere, the less it seemed possible.

A sudden flash of inspiration and she was over at the sleeping bags. She pulled them up, shaking them out over the bothy floor. A massive spider fell out of one, she wasn't sure which and didn't want to think too deeply about it. But there were no phones, no stove. The tiny gas cooker's absence made even less sense. They hadn't used it since yesterday, when it had run out of gas in the middle of boiling water for tea. She remembered that clearly. Martin banging it against the wall, trying to eke out any last bit of fuel. Him throwing it hard at the rucksacks so that it bounced off and made a clattering sound before falling still on the floor. She hadn't moved it since and Martin said he hadn't either. She was at a loss.

There are more things in heaven and earth, Horatio, she thought, *than are dreamt of in your philosophy*. Despite Martin's lack of faith, she did know the whole quote, and she knew the context. She liked paraphrasing, that was all. She looked around the room and wondered what was in here with them. There was something; she was certain there was. Not a person, like she had first thought, but something much less easy to deal with or understand. She touched the wall and shivered. She whispered as quietly as she could, 'Jules?'

There was no reply from the wall. Martin had turned. 'Did you say something?' he said.

'No,' she said, 'just muttering to myself.'

Martin caught her gaze and held it, and she wondered if he had heard what she had said all along.

13

One of the hardest things about Jules dying, apart from losing him, had been the aftermath of his death. Susie had not lost someone close to her before. Both her parents and even the three of her grandparents she'd known, back then, were all healthy and looked like making ripe old ages. So Julian's funeral was the first she had ever attended. She had no idea what it would be like or how to behave at this kind of event. What she wanted to do was throw herself into the ground with the coffin and lie there with it, waiting for the earth to close up over her. She'd had suicidal thoughts like this a great deal at the time although, looking back, she wondered if she'd been dramatising everything inside her head. It was hard to remember it all clearly and really know.

On the day of the funeral she'd referred to him as Julian, rather than Jules. It brought her some removal from what was going on. She had sat quietly at the back of the church through the whole ceremony. His parents had asked for her opinions on what they should do, what music to play, cremation or burial, that kind of thing. She didn't have a clue and thought it was their call anyway. They had never imagined they would have to make decisions like this for their son, she could see that in their faces. Susie and Jules certainly hadn't wasted any of their time together discussing funeral songs or flowers, any of that angsty stuff some teenagers did. She was glad they hadn't; it was good to be able to say she didn't know and for it to be true. Choosing anything felt too hard. Worse, it felt like admitting he had died, accepting it, and she wasn't ready to do that.

The medical facts were that Julian had had an aneurism. This meant there was a blood vessel in his head which had burst. The doctors said it had been waiting for him there most of his life, a time bomb set to go off at any moment. It could have been much sooner; it could have stayed intact until he died much later of old age. It was impossible to know. If they had found it, they could have operated or tried to treat it but there would have been no guarantees. She told people these facts, recited them like they meant something. Those around her always had the same type of response: perhaps it was better this way, he had never known, he was able to live his life. He hadn't spent his last days in hospital or worrying about surgery. But Susie struggled to see what could be better about anything. The fact was that he was gone, and nothing anyone could say would do anything about that. She acted up; was rude to people who asked stupid questions like how she was. She'd never been a moody teenager but now she was making up for it. She remembered the pale face of her father, desperate to say the right thing, but she wouldn't let him. Every little nuance of what he said she'd jumped on and bitten. She regretted that now, but she couldn't take it back.

The funeral had felt like a dream. Everyone there, all in black, sitting in a chapel at the graveyard. They'd gone for a burial in the end, in the same plot as his grandfather, who'd died when Julian was still a child. She couldn't help but think about the details of the disposal. Her nightmare scenario was seeing his grand-dad's coffin down inside the grave before they put Julian with him or, worse, bones or a dead body. She couldn't bear that. They would have to remove the body that was already there first, her mother had told her when she'd asked. Where would they put it? What kind of state would it be in now? It would stink, she guessed, and the coffin might be ruined by damp and fall apart, spilling its contents. These horrifying pictures haunted her everyday thoughts although, strangely for Susie, she didn't dream about them. It seemed she was torturing herself enough during the day.

The funeral wasn't hard. She'd sat there at the back of the chapel between her mother and father. She hadn't slept for days and the world was misty around her. Her dad put a gentle hand on her elbow but she looked up at him, confused, and he moved away. The vicar stood at the front of the room and spoke about Julian. What a light had gone out, what a future had been stalled, how it must be a grand plan we could never understand. They played hymns and slow music. None of it was anything to do with her, to do with her Jules. She could not believe that the box at the front of the room contained his body. His remains, they had kept saying at the funeral house. But she had seen the body on the day he died and nothing of him remained there, she could guarantee it.

By the grave, she was offered soil to throw on to his coffin but she wouldn't do it. She wouldn't have a part in burying him, be implicit to that task, because it would have knocked a whole layer off her ability to deny. This way, she could pass this day off as one of her more vivid dreams, and watch for the door to open, for Jules to walk in and hold her in his arms again. She could close her eyes and will him to return. She willed it hard, screwing up her face and eyes, chanting like a mantra that it was all a dream, but nothing brought him back.

Weeks later, she would wake from the stupor of lack of sleep and something odd the doctor had prescribed for her and realise that she had missed it all and feel regretful. She had understood, then, what funerals were for. How throwing that soil into the ground and hearing it bounce against the wood was part of the process of letting go. She would eventually talk to counsellors about closure and moving on. She had thought she had managed that, in the end.

Now, though, she looked around the bothy and wondered. She thought she could feel him here, her Jules, in a way that she hadn't anywhere since the night before he died. She had listened for him everywhere, kept a vigil for so long; every time she closed her eyes to go to sleep she had made a wish that she would wake up to find him there. And now, so many years after she had given up and moved on with her life, she could feel him again. She was almost sure he had come back to claim her. Hiding the phones would be just his style. He was always very playful, and he liked to tease.

The opposite of Martin, she thought. She looked right around the room and closed her eyes. She willed for him to come again for the first time in years.

The day was going pretty slowly. In the afternoon, Susie's hunger came back with a vengeance, and she was bent double with pain. Nausea hit her in waves and she thought she might throw up, which seemed a strange way for her body to deal with not having food. Nature has some mysterious habits. As the day passed, her ideas about Jules coming to find her at the bothy began to feel ridiculous. Why would he come here of all places, and now of all times? If he was going to come and rescue her from this life he had left her to, surely it would have been before now, on her wedding night, before her honeymoon. Before 'the weekend'. If Jules could come for her, he would have saved her from all of that.

Susie wondered how long Martin had felt suspicious about another man. Saying something about it had seemed to get it off his chest. He cheerfully collected more peat for drying, whistling as he brought it in. He didn't comment about things he might have mentioned in the past. He didn't even go on about the phones being missing, although she knew for sure that this must bug him. She wondered where he had buried it all. She knew about burying the way you felt about something, how it made you feel. She was the expert on this kind of burial.

As the day progressed, she tried to think of something to do. Even walking didn't appeal. She didn't want to leave the hut. Whatever was there, it felt more real by the minute but it wasn't something she was afraid of any more. The fire stayed warm and they took turns to pile on peat to keep it burning. Towards the end of the afternoon, as the light started fading, Martin fetched a last lot of water and they settled for the night with mugs of tea. 'At this rate we'll have to stop using the peat,' Martin said. 'We're taking too much.' He didn't sound too committed to the idea, though. Susie couldn't imagine he would insist on it. That would be a bad thing to do; the fire was the only thing they had in this disaster. That, each other and whatever else was staying here with them. It struck her now that she wasn't that bothered if the river was likely to be passable or not tomorrow. Whatever drove her before was gone. She was happy in the bothy now with her lover, with Jules, she dared to think. It could be Jules. She shook herself then and sat upright. This was like being surrounded by poisonous gas and slowly surrendering. She needed to remember that it was important to leave here, that it mattered if they could get across the river. She breathed deeply. She felt like she'd had a close escape. She was wrong not to be scared; it was all part of the power of this insinuating presence.

The day faded outside and the room turned orange. Susie settled down in her sleeping bag, as close to the fire as she thought safe. She had hardly talked to Martin. She lay and watched him as he paced and whittled away at a stick he'd found. He didn't seem to be making anything with it, just cutting at it with that horrible knife. She suspected the action of cutting the wood was calming for him, like when she had stomped through the bog, but it was unnerving to watch. His movements got harder, faster, began to look frantic. She was concerned he might chop through a finger or start hacking into flesh. She thought about starting up a conversation then, talking to him about something, anything. But she couldn't think of a thing to say that they hadn't discussed a million times before. She was at a loss to explain how they ever found things to talk about these days, after all these years together, when she really thought about it. But then, she hadn't exactly talked lots with Jules when they had been a couple. Whatever it was they had conjured up between them had been beyond words.

Her relationship with Martin wasn't, though, so she made an effort. 'Do you believe in the supernatural at all, Martin? Anything unexplained, or do you think science has all the answers?' It wasn't a question she'd asked him before but it was close enough to old territory for her to have a fair idea what the answer would be.

'I think it's all claptrap. The lot of it.' He stopped whittling at the stick. 'Don't get me wrong, I don't think science has all the answers at all, not yet, but I think it's the right direction. I don't believe in magic or the bogeyman.'

She looked at the ceiling and thought about how to frame what she'd say next. There was no good way to argue against Martin. He could twist anything and make her look stupid so she might as well just say what she thought. 'I don't think that makes sense,' she said. 'Not entirely. I'm not saying I believe in any of the myths and legends that you hear about, vampires and ghosts, that kind of nonsense. But that this is all there is, solids, liquids and gases, the things we can see and touch. It seems small-minded to imagine the human experience can see and feel everything. What I mean is, there has to be more.'

Martin shrugged. He blew on the wood and dropped it on the floor next to him, kicking it into the corner and making a banging that jarred at Susie's nerves. He kept hold of the nasty hunting knife as if he hadn't finished with it yet. 'Maybe there doesn't. Maybe reality is just . . . reality.'

The wind outside was kicking up a storm and Susie could hear it battering the window in its frame. It sounded like nature itself was protesting at what Martin was saying. Nature or something even deeper than that. Wrapped in her sleeping bag lying close to the fire, Susie felt a cold flush sweep her body. A draught in the hut blew on the fire and made the flames leap. She closed her eyes. She could feel Martin in the hut but she could feel another presence. Someone else. Something else.

She sat up and opened her eyes wide. 'Did you do something then? Sit across the fire or something?'

Martin looked at her as if she were crazy.

She shuddered. 'The room went cold, just for a moment.'

Martin was smiling and shaking his head. 'A bit of talk about ghosts and you're suddenly seeing them,' he said, dismissively. 'You've got such a vivid imagination, Sue. You should have done something creative instead of social work.'

Susie tried to smile but she was riled about what he'd said. He had it all wrong. How could he be so dense? Could he not feel anything here? She knew he had a thick skin about anything he didn't want to know about but the way he closed his mind so tight shut was ridiculous. It was fear, she decided. People like Martin, who wanted to believe in only what was solid and in front of them, were scared of everything else. They accused religious and spiritual types of looking for a safety blanket because they were scared of dying, but they were just projecting. They were the kind of people who found oblivion preferable to the idea that there are infinite possibilities.

She watched the fire crackle and die. Martin came over to her, placing his sleeping bag near to hers. He lay down and climbed in, moving closer. She didn't really want to sleep right next to him tonight. For some reason, it felt like being unfaithful. She knew it was ridiculous; Jules died years ago and she was married to Martin. It was what she felt, though. Martin leaned in to kiss her and she let him, but she pulled away quickly, feigning a yawn and turning her back on him. She didn't want the kiss to lead anywhere. The hunting knife glinted at her from the floor beside Martin, where he'd placed it before climbing into his sleeping bag, way too close for comfort. She told herself she needn't worry; Martin was her husband and he loved her. What happened on 'the weekend' was an aberration, not typical of their relationship, not really.

'When did you start thinking I was seeing someone else?' she said, coldly. Part of her wanted to cause a row and make distance between them so that she didn't have to pretend, to kiss or make love. The other part knew that she was playing a dangerous game.

'When you said Jules in your sleep.' She could hear the smile on his words and tell it wasn't a good-humoured one, somehow. She wondered how that worked.

'Hmm. It seemed more deep-felt than that, like you'd been thinking it for a while.'

'You're good with people, Sue, but you don't know everything. I was concerned because you were literally moaning a man's name in your sleep. We talked about it, you explained, we're all fine. Okay?' The tone in his voice invited no questioning. Susie wanted to argue, but the way he had spoken stopped her and she resented it.

'I don't know why he came into my head. Why I was dreaming about him or whatever,' Susie said. She was trying to be reassuring but her voice was all wrong, too stressed and uncomfortable.

Martin snorted. 'Whatever. It must be this place or something. When I came with my parents they did nothing but argue and I'm sure they never did before. It was here that the rot set in.'

Susie sat up in her sleeping bag and stared at her husband. A massive shiver passed through her. The same thing had happened to his parents when they came here and now even Martin was making concessions to the bothy being somehow to blame, despite all of his doubting ways about these things. She couldn't see him clearly in the light of the dying embers and was not sure for a moment that it was really him. Martin would never suggest anything as irrational as he just had, blaming the bothy for the problems in his parents' marriage. But it made sense, the fact he'd wanted so badly to come back here, as if he'd been compelled to. Whatever evil was at work here had taken Martin, too. 'Martin?' She breathed his name. She wasn't sure what she expected in return.

And then he was on top of her, grabbing her wrists and pinning her to the floor. The look on his face was alien to her, not like the husband she knew at all.

'Stop it, Martin. You're frightening me.'

He grinned manically, and brought his face close to hers, their noses touching but not in any tender or affectionate way. 'You know, if a person wanted to kill someone, this would be a good place to bring them. No one to hear the screams. Buried in that bog they'd never find you. Not in a million years.'

Susie struggled and squirmed underneath him, trying to get free, but he was far too strong.

'Martin?' she said, pleading with her eyes. She remembered the knife he had, the big, sharp, serious blade that he had placed the other side of his sleeping bag.

He held her there with that crazy look in his eyes for a few more moments. Then he let go and rolled on to his back, laughing.

'That wasn't bloody funny, Martin.'

He stopped laughing. 'Oh, stop being a baby, Sue. You wanted to be scared.'

'What, by a ghost story? I never even said that. And I definitely didn't want to be scared for my life.'

He brought his hands to her neck and wrapped them around it. 'All I'm trying to make you see is that real things are more frightening than the stuff in your head. Like if I squeeze now. Squeeze and squeeze and, pop, you're gone.' He mimed this action but didn't apply any pressure.

'Stop it, Martin.' She wriggled free from underneath him, and sat up.

'Oh, honestly, as if I'd ever hurt you, Sue.' He rolled over, ready to sleep. Of course he wouldn't hurt her. She knew that, right? She lay down again. But, as he reached his arms around to hold her again, she couldn't settle at all. His arm and hand seemed to burn into her side. She thought about 'the weekend' again, the bits she usually pushed so far to the back of her mind they were almost forgotten, faded, like dreams. But she couldn't dismiss them so easily now because what he'd just done had reminded her so strongly. How could he think any of this was funny? He had pinned her down then. He had wrapped his hands around her throat and squeezed too, for so long that her sight had blanked out in a neat half a line down the middle and half of the world totally blacked out. She remembered she had felt strangely calm as she heard his voice, urging her to die. But he had stopped short, and she hadn't died. He had hardly spoken for the next three days and, although he didn't apologise, she knew he was sorry. She knew in her heart he would never hurt her. She wouldn't have stayed with him if she'd have thought there'd been any serious intent and she'd made a promise she'd leave if he was ever violent towards her again. She was determined she would keep that promise.

Soon, Martin was snoring. His hands were wrapped around her chest but she didn't like the sense of them there. It felt as if they were stopping her breathing. She pushed them off and on to her waist, moving away from him a little but not so much that she would get cold. The last embers of the fire had died in the hearth. She thought about what it might feel like if she woke with Martin cold next to her in the morning. If this situation continued much longer she might find out as they slowly starved or died of the cold when they got too tired to get peat. She couldn't feel anything about that; she put it down to not taking the scenario very seriously. Lightning in the same place twice and all that.

A silence came over the room, along with the pitch-black. She could hear the slight whistle of the wind outside the hut but that was all. Martin had stopped snoring and, for a moment, she was concerned her daydreams had come true. She had to place a hand across his mouth to check that he was breathing. He rolled on to his back, then, and the snoring began again with a vengeance.

She closed her eyes but everything felt wrong. She opened them again. Not being able to see a difference between her eyes being opened and closed was a strange sensation, something city dwellers aren't used to. She thought about how she could tell whether her eyes were open. Maybe she got it wrong some of the time, or had it totally the wrong way around. She lifted her fingers to feel her closed eyelids, to check.

There was a noise from the corner of the hut, the sound of objects resettling. She started, and then she was sure that her eyes were wide open. She couldn't see but she could feel something. That presence again. She wondered if it would come to her, touch or kiss her, pin her down and squeeze the air out of her. She wondered what it wanted. It stayed where it was, though, rattling around near their possessions. Perhaps it was having a go at finding the phones or putting them back exactly where they should be for the next day. That would be Jules's style all over.

She reminded herself that Julian was dead. She had held him, cold in her arms. She had seen him buried in that Surrey churchyard. He couldn't be here in the bothy. Even if you believed in ghosts and fairies, that wouldn't make sense. Why on earth would he come to find her here? Except that she could definitely feel something and whatever it was reminded her of Jules. Why had he come back so vividly all of a sudden? The feelings were so raw, as if it had all happened yesterday. It was too much of a coincidence to ignore when she really thought about it.

Susie tried to close her eyes and go to sleep but she couldn't. All she could think about was being touched so tenderly, here in the bothy, and how different everything had been with Jules. She began to cry without making any sound, water leaking from her eyes and over her face.

14

The next morning, Susie got up and dressed, then went for a walk. She didn't go down to the river; it didn't even cross her mind. She was no longer thinking of escape from the cottage. She felt a sense of surrender, like she'd been overcome by those gases, and it was frightening but she had no fight left in her. She tried to remember how many days they'd been trapped but found she couldn't. She thought it was about a week but when she tried to count the days she got stuck. Her life before the bothy felt misty, like a distant dream. It was as if the place itself had grown right through her like a creeping plant, taking over her body. She felt as if she'd been possessed. Hunger had set in like a disease and all she could think about was food. Not fancy food; not roasts or steaks or big chunks of cake. Any food. Plain white bread with no butter. An apple. She stared at the land around her as she walked, wondering if there was anything growing nearby that could feed them. It wasn't a great time of year for fruit or berries, but maybe there were plants they could eat, some kind of wild grasses or salad leaves. Maybe the last remnants of fruit too. It didn't matter if it was soft or old. She was tempted even by the leaves on the few trees around about. Anything at all to fill her stomach, even if her body was unable to digest it.

She walked, hoping the feeling would abate. It was strange that, despite the burning hunger, she wasn't driven to try to get back to civilisation. She explored the land around the crofter's hut and the only call she felt was one summoning her back inside. It was a strange, crawling sensation. Something outside of nature was attached to the bothy, of that she was sure, and her reluctance to leave was connected with it but she didn't know how. In her most optimistic moments she allowed herself to believe it was her Jules, come back to her. There were other moments, though, ones of creeping doubt that sent ice right through her. Despite this, she was beginning to feel at home in the bothy and was enjoying the rhythms of living there: sleep, walk, sit in front of the fire. She was getting more sleep and deeper than she had in years and she felt good for that at least. People should do this kind of thing more often, she thought. Get themselves trapped in huts in the middle of nowhere, half starving. Like a forced fasting time. Going without food brought you closer to your spiritual side. This was what had brought the night-time visitor who kissed like Jules.

Thinking about those kisses and that touch, a thrill shot through her body. She thought of Jules, let herself believe that what she'd experienced was her lover come to claim her. It didn't last long, this delusion. She remembered the facts. Julian was dead and gone and if he could have come back and found her he would have done it years ago. She desperately wanted to believe that her young lover had found her but she wasn't so disconnected from reality that she could. She stood looking over the bogland and realised that. She would have sold her soul to make it different.

On the way back to the hut, she picked up the saucepan and took it to the river to fill. They had run out of milk now but needed to keep drinking. The river water was safe to drink as it was, so close to the source, but it didn't look appetising: it was slightly discoloured and muddy looking even in this pure part of the world. Boiling it and making tea was her preference, although Martin had drunk some cold. She headed back to the bothy.

Martin was emerging from the hut, stretching and yawning as he came out of the door. He smiled at her and walked off without talking, on his way to the toilet or just to get peat or perhaps both. She watched the way he walked, his long legs so sure and capable. He was capable, she realised then, and very healthy looking, vigorous. She wondered if that was one of the main things that had attracted her to him. Jules had been darkly moody to look at, with shadows around the eyes. In hindsight he was the kind of man she could imagine Hemingway describing as 'marked for death'. A romantic choice, but not very practical.

She shook her head. She needed to stop thinking about Julian. She called him that now, in her mind, Julian, to try to remove the connection she had been feeling with him. It was the only way, to stop thinking about him. It was how she had dealt with things before.

It was how she worked her life out and coped with losing him. She had blanked Jules out so strongly that she had almost forgotten all about him until they had come here. She was good at blocking things out, had become an expert.

The hut door was swinging open like an invitation. She went in, found her sleeping bag and wrapped herself up in it. She quite fancied going to sleep and not waking up, the way Jules had. Maybe she would wake up where he was now, then they would be together. She could help herself get there. Martin's knife glinted at her from where it still lay on the floor. She shivered. Why was she thinking this way? She was tired, and lay down on the floor. It was cold in the bothy but she knew Martin would be back soon and that he would set a fire.

The door blew open, letting in a very cold breeze. She wondered how that had happened; she could have sworn she'd closed it firmly. She got up fast and was dizzy for a moment. She steadied herself against the wall, enjoying its firmness against her hand. The room spun. She sensed something like a whisper near her neck and did not feel alone. Then it passed, along with the dizziness, and she decided it was probably all to do with the lack of food. She walked to the door and went to close it. It was unfortunate timing and she realised too late that Martin had just made it to the threshold, seeing a flash of his exasperated face as she pulled the door shut in his face.

'Sorry,' she said, opening it again. 'It blew open.'

Martin didn't respond but pushed past her into the room a little roughly. Susie was a bit shocked at being pushed aside but she didn't say anything. He was carrying several carrier bags full of peat and busied himself moving what was dried and making new layers near the fire. Then he set to filling the grate with the older fuel that was dry and ready. Susie watched him, thinking again how capable he looked, how hardy. He turned and caught her watching. He gave her a tight smile.

It was then that Susie remembered she had fetched water and left it outside, by the wall, rather than bringing it in to heat on the fire. She went out to get it. The saucepan was exactly where she'd left it except it was empty. The heart dropped out of her as she realised she would need to make the journey to the river again. Not yet, she decided. It would have to wait. She walked back inside.

'Did you empty the water out? Or knock it over?'

Martin was stuffing dried-out mud into the fireplace and turned towards her, his attention split between what she was saying and the task. 'Eh?'

'The water. I fetched some water and it's gone.'

'Well, it wasn't me.'

Susie paused. She would normally have left it like that, but these weren't normal times. Right now her body was eating itself from within and she couldn't help but blame Martin for bringing them here, even though she was trying not to see it that way. 'Who else could it have been?' she said.

He shrugged, and moved away from the fireplace to set it alight. 'I have no idea. Maybe you're mistaken about getting the water in the first place.'

She was incredulous. How could he possibly think she could have made a mistake like that? Did he think she was stupid or had early onset Alzheimer's or what? She could feel anger boiling up from the bottom of her and taking control. She took deep cool breaths to try to stop it. 'I did fetch it,' she said. 'I can't believe the way you doubt my word the whole time, Martin.'

Martin was sitting on the floor in front of the fireplace now. He was watching the burgeoning fire as it grew and not looking in Susie's direction. The orange of the flames lit his face and made him look demonic. 'I don't know, Susie. All I know is that I didn't do anything with your water.' His Yorkshire accent ground up the words and made them resonate. Susie watched his face and felt afraid. Something about it reminded her of other times: bad times. He didn't look like her husband any more and she could hardly hold his gaze. She had thoughts she tried to quash, about Martin, about why he'd wanted to come here, to somewhere so remote. That remark he'd made, about getting away with murder. Had he meant it? Was this place doing something strange to him as well? He looked like he was thinking for a moment and then his eyes narrowed. 'You know what I think? I think you fucked up with the water.' His lips curled and the way the fire shone in his eyes he looked thoroughly evil.

A sudden fury took hold of Susie then, a feeling she wasn't used to and didn't think she could control. She wanted to scream and tear at his clothes. She gritted her teeth and clenched her fists. The warning was there in his eyes, though, and she held back. The soles of her feet buzzed with her anger and her fingers shook, but she said nothing. She wondered what all this holding in would do to her in the long term. She suspected it could make a person ill.

Day turned to night almost indeterminably. Susie found it was soon dark, and that she hadn't noticed the light changing. The days in Scotland passed quickly this time of year and the dark arrived fast. She felt like she was going into some low blood-sugar trance and nothing seemed real any more. She and Martin had hardly spoken, but just sat, both watching the fire as if it were a television. Susie felt hypnotised by its flames as they licked the air above the hearth. She thanked God for the fire. As Martin had said before, it was the only thing they had.

It had gone completely black outside the hut. Susie needed the loo, and she got up to fetch the torch. She searched the room for it, digging through her bag and then Martin's, rifling through the pile of belongings they had made. She couldn't find it anywhere.

'What's wrong?' Martin asked, looking up sleepily from where he was perched on the floor, his body propped up by the shoulders.

'I can't find the torch,' Susie told him. She was

getting increasingly flustered, pushing items around at speed and messing up the corner.

'Well, that isn't going to help,' Martin said.

Susie stopped for a moment, staying very still. That way she might not do or say something she could regret. She bit her lip, breathed deep, did all the things that were supposed to help you keep your temper. 'It isn't going to not help.' Even to her, the response sounded pathetic.

Martin was on his way over; coming to take charge, to take over and sort out what she was not able. It annoyed Susie, the conceit of it all, that he thought she was just missing something. She'd spoken to him about this before; the conclusions he seemed to draw about her. It always seemed he assumed the worst, that she had done the most stupid thing, was missing the most obvious thing. He had responded that he was just look-ing at situations in a logical way and had quoted Sherlock Holmes. *When you have eliminated the impossible, whatever remains, however improbable, must be the truth.* She wanted to slap him very hard as she thought about it now.

He reached her side and put a hand on her shoul-der. Its presence there did not feel like someone trying to comfort so much as control, standing over her and making a point. She wanted to bat it away but she resisted, leaving it there and moving aside. He came past her and dug through the bags and the pile of things. His movements got faster and faster; became frantic. She watched as he pulled and pushed and searched and finally came to the same conclusion. 'It's not there.'

'I know,' she said, bouncing down on to her sleeping bag. On the one hand she was pleased he hadn't found it. On the other, she didn't really want to go out of the hut in the dark. Even if there was no one for miles around it wasn't nice, walking into the black, not knowing what you might step on, what might be standing there waiting for you. No matter how improbable it was that there was anyone or anything that could harm her there, it was not impossible, and there was no way of knowing the truth. She pulled her coat hard around her and headed for the door.

Outside the sky was as black and uncompromising as the peat bog. Susie shivered as she headed far enough away from the hut. She hated this about being here, the lack of civilisation that meant no flushable toilets. She didn't see the need in dealing with this, ever. She tripped as she walked a short distance from the hut. She removed her trousers and crouched on the moorland. The cold hit her in waves, together with the hunger. She hoped this would all be worth it, that there would come a time when she would be able to look back on the whole experience as one that had been valuable and character forming. Right now she couldn't see it; it was just unpleasant.

She stumbled back towards the orange glow of the hut and wondered where the torch had gone. The mobile phones were next to useless out here so it didn't really matter about no longer having them, but the torch was a real loss. She couldn't see that Jules would take that. It didn't make sense as a prank the way the other things had. It would cause too many problems. She felt strongly that it was more likely Martin had hidden these things. Did he have a plan? Had he brought her here for a reason and were the disappearing things all part of that? She hugged her coat around her and tried to make sense of it. She put it down to the lack of food and stimulation, sending her a little insane.

She ducked under the lintel and inside again. Her husband couldn't be planning to hurt her. He loved her and, if he didn't, he was the kind of man who would have just told her bluntly and walked away. She was forgetting who she was married to. As she walked into the hut she saw Martin, just a flash of him in the firelight, sitting up and writing in a red notebook. It surprised her; he wasn't the type to make notes or records of things. He'd always said he would rather live them. But when she closed the door and looked a second time he was sitting staring at the fire and there was no sign of the book. Had she imagined it? She sat down too and joined his meditation. She was due back at work in a few days' time but that didn't seem real at all. How could she possibly ever go back? She had to admit that this holiday had made her disconnect from the rest of her life in a way none ever had before. The real world where she worked as a social worker was a million miles away, not just in the next-door country but another dimension. Despite being trapped in the middle of nowhere without food, she felt strangely calm. She lay on her sleeping bag and her eyes relaxed, unfocused on anything in the room. There was nothing she needed to see.

'What have you done with the torch? And the mobile phones? Do you think this is all a big joke, Sue?'

'I beg your pardon?' She pulled herself up on to her elbows, genuinely surprised.

'I know I didn't move them. So, therefore, I can only assume you did. I've searched up and down for those phones and they're not anywhere. And now this.'

She tried to work out why he was bringing this up, trying to push the blame on to her. The way he was going on about it made her wonder about him again. Was he trying to distract her attention from the fact it was him all along? Unless it wasn't him and there was an altogether stranger explanation, something that would always be missing from his deductions, dismissed in the 'impossible' category. 'On what planet do you think it makes sense for me to hide the phones or the torch or the stove?' she asked him.

'I'd forgotten about the stove.' He said it as if it proved something.

'Martin, I've been here with you and sat watching the fire. I've been out for a wee and I've been out and walked across the bog. That's about all I've done for days. That and fetched water from the river. I don't know when you think I'd have found the opportunity to move those things and you not see, or why on earth you'd think I'd do it.'

'It has to have been you. There isn't any other explanation.' Martin made it sound like it was final.

Susie sighed. 'Let's try your Sherlock Holmes logic. It wasn't you. Your wife, who you know to be an honest, sensible woman, says it wasn't her either. So it must be something else. However improbable.'

'Oh, for God's sake Susie, not this nonsense again.'

There was a silence then, broken only by the crackling of the fire. There were so many answers to what he'd said but Martin's tone had done it again: shut her up. He knew how to put a warning in his voice and it was bullying, now she thought about it, now she noticed it. The only thing she could think was how she wished she was not here with Martin. She wished she was with Jules. She really wished it. She screwed up her face with the effort of wishing it. If she could have one wish come true her entire life she wanted this one to be it. She poured her soul into wishing.

The bothy door flew open with a big gust of wind. Susie was startled; this had happened more than once now and it was unsettling. Martin tutted and stood up. He walked over and slammed the door shut, taking time to make sure it was jammed in place. 'You need to shut the door properly when you come in.'

She stared at him. She was certain she had shut it properly. She had pulled it to and heard the click. She thought about it carefully; she was absolutely sure. 'I did,' she said, quietly. She didn't want to provoke him but she couldn't help it. It was true and she was sick of being accused of things she hadn't done.

All at once the room changed. The flames in the grate flickered dangerously as Martin flung himself across the room. Then he was by her side, his hands on her shoulders, pushing down. She was on her back, landing hard on the floor and rebounding, seeing Martin staring at her from above, his face like fury. All of his features had contorted as he held them angrily and began to shout, inches from her face.

'Why the fuck are you lying about it, bitch?'

As he screamed, he splattered her face with saliva. She moved her head to the side, away from it, trying to avoid not just his spittle but his fury.

'Why!' he hissed into her face. 'Why. The. Fuck.' Even though she was scared she could hear in his voice that he sounded like a wounded animal. If he was a danger to her, it was because he was broken inside.

'I'm not lying.' Her voice was small and pathetic. His hand flew back, a fist forming above her. He shook his hand in the air as if it was all he could do to hold back from hitting her. Then he stopped. It was as if someone had grabbed him from behind as he fell backwards and away from her. Susie looked up at him. He looked upset, like he might cry, and he was shaking. She stayed lying where she was. She couldn't quite believe it was over. She felt for her face, for her neck, checking that something hadn't happened or that she'd blanked out.

She sat up, breathing hard and taken over by tremors from head to toe. She looked at Martin, who was lying very still on the floor now, moaning lightly. A thought came into her head, a name. *Jules.*

She couldn't help coming to a conclusion that she knew wasn't logical and yet, to her, on some deep level, it made sense. She thought that Julian had come and saved her from what might have happened next, stoppered Martin's anger. She could feel something in the room, that presence again. *His* presence. She refused to deny it any longer. Jules was here. He had somehow done what she had willed him to do all these years and found a way back to her and he was protecting her from Martin. Maybe that was what had brought him here at last – the need to protect her. Being at the bothy had changed Martin. Maybe it was all the bad memories from his first trip here that had done it. It struck her then that the other Martin was an act and the one who screamed in her face and pinned her down, wrapped his hands around her neck and squeezed, that was the real person. The man she was really married to was the one who talked about burying her in the bog. She shuddered.

But it was all okay because Jules had come and would make sure she was all right. She shivered as he flew through her, dancing with triumph that she had worked it out.

15

Susie arched her back as a soft hand ran down her side towards her waist. It moved oh so slowly in small circles around her belly button, it stroked her face. She moved her hips to take in more of him. She was being made love to, slowly, firmly, wonderfully, and it was delicious. It was not Martin; of that much she was sure. But every time she tried to look at her lover's face, find his eyes, that part of him blurred then disappeared. All she had were the feelings and a faceless lover. She called to the man she hoped it was, wished for it to be more than anything in the world. 'Jules,' she whispered. 'Jules, is it you?'

There was no answer except more movements of the hips, hands reaching round to take hold of her back then, in a sudden change of heart, to pin her arms. She gasped. His weight on top of her was almost overwhelming. A moment passed and she came, a powerful orgasm that shook her all over. It had been a while. Her toes curled and her fingers tingled and then she woke up.

The room was deathly cold as she came to and realised she had been dreaming. An intense and vivid dream, but a dream nonetheless. She opened her eyes and assessed the situation. She felt the rush of blood in her stomach and legs, the familiar light contractions just below her belly button. The lovemaking might not have been real but the orgasm had been. Despite the cold, her skin was flushed and rosy. Inside, though, she felt frozen. She wasn't sure why but the dream had sent her stomach churning. She turned on her side to look for Martin, watch him snoring. Even if his amazing capacity for sleep annoyed her sometimes, watching him was a morning comfort, part of the rhythm of the day. She turned and reached with one arm to hold on to his shoulder. But he wasn't there. This was so unusual it made her sit up.

Susie dressed quickly, tripping over her feet as she pulled on her jeans in a rush. She grabbed her fleece and without even putting her coat on she was out into the cold morning. Martin was there, sitting outside with his back to the hut and his head in his hands. He looked old, and lonely. It was raining on him, not hard or fast but relentless, and yet he made no effort to shelter from it.

'Hey,' she said, leaning down to him. He looked up at her, giving nothing away. 'Is something wrong?'

He shook his head from side to side as if he meant no, but then he spoke. 'You were calling for him again, for that Jules bloke.' He looked close to tears. She had never seen him so affected by anything, not even on their wedding day when he'd been unusually emotional. 'How can I compete with a dead man?' he said.

She paused and looked into the middle distance. Now she was no longer panicking, she began to feel the chill in the air and she pulled her fleece as tight as it would go around her. 'What was I, er, doing?' she asked at last, feeling slightly uncomfortable with what the response might be.

'You were calling for him, and moaning in your sleep.'

'Nothing else? I was just making noises?'

Martin nodded, a glum expression on his face. 'Just making noises about your young romantic lover who never did you no wrong before he popped his clogs.'

The way he'd worded it made her smile. She reached a hand to his back and rubbed it gently. Despite his bad behaviour the night before, empathy kicked in; it must be hard for Martin to bear. Maybe that was what had caused him to act so out of character. Jules had come back, of this she was sure now. The pinning of her arms was just his style. He liked that, to inflict just a little pain, just a little control so that it was sensually edgy but nothing too heavy and she had liked it, too. Very much. Only Jules had hit a nerve with her that way in his lovemaking and now she was certain he was here. And Martin knew too, she thought. Despite the apparent strength of his disbelief in anything outside of the norm, he did have a side that sensed things just like she did, and she could see from the state of him that he knew about this somewhere deep inside, somewhere denied.

'We should check the river,' Martin said, half-heartedly. She was surprised he mentioned it at all. Before now he had seemed happy to stay here as long as it took, in no rush at all to get out of the place and enjoying 'the adventure'. Susie didn't want to check the river today. If they did and it was passable they would leave the bothy behind and leave Jules behind, too. In a deep place a voice said, *Why would it be Jules?* But there was a part of her that didn't care, that was prepared to take the risk because what she'd had with Jules was worth it. She felt like she was being sucked in and held fast, just like she had been in the bog, but she couldn't fight it.

'We should look for berries, or grasses we can eat. Mushrooms. There must be something edible on this land. I can't believe it's completely barren,' Susie said.

Martin looked at her as if this wasn't something he'd considered. 'Possibly,' he said. 'Mushrooms or some edible berries. Food of some description.'

The mellow smile across his face melted Susie inside. She reached for him, grabbing his hand and pulling it towards her. 'I'm starving but I'm glad to be here with you. I have no idea why I'm calling out that name. It's years since I thought about him, and I don't miss him any more.' The lie came easily.

Water bubbled above the fire. Susie had been for one of her walks and was feeling refreshed but her hunger was coming back with a vengeance. The walks would have to stop unless they found a source of food, and soon. It was getting harder to put one foot in front of the other every day; she was losing strength and the weight was beginning to fall off. She would soon look willowy again, like she did when she was young, so she didn't think this was altogether a bad thing, but she also knew she would be ill soon if their situation didn't improve.

'I've been thinking,' Martin said. Neither of them had spoken for ages and the sudden sound of his voice made her start. 'You really believe you didn't move those things, don't you?'

'Never mind believe,' Susie said, 'I bloody didn't.' She narrowed her eyes as she looked at him and he stared back as if trying to work something out.

'You know what? I believe you. Which means either I'm going mad, you're going mad, or something is afoot here.'

Susie was glad to hear Martin include himself in the list of things that could be going wrong, but wondered why the sudden change of mind about it. And then she knew. It was because of what he had worked out, deep in his heart. He knew they weren't alone in the bothy, although he could never admit to believing something like that. He would have to deny it all, even to himself.

'Perhaps you were right all along,' he continued. At this point Susie wished she had her Dictaphone handy to record this historic event. Like so many of her possessions, it was back at the hotel sitting lonely in a suitcase. Martin had said she might be right, though, and that was enough to lift her day. 'Maybe there's someone nearby, camping. That man you saw could have been real. We should look.'

'But you already did look,' Susie reminded him. 'You went on a really thorough look around everywhere that first night when I saw him. And I've walked all around – there's nowhere anyone could hide.' She didn't want to send Martin chasing after something he'd never find. She knew the man she had seen was not real now, that he was something else, something more than real. 'I don't think we'll find anything now. Maybe someone was here but they went.'

Hand on chin, Martin puzzled over this for a few moments. Then he raised his head. 'How could they have gone anywhere? There's no way out, remember? If there was someone here – and you were pretty sure you'd seen someone – then he would have to still be here. Somewhere.' He stood up. 'We could look,' he added, his voice steady and very serious. 'The thing is, it was all right at first when it was just someone smoking outside the hut, but now they're taking important things.'

His level stare made Susie self-conscious. She half imagined he wasn't talking about the torch or the phones, but the lovemaking. He couldn't be, she knew, but the way he was looking at her was rather odd. In fact, it was all quite strange, really. Martin changing his mind like this, and actually saying that she might have been right all along. Martin questioning his own sanity in the same breath as hers when this was usually the one thing he was completely sure of, that Susie was a little manic and he was the steady one. His sudden doubt in himself made her all the more certain that they were being haunted, and she shivered. What if she was wrong? What if this wasn't Jules but something more sinister? It was already putting her in danger, making her reluctant to seek out the safety of the civilisation a few miles away. 'We could look,' she said, after a pause. 'And we could look for some source of food while we're at it.'

'That sounds like a good idea,' Martin said, smiling

broadly at her. 'A spot of foraging.' Susie studied his face looking for signs of cracks. It could be the hunger or the being cut off or even the idea of a rival, but something was changing in Martin.

The part of the bog nearest the hut was almost dry. It got muddier the further they strayed. Martin walked, swinging a huge stick he had found to help him on his way. He said this would ease the pressure on his knees and that this was why serious walkers used those sporty-looking poles that brought to mind skiing.

Susie looked out ahead of her as they made their way across the landscape. She really didn't see anywhere someone could hide. There were no woods immediately nearby and the flat land stretched out for miles ahead and behind them along the banks of the loch. On the other side of the loch, a densely wooded hill stretched upwards not far from the bank, but to get to their side of the lake would take more than a swimmer, especially in November weather. Martin had gathered momentum about this task and it had given him a new purpose. He walked with a spring in his step that she hadn't seen for ages.

Most of the land around them was bare and muddy:

barren looking. There was the odd little clump of bushes, mostly stripped bare of leaves by the winter, with black spiky branches poking severely into the frosty air. It was here there might be food, of a sort, if they looked. Martin had mentioned grubs since they'd left the hut but Susie wasn't so sure. She'd have to be much hungrier than she was just now to countenance that. There might be the odd bramble, though, small bullets of fruit gone hard in the frost but more or less edible under the circumstances. And mushrooms. Mushrooms grow anywhere, especially in damp places, Martin had said repeatedly since they set out. It was just a matter of which species they could find and whether they were edible or not.

A haze loomed over the loch as they walked towards it. Susie wondered what lurked in that mist. Martin walked to the edge of the water and surveyed it. 'Unless they've got a boat,' he murmured to himself. Susie watched him as he poked the ground with his stick, to what end she was unsure. He really was so capable; she could see why a woman might go for that. It just puzzled her why *this* woman had when it was the opposite of what she really longed for in someone. She had forgotten somewhere along the way that she was a romantic, needed the angst and agony of that in her life. She didn't know how to solve this problem now. Ten years into a marriage with Martin she was too far down a path to turn back, too lost.

Having satisfied himself that there couldn't be anyone camping outside, Martin turned to the plant life they could find. They toured the small clusters of bushes and heather. They had brought carrier bags with them, ones they had used to collect peat but all they had. They could take the pot and clean things in the river before cooking them anyway. Martin led the way between the small islands of life in the peat bog. He told Susie what to pick. They did find some berries, small round purple things that Susie didn't recognise but that Martin said he'd eaten before and were related to blueberries. There were mushrooms too, mostly hidden when you looked under and around the plants, and other fungi. Martin suggested that some of the slimier looking matter might be edible but, like the grubs, this was another place at which Susie drew the line. None of the mushrooms they came across were safe, Martin said. There were some that looked to Susie like the ones they sell in shops but she didn't know enough to be sure and certainly wasn't going to take a risk on it. They did collect some leaves, though, that Martin said were fine to eat and would taste like salad. She had no idea where he had got all this outward-bound knowledge from but he seemed to know what he was talking about.

Back at base, they headed down to the river with the berries and some of the leaves. Susie washed everything in the fast eddies of the stream while Martin looked on, commenting that the water flow had waned just a little and that the situation as regards getting back might change soon. The stepping stones were visible below the waterline now. Susie found her heart was beating faster. She felt something close to fear at the idea of leaving and tried to change the subject.

Back at the cottage, Martin added more fuel and prodded the fire into action. Susie used a camping knife to cut up the leaves. She looked around for the other knife, the serious, heavy-duty one, but she couldn't see it anywhere. She chewed on the berries but they were very sour. They hit her stomach with a twist of acid and made her feel a little sick. 'Probably better with a little sugar,' she told Martin. He turned, looking confused, and she pointed at the berries, passing him one so he could taste it himself. His palate must have been more sensitive to the bitterness, as he spat his out into the fire pulling a very ugly face.

Soon the fire was roaring. They sat with their backs against the wall and plates on their laps. The leaves didn't look too appetising but they tasted fine, as Martin had predicted. At first, Susie found it tempting to shovel the food down her throat as fast as it would go but found the sensation of her stomach being filled a little uncomfortable after so long. She picked at the leaves and placed them one at a time into her mouth. It was the most delicious meal she'd had for years. She felt full when she finished and the sense of satisfaction was extremely pleasant. She sat back, her face slightly flushed, and took a big mouthful of tea. She was smiling.

'Good?' Martin said, catching her mood.

'Too good to say,' she replied.

He grinned at her then, looking very self-satisfied. He looked as though he thought he had done it all himself, even though foraging had been her idea all along. She thought about mentioning this but it didn't seem very important, not in the scheme of things. She was alive and not about to starve any more. They were safe in the bothy and no one was in a rush to leave. Jules might come back again tonight, or the next night; she was sure if she was patient enough she would feel his touch again. Her real life, her job, the house she and Martin had bought together and the life they shared, were a million miles away. She couldn't imagine for a moment going back to them ever again.

16

It was about an hour after eating that Susie's belly began to rumble and burn. She wasn't sure if it was the fruit, the leaves or just her shocked and shrunken stomach on being presented with food for the first time in days. A deep nausea set in soon afterwards and she knew she was going to be sick. When it became impossible to hold out any longer, she ran out of the bothy and as far away from its walls as she could manage. She was too busy vomiting at first even to think about the consequences, throwing up the contents of her poor, starved stomach. She was dry-heaving for a while before the nausea abated. She wiped her mouth and headed back to the hut, suddenly concerned. What if Martin had made a mistake with one of the foods and picked something poisonous? They could die. What if he'd done it on purpose? They'd never find her buried in the peat. She tried not to think about the things he'd said when he'd pinned her down and made that threat.

Back inside, Martin was looking pretty green too. She didn't wish him ill but it did alleviate her worries a little to see that he was suffering as well. Of course, it could all be an act. Again, she dismissed these frightening thoughts. He was prodding at the fire and she suspected this was a good distraction for him. She didn't feel sick now; better out than in, as they say. She didn't think she would throw up again. Martin sat down and put his head in his hands. Her thoughts towards him were venomous. He always thought he knew enough to make decisions and most of the time she understood he didn't, but she had trusted him on this and it had turned life and death. She made a note not to accept Martin's all-knowing on anything of any importance again. She watched him pretending to tend the fire; and if she could have made a bullet fly from her eyes into the back of his head, she would have.

'I threw up,' she told him. Her voice sounded flat and lacked emotion; she wasn't sure why because she was certainly feeling it inside.

'I wouldn't worry about it. It's probably just your stomach reacting because it had been starved for so long. It's extremely common.'

Susie wanted to shout then about what he actually knew about it. How many times had he been out there foraging for wild food before without a book or an expert or the internet to guide him in the right direction? She took deep breaths and tried not to let her temper rise. Her throat was dry from the vomiting, scraped and raw. Her mouth felt dirty and spoiled and she didn't even want to think what her breath must be like. It had been a few days since she had brushed her teeth because she hadn't been eating, so figured there wasn't much point. The mix of stomach acid and undigested food would no doubt make her hard to kiss but, luckily, there was no one living she wanted this from.

'Am I going to die?' she asked Martin. She knew it might happen, that throwing up could be the first sign of proper poisoning. But she wanted Martin to say it out loud, to admit the situation he'd put them in. She wanted to see the look on his face so she would know, for sure, if he was trying to kill her.

'Don't be ridiculous,' he said. 'Not from eating a few leaves and the odd berry.'

It sounded reasonable enough but Susie frowned. She'd heard the exact opposite before and been warned about wild food; never to eat anything unless she was totally sure about identification. She supposed beggars couldn't be choosers, though. To be fair to Martin, they either had to begin foraging from the land or starve. Even after all the vomiting, she felt better than she had before. It was horrible being hungry, truly hungry. Only now that the empty feelings had been assuaged did she realise how unpleasant it had felt.

The room was warm but Susie felt quite chilled, a cold sweat soaking her T-shirt. Martin was curled up in a ball, away from the fire. Shadows danced around the room and the colours of the fire looked brighter than usual. She was a little light-headed and her senses felt slightly out of balance. 'How are you feeling?' she asked Martin. In all honesty, she wasn't that concerned except to find out what he might have fed them both.

'Fine.' He didn't sound fine, though. He didn't look

up from where he was curled in a ball. 'Still a little nauseous,' he admitted.

'Maybe you should make yourself sick. I'm feeling so much better than I was.' She thought it was a good piece of advice.

'You made yourself sick?' He looked up through his fingers. He did not look well at all.

'God, no,' she said. She was beginning to feel quite cold and climbed inside her sleeping bag. 'But I threw up quite a lot.'

This confession sent Martin off heaving for a while. He made a big fuss of breathing in and out and collecting himself. 'Thanks for the info,' he said.

'Well, you did ask.' Susie hugged herself. Inside her head she imagined pushing a sharp knife through his spleen. This picture came to her as vividly as if she saw it in the room in front of her and it shocked her a little that she could visualise it so easily. She closed her eyes and tried to make these images go away. She didn't want to hurt her husband. She tried to think of Jules, to conjure him up, but it wasn't working. Martin came out of his foetal position, running out through the door, finally going off to throw up like she had.

The fire danced and made shadows around the

room. Susie felt hot and then cold. She thought about Jules, and whether he might come and see her that night. And then her body chilled again as she allowed the thought that it might not be Jules at all.

The flames in the hearth had almost died. Martin had been gone an awfully long time and Susie was beginning to get freaked out. A cold sweat spread across her body again. Even though the fire wasn't raging, it seemed to cast long shadows. She hoped Martin was okay. She hoped the bloody food he'd found had killed him. All the contradictions of her feelings about him played games in her head. At least the violent thoughts she'd had towards him had eased; that was a side of herself she didn't like, one she'd never imagined existed before she found herself trapped here, in the bothy.

She heard someone whisper her name. At first she thought she had imagined it, then she heard it again. 'Sssssuuusieee.' The voice stretched the s sounds and lisped a bit. It was not a voice she recognised and yet she still found herself calling out her lover's name. 'Jules?' In return, the voice laughed, a cruel sound. The sound of pure hate. The cold spread and crawled over the top of her head then down her back.

She did not feel alone but this time that wasn't a good thing. Whatever, whoever had been here in the bothy before, it hadn't seemed to wish her harm. It had made love to her, touched her in gentle ways and reminded her of days gone by. Now things had turned. She didn't think it could be the same presence that had been here with her before. This was a dark and ghoulish thing, and it lurked in the corners. It wanted to hurt Martin; it wanted to hurt her. It was this presence that had put the bad feelings towards Martin in her head, she was almost sure. Malevolent, it danced in the corners of the room and taunted her.

'Ssssssuuusieee.' The voice came again, like a viper hissing. She was shaking all over and tried to take control of her body. She squeezed her eyes tight shut and told herself it would all be all right. 'Susieee!' Quieter this time, and yet it seemed closer.

The door banged open and Susie was so stirred she jumped right to her feet, sleeping bag still wrapped around her body. But it was only Martin, back at last, slamming the door behind him. The hut had grown quite dark but even so she could see he looked very pale. He didn't say anything as he came in, but moved slowly to the side of the room and sat down with his back to the wall. She saw him shiver, then push his knees to his chest and hug them.

'You okay?' she said.

Martin let out a bit of a moan then said, 'yes', but wasn't exactly convincing.

Susie wasn't happy. She wanted Martin to be strong. That was his job; it was why she had married him. He was the one who was strong and in control, even if it wound her up sometimes. She wanted him to come and hold her tight and make it all feel better. 'I'm a bit freaked out,' she told him.

'For God's sake, Sue. We aren't going to die or whatever it is you're obsessing about.' There was a note of pure disdain in his voice and this set Susie even further on edge, even more against him.

'That isn't what I meant. It's this place. The bothy. It feels . . .' She was struggling to describe it in a way that Martin would find palatable. Haunted was the wrong word; anything that implied the supernatural so strongly would just get him going on his pet subject. 'I don't feel alone here.'

'Well, you're not alone here.' Martin was obviously amused and it carried in his voice. 'You're with me.'

'I'm not talking about when you're here. When

you're not. And when you're sleeping. It feels like there's something here, someone else.' She couldn't hear anyone whispering now Martin was back but she could still feel it, that presence. It made her want to sit close to the wall and not turn her back on anything.

'For goodness' sake, Sue. We've searched the vicinity. There's not a living person for miles. You know that. Christ, it was you telling me that earlier today.'

Susie paused. She almost didn't say it. Then she started speaking again. 'I guess I don't mean a living person,' she said.

The response from Martin was fast and predictable. Susie realised as soon as he laughed that she shouldn't have told him. He still looked weak, his head rocked back and against the wall, but his laughter came out strong and then the words. 'Sometimes I just don't know what we're going to do with you, my dear, darling Sue. Such ideas.'

There was a silence then. Susie didn't even feel angry at first, just a bit silly for saying anything to Martin when she could so easily have guessed at this reaction. She sat and tried to will herself warm but no matter what she did she was cold all over. She supposed it was the bad food, the slight poisoning. She saw something move, in the corner, fast, perhaps a mouse. Then again, in another part of the room. She turned quickly to see what it was. She didn't catch it, though. Over and over this happened, a swift movement on the edge of her field of vision that disappeared when she focused on it. She felt dizzy trying to follow its tracks.

'I think there might be a mouse,' she said.

Martin laughed again but in a more sane way; he didn't sound like he was making fun at all this time. 'Okay, now I see. Sorry. I thought you were being insane for a moment then.'

The atmosphere cleared a little between them. Susie was sweating and her forehead felt clammy to the touch. She didn't feel at all nauseous any more but still had a sense that everything was strange. She shook herself and looked at Martin's self-satisfied smirk. That was when the proper anger hit her. She couldn't even say what she thought, what she felt, not about anything. He had laughed and his reaction had shamed her. When she saw the mouse and he'd made the assumption that this was what she'd been talking about all along, she hadn't spoken out and put him straight because of this attitude. The black shadow shot across the corner of the room where she wasn't looking again and she closed her eyes. Martin left the bothy without saying a word and she didn't know if it was to throw up again or for the toilet or some other reason.

All sorts of dreadful pictures came to her again. Martin, shot in the head. Martin, dead in the river. Martin, a stake through his heart like a dead vampire. Martin's head in the fire, detached from his body but still screaming as the flames burned his hair.

And then other images. Martin screaming in her face, his mouth so close to her that spittle hit her hard as he shouted. Her husband leaning over her, pinning her to the ground but not the way Jules had. There was nothing sensual about this particular memory, nothing nice in any way whatsoever. This was just control. Just a man, exerting himself over his woman and telling her what was what. Martin, sitting on top of her in that cottage in the middle of nowhere, holding her wrists so hard they had bruised later, and looking her straight in the eye saying, 'I wish I'd never met you, Sue.' Martin's hands around her neck and, when he stopped, her gasping for breath and shaking all over. Him, standing whistling in front of the mirror, later, shaving, acting like nothing had happened.

These pictures were 'the weekend', playing out in

her head as if she had captured it on film. She didn't know why it had come to her so strongly right there and then but it had. These were memories she tried so hard to push away, to pretend they didn't exist or hadn't happened, but she found she wasn't able to now. It was like someone had turned a switch inside her and made her look right at them, at the sores and blisters of her life with Martin. She wanted to look away but someone was holding her head still, holding her eyes open. They wanted her to see it and to take it in, to remember what Martin had done and how bad it had been. And it hit her, just how terrible the weekend had been, and how stupid it was of her to have stayed with him. How had she not seen that before? And now he had her, in the middle of nowhere, beside a peat bog.

It had all started over something stupid. She couldn't even remember now what had provoked the row; the issue hadn't stayed with them, just the aftermath. They had been drinking. This never helped their rows and had contributed before to things going too far, but this time she hadn't seen it coming. Neither of them had appeared to be drunk by any stretch, just a little lubricated. At first it had been good; loosened them up and got them giggling. Susie particularly remembered feeling able to be more honest than usual and was saying what she thought. She wondered now if that was exactly the problem, the thing that had tipped the row over the edge.

That and the baby thing. Whatever they had started rowing about, she had turned it to this. In hindsight, it was clear why. She had wanted to talk about it again, to resolve her feelings. No, more than that: she had wanted to change his mind. She hadn't exactly gone about it the right way, though. They had been screaming at each other already about whatever the hell petty thing they were rowing about and she had brought this into the equation out of the blue.

'A real man would give me a baby!' she had shouted.

He had stood for several moments, staring at her. He had hardly moved a muscle. 'It's not that I can't. I won't.'

'That doesn't make any difference to me. A real man would give me the thing I need more than anything else in the world.' She had stopped shouting and was talking in a low voice, almost menacing.

'Maybe I just don't want to mix my genes with yours,' he said, in a similar kind of voice.

The coldness in the way he spoke had touched and chilled her. She had known immediately that he meant it. She couldn't respond to that with anything that would make sense because her world was so rocked. That was when he said the next unforgivable thing, about killing the other baby. Jules's baby. He really shouldn't have gone there but he didn't know. He had no idea of the danger in the territory he was broaching.

Susie had flown into a rage. She wasn't usually a violent person, despite the visions she'd been getting in the bothy. In fact, she had never been in a fight in her life. But she couldn't even see for fury when he brought that up, about her baby. About the little boy her mother had convinced her to dispose of one bleak March night back when she was so young and such a mess. *You could hardly say there was something active about that decision*, she told herself now. You couldn't say she killed anything because she was hardly involved, just her body being moved from place to place and doing what it was told, going through the motions, that was all.

Martin had flung her down like she was made of paper. He had pushed her to the floor and he had pinned her there, sitting on her middle so she couldn't move, his face millimetres from hers, and at that moment she just hadn't known what he was capable of. Then everything had gone still between them. The cold of the silence made her quake with fear. He was quiet, unemotional, measured like he normally was. 'I wish I'd never met you, Sue.' She could tell these words came straight from the heart. Then the rest. She had never thought she was going to die but, looking back now, she was chilled to the core about it. He might have killed her. She had no idea why he had stopped.

He apologised, later, for pinning her to the ground. He had needed to calm her down and keep her still, though, he said. She would have hurt herself if he hadn't. But he didn't say sorry for what he'd said. She had pressed him on it but he had refused time and time again. 'I'm not sorry and I won't lie about it,' he repeated, every time they had the same conversation. 'I meant it when I said it.' These words, the ones he repeated over and over in the cold light of day, they burned away at her over the years. As for his hands around her neck, he denied that had ever happened. She couldn't get him to admit it, never mind apologise, and as time passed she had begun to wonder if she had imagined this bit, or dreamed it, his insistence was so impenetrable.

She sat shivering in the hut, thinking about that night in a way she hadn't for ages. She thought about the terrible things people do to each other and how they manage to live together afterwards. The way some women go back again and again to their men no matter what they do. Worse, the ones who get killed every day by men they love and can't break free from. Was she in the same danger? She knew in a way that hadn't been clear to her before this moment that she should leave Martin. She knew it but she wasn't sure she felt it yet.

She wondered what it was haunting her; sod what Martin thought, haunting was the right word. She puzzled over it. Why did it make her look at this picture, remember the worst moment of her marriage and in such detail when she'd gone to pains to lock it away securely, right at the back of her mind. When she thought about it, 'the weekend' had been preying on her mind since she got here. It was all related somehow, all the same thing. She closed her eyes. She felt slightly nauseous again but didn't think it was anything to do with the food. This time it was a physical symptom of what was going on inside, a reaction to the feelings that came up with the memories.

She saw a light moving outside the hut then. Martin with the torch, she assumed. She watched the light and tried to calm her thumping heart. Then she remembered they had lost the torch. She was too scared even to scream. She hugged her knees and forced her eyes shut, chanted to herself that he would be back soon, everything would be okay. That he must have found the torch and be shining it around outside the bothy. This had to be the reason.

17

The door opened and Martin came back in. Susie uncurled herself and forced herself to look up at him. She was relieved to see her husband and not an intruder, or some ghoulish thing, whatever was haunting them.

'Did you find the torch?' she asked, praying he would say yes.

Martin looked confused. 'I wasn't looking for it.'

Susie thought about explaining what she'd seen but decided there was no point. He would have some logical explanation for it, something that made sense but did not explain anything as far as Susie was concerned.

That was the problem with logic. She thought about the quote again, from Hamlet. She didn't think the prince was mad but it was the world that told him his visions of his father were in his head. All of this denial was enough to send you crazy when you knew better, when you had experienced the other side of life the way she had.

Martin braved more leaves, munching them loudly and making Susie feel nauseous again. They sat for a while making small talk. The weather was clearing up. The river was still quite swollen. The food might not make Martin sick again now his stomach was recovering. Susie joined in the conversation half-heartedly and wondered if they ever had anything real to say to each other these days.

The door blew open and slammed shut again, startling them both. Martin stood up and walked over to investigate, unsteady on his feet. He pulled on the door and examined its joints, the handle, the small metal catch that should have made it stay shut.

'You can't have closed it properly,' he said.

She laughed. It was just so typical of Martin to come to this conclusion that she found it genuinely amusing. She might not have if she hadn't had him bang to rights this time. 'You were the last one to come through the door,' she said. She couldn't help grinning and the pleasure told in her voice. 'You must have not closed it properly,' she said. Martin turned towards Susie and glared but he didn't say anything.

The door slammed shut again; he had finished examining it and gone outside. Not being able to see him unnerved Susie. She remembered the light she had seen outside when he'd been gone before. She shouldn't have said anything. She should have taken the blame and then it would all have been fine. When would she learn it wasn't worth contradicting her husband, that the consequences were always too hard to take?

'Ssssuuuussieeee!' It was that voice again, the hissing, nasty voice. She sat up and pulled the sleeping bag tighter around her. 'Sssuuuusieeee!' She wished Martin would come back quickly. She shivered. She wondered about getting up and investigating the sound, but she was glued to the spot. She didn't want to know what was haunting her. Despite her fear, she worked against her paralysis. She made herself move, stand up and walk towards the door. Whatever it was, she would face it, now.

The door opened sharply towards her and she squealed. Martin came into the room, grinning.

'You bastard. Trying to scare me like that.' She batted him on the arm but was too relieved to be angry with him.

'What?' he said. He was still grinning. 'Scaring you like what?'

'Oh, come on, Martin. I know it was you calling my name trying to freak me out.'

His face went serious then. 'I don't know what you're talking about.'

Susie studied his features, trying to read him, trying to work out if he was telling the truth. He was giving nothing away.

Martin smiled then, the grin spreading across his face in the warm light of the fire, making him look like the devil. 'Was little Susieee hearing voices then, poor Susieee is losing her mind, we'll have to lock her away . . . Poor, poor Ssssuuuussssiee!'

It was the same voice she'd heard, whispering from outside. It had been Martin all along. She stood there, looking at him now, taking it in. He looked like he might pounce and kill her as soon as glance at her. She sat back down and pulled her sleeping bag around herself as tight as it would go.

'Jesus, Sue, I was just having a laugh,' he said then,

turning back into sensible, capable Martin in front of her eyes. But she knew what she had seen.

Susie had no idea how long she had been sitting staring at the fire. All she knew was that its flames were fascinating, beautiful. She was tempted to touch them, feel their embrace, but she knew better. They looked like the petals of an exotic plant but she kept in her mind that they were flames and that they would burn her. She no longer felt sick at all but a slight state of euphoria had set in with renewed hunger deep inside her. She began to giggle for no reason whatsoever.

'What?' Martin asked her. He looked very confused. 'What's so funny, Sue?'

She couldn't explain because she didn't know. She shook her head and convulsed with laughter. Martin would get annoyed if she continued, of that much she was sure, but she still couldn't stop and, if anything, that made it funnier. To her surprise, though, as she continued giggling Martin joined in. It was like he'd caught it off her, and he was laughing just as hard, rocking backwards and forwards and holding his stomach like he might laugh himself a hernia.

Finally, they stopped laughing and looked at one

another. Martin came over to Susie and kissed her hard on the lips. She was a little shocked by the passion in his kiss. Despite everything, she held him tight and thought of the feelings she had for him. She didn't want to lose him. She wasn't ready to leave him. He would never hurt her, she told herself. But she couldn't feel certain she was right about that. Holding on to him, she saw behind them both, against the far wall, a pile of items arranged jauntily. The cooking stove was there, and in the prongs of the one gas light were both of their mobile phones. Leaning against the stove, switched on projecting its light on to the wall, was the torch. Susie couldn't help but let out a gasp and Martin turned.

'What the . . .' He let go of Susie and moved towards the artistic arrangement of their missing things. He turned to Susie. 'It's the stuff that went missing.'

'Yes,' she said. She remembered what she'd thought before, that a daft but harmless practical joke would be typical of Jules. When the torch had gone missing that had thrown her, but now it had been given back before the next sunset, it all made sense again. Jules had been an artistic sort, and he had often tidied Susie's things into what he called 'sculptures'. She grinned at the recognition of his work. It felt like sharing a secret joke with him. Martin turned and caught her grinning.

'You think this is funny?' he said. 'To hide important stuff like the phones and torch and get me worrying about people camping nearby? Or are you just trying to prove your point about the man you thought you saw smoking?' He paused, and blew out air as if it was full of poison. 'You really are a piece of work sometimes, Sue.'

'I didn't do it.' The words felt wrong, though, like lies, although she was certain they weren't. Was she going mad?

'Well, I bloody didn't.' Martin's voice sounded stung by betrayal.

'I know.'

Martin was shaking his head. 'You're making no sense at all.'

'This isn't about me. It's the world that's not making sense. At least, the world the way you see it. To me, this makes more sense than anything that's happened for years.' She felt suddenly free to say exactly what she thought about everything. Martin could like it or not like it, but she would tell him what she thought.

'For such an intelligent man you have a very closed mind. I think it's fear that closes it so hard shut.'

She would have liked to have been able to bottle the look of shock that took over Martin's face then. It was utterly brilliant. He was too confused to be angry. She saw all the emotions as they hit his forehead, one twitching into another, morphing into the next. She had never noticed before how expressive he could be.

Finally, he appeared to have worked out what he thought about it. 'How exactly do you see the world then, Sue?' he asked her. 'What on earth do you think has happened to cause these things to disappear and then get themselves into such an arty arrangement? Pray, do tell.'

She smiled like she knew a secret. She wasn't going to mention Jules, that was for sure. Despite her feeling of openness and her lack of fear over his reaction, she didn't want to share Jules with him. It was as if saying it out loud could scare her lover away. 'There's something here,' she said. 'Someone. Not a living person camping out but something else. A presence.'

He looked back at her, incredulous. 'You mean a ghost?' He ran his fingers through his hair. She noticed he was sweating.

'I don't like the word ghost,' she said. 'It's too limiting.'

'Limiting . . .' he said, his voice trailing off. 'There's no point arguing with you. There's no logic to your opinions and you're not prepared to listen to common sense.'

'To your sense and your logic, Martin. But do you really think that we know everything, experience everything? Human beings? I don't know. I think that we're really limited.'

'Right, so the entire human race is limited too.' He sat down and crossed his legs, facing her. He looked up through his fringe. 'You're sounding like some crazy hippy person.'

Susie shrugged. 'I'm as sane as you. I just see the world a little differently.'

'Yes, I'll bet you do,' he said. He started laughing, very pleased at some private joke.

'Now what's funny?' she said.

He shook his head vigorously from side to side and wouldn't say.

Susie woke with a start. Her head was throbbing. She didn't remember dropping off to sleep and so she was slightly disorientated as she came back to consciousness. Martin was asleep, leaning against the wall rather close to the fire. His face was flushed a healthy red but he wasn't snoring. She had a sudden fear that something had happened. When she was first with Martin she used to wake up most nights and feel compelled to check he was breathing, feel his skin so she could be sure he was warm and alive next to her in the bed. She walked over to Martin and waved a hand in front of his mouth and nose, feeling his gentle breathing with some relief.

His eyes opened, as if he had been lying in wait. He started slightly on seeing her hand so close to his face and batted it away. 'What are you doing, Sue?'

She was embarrassed. 'Just checking you were well, you know, okay.'

'Of course I'm okay.' The words of someone who took his being for granted, his health as a given. Day-to-day living could never be the same after the kind of loss Susie had suffered with Jules.

The fire had gone out. Susie got up and added more fuel. She threw on a couple of twigs, then a lit match and poked it alight. The peat gave off a lot of black smoke as it burned. It was getting dark now but at least they had the torch back and the fire was warming the room nicely. Martin was sitting up, wrapped to his neck in his sleeping bag. This position reminded Susie of dead people; funeral pyres. It brought to mind Egyptian mummies and sent a shiver down her spine. She went over to Martin and sat close behind him, as if she still needed to prove to herself that he was alive. It was then that she saw the red notebook again, just its corner, poking out from under the bottom of Martin's sleeping bag. She only caught a glance of it but it was enough to make her sure of what she'd seen. Martin was writing about something, which was unusual enough, but even more strange was that he was hiding it from her. She had to know what he was writing about inside the book. She had to get a look at it, sometime when he wasn't there.

'You hungry?' Martin asked her.

'Not really,' she replied.

'No, me neither. But if you are we could have more leaves. I mean, they didn't kill us and the second lot didn't make me sick so it must have just been our stomachs in shock.'

Susie shrugged. 'Yes, I guess you're right.'

'Better than starving, right?'

Susie considered this for a moment. 'Not if you just puke them right back up again.'

'Hmm. Well, I'm sure we took in something from them.' There was a smile on his voice. 'Anyway, it could just have been something unsavoury that had got on to one or two, animal droppings or some such.'

That thought brought the sense of nausea back to Susie and she was certain she would not be eating anything any time soon. 'Were you very sick?' she asked Martin.

'Nah,' he said, shaking his head. He seemed very casual about it but she knew him better; he was lying about something. Maybe it was about being sick at all. She wasn't sure she should let him give her more food.

'I was really very sick.' She rocked a little, her foot dancing on the floor.

'Really?' He sounded hostile.

'Well, quite sick,' she said. 'I've always had a strong stomach but something in those leaves was not very good for me.'

Martin didn't say anything. He was staring at her. Her foot began to move faster as she felt nervous under his scrutiny. There was the sound of deep breathing and then, 'Can you cut that out?'

'What?' Susie said, genuinely confused.

'Your foot going like that. It's making me feel edgy.'

Susie was embarrassed. She was only half aware of her fidgeting and it always mortified her when people pointed it out. 'Sorry,' she said. But she didn't mean it. She was sorry he had felt the need to point it out, perhaps, but it was hardly her fault. She didn't choose to shake her foot or bang it against the floor. She'd noticed before that, when anyone pointed it out, she would make an effort to stop that part of her moving like crazy, only to have the movement take up in another part of her body. It was as if she had a restless soul, a force inside her that was trying to burst through her skin and get out. Martin was surely used to this about her, though. It certainly wasn't something he'd mentioned before.

The room went quiet as Susie held her foot still and tried to focus on not letting another part of her body take over. She stared at the fire. There was a pain she felt, not a physical twinge but something deeper. Her husband was supposed to love and support her, not point out things like this and make her feel bad about herself. She was irritated. In fact, the feelings rose higher than that to a soreness inside, almost anger. She realised she felt edgy as well. She wasn't sure exactly why. She figured it probably had something to do with the stomach upset she'd had but couldn't quite work out exactly what.

The fire was just a smoulder now and Susie and Martin were lying close. Martin hadn't spoken for ages but she knew he wasn't asleep by the shallowness of his breathing. She thought a couple of times about trying to make conversation with him but then remembered how he'd been the last hour. Every time he'd spoken it had been to snap or correct. He had been very irritable and difficult to get along with and the last thing she wanted was more of that.

The room began to get cold. Susie got up and set a fire, considering whether she ought to go and get more peat; the pile of dried fuel by the wall was looking depleted. She wondered what time of day it was. It wasn't completely dark outside. It felt as if time was stretching. She thought about what day it might be. She had no idea how many days had passed in the bothy. A week and a half, she thought, but not with any clarity of vision about it. She wasn't even sure if it was a weekday or the weekend. It must still be November, that was what she thought. She needed to know, though. She scrabbled around on the floor for her watch and checked the date. Her brain was on go-slow and she had to count on her fingers to work it out. Eight days; she hadn't been far off. That meant half-term was almost over and Martin would be expected back at school. Then they would be missed and the hotel might wake up to their absence and send someone to come and look for them. Would they have any idea where to start?

For a moment, she had forgotten about feeling haunted and was back in control. Her real life did matter. She liked her job and the people she worked with and Martin was going for a headship so needed an unblemished record. Just for a second, she was her old self: capable, organised and practical, rather than some dreamy romantic hanging on the ghost kiss of a dead lover. She walked across the room. She grabbed the mobile phones and took them back to her nest.

Susie switched on one phone and then the other. She didn't understand how but hers actually appeared to have gained some charge and almost made it on, fading out at the last moment. There was still a little life left in Martin's phone. It played its welcome tune, which Susie couldn't help but think was a bit of a waste of its battery, and then flipped to searching for a signal. She watched as it did, willing it to find something. For the first time in a couple of days she thought of hot baths and showers, a big fluffy bathrobe. Her stomach still felt a little delicate but that didn't stop her thinking of stodgy lasagne with a large glass of good red wine. She savoured that fantasy.

And there was a signal. She could not believe it. She didn't get this about mobile phones, how there could be nothing one minute and then, in the next, in the very same place, you'd catch the edge of something. She knew how fragile this could be and panicked for a moment, trying to work out the best number to dial. In the end she went for 999. She was about to press 'call' when the phone was knocked from her hand, making her shriek. She turned to check on Martin but whatever trance-like state he had entered he remained there.

It was Jules who had her, though. Unlike her experiences of his touch before, this time the feel of his fingers against her made her skin warm up. She was lifted upwards too, as if he had grabbed her by the waist and was pulling her to him. His touch was still loving but not tender this time. There was more urgency to his movements, a passion. She responded by lifting her head for a kiss and felt his lips on hers.

Then she could see him. It wasn't clear. She couldn't see a face or body but a shadow of something, wrapping around her, enveloping her completely. 'Jules!' she whispered, sounding breathless. There was a loud tut from under the soft blue cocoon right next to her but Martin didn't bother to look and find out what was happening. He certainly would have been surprised to see her wide awake and sitting up as she called for Jules. She wondered if he would have seen the shadow there too, holding her, the shape of a man.

Then, as quickly as it had come, everything disappeared. The shadow and the feeling of being held fizzed away like static. The body she had felt so solidly, arms and legs and chest, dissolved into the air. Susie was sitting very upright and stretched as if he was still holding her, but his hands had gone, and his lips. She felt very cold. She shook herself. She remembered the phone and the signal.

The mobile had clattered over the floor and she could see its light a few yards away. She crawled over and grabbed it up, hungrily looking at its display. The numbers she had dialled were still there, ready for her to press 'send', but the signal had gone. She clicked off that screen and on to others but it just confirmed what she knew: the lines of communication had closed down before she'd had chance to follow through.

She walked up and down the room, holding the phone above her head, around her back, at all sorts of angles, but nothing. *It's okay*, she told herself. *It's fine*. If Jules had knocked the phone from her hand and prevented her from ringing he must have his reasons. She had been right before. They were meant to stay. They were supposed to be here so that Jules could come to her and they could be reunited. She tried to believe it but something inside said she was kidding herself and she felt scared. Because if it wasn't Jules who was keeping them here, then it was something else, something dreadful. A presence that pretended to be her lover to ensnare her. Insidious, like poison gas, it had overwhelmed her and it would win. She could feel it winning.

Jules wasn't here now. She wished with all her heart that he might be but he wasn't. She wanted him to come back and kiss her then make love, like he had the other night. She had woken up after that, she knew, but that didn't make it a dream. Her pulsing stomach had been proof of that. No, Jules was real and he had been here, he had to have been because the alternative was terrifying. She had to believe it.

18

Sun coming through the window had woken Susie up. The first thing that came into her head was that Jules hadn't come back in the night. This thought made her skin crawl with the cold. She sat up. She felt dehydrated, as if she'd been drinking alcohol. There was a strange absence in the room that she couldn't work out to begin with. Then she noticed that Martin's sleeping bag was flat to the ground: empty. Her first thought was that this gave her a chance to look for the book he'd been writing in. She pulled his sleeping bag from the floor but there was nothing in there. She looked for his rucksack but it was nowhere to be seen.

For a few moments she was disoriented. Then fear set in. Her first thought was that Martin might have gone back without her. She grew colder still. Even if this meant the river was now crossable, she wouldn't fancy attempting that on her own. Besides, she knew Martin and she knew what it would mean if he had gone without her. It would be a statement of intent; a bell tolling on their marriage. On one level, she wanted a divorce; she did when she really thought about it. On many others the idea was completely terrifying. She looked around the room for signs that would tell her if he was still around or not.

She got up and pulled on clothes, finding her jacket and putting that on too. Even with all those layers, she felt the chill in the air. She was so hungry she felt hollow inside. She didn't know how much longer she could go without proper food and was already thinking she would risk being sick again rather than starve. Like Martin said, it hadn't killed her and a full stomach felt like a good idea. All thoughts of getting back to her job, of Martin and his headship, had gone right out of her head and blown away with the cold north wind.

The door swung open easily, as if it hadn't been closed properly at all. The air outside was crisp and cool but the wind, when it hit her face, was freezing. With some relief, she saw that his rucksack was outside, placed to the side of the bothy's doorway. He hadn't gone after all. She breathed in deep and tried to bring her heart rate back to normal. She couldn't see any sign of Martin from where she was standing in front of the bothy and she continued to look around and over the bog for him. Then she turned and caught site of a figure a little off in the distance, rifling through undergrowth. It had to be Martin.

The wind howled across the flat bog as Susie set a brisk pace over to where she had seen her husband. It took her a few minutes but she was soon within shouting distance. This close up she could see it was Martin. She could read the brand name on his coat and see how its red hood flapped in the breeze. 'Hello!' she called and he looked up with an expression on his face that might have been a smile or a grimace, screwed tight against the wind.

'Hello,' he said. 'I'm foraging.'

'So I see.' She came closer. He was on hands and knees pulling at the earth. 'What's on today's menu then?' she asked him.

'I've found some brambles this time. They're old and shrivelled but pretty well preserved by the cold.

They won't be so sour like the other berries. And plenty more of those leaves.'

Even a few hours ago she was sure that the idea of more leaves would have turned her stomach but, for now, it was still appetising, despite the bad experience of the previous day. 'Do you think those other berries might be what made us ill?' she asked.

He shrugged. 'I still think it was our shrunken stomachs,' he said. He held out the carrier bag with his pickings for her to inspect.

She took the bag from him and began to look through, moving its contents around in the bottom. Then she handed it back with a smile. 'I don't know why I'm bothering,' she admitted. 'It's not like I know anything about these plants.'

Martin smiled and added another handful of his crop to the bag. 'What doesn't kill you only makes you stronger,' he said.

The wind blew across Susie's face so that her view was blocked by her hair. She wasn't at all sure about Martin's assessment of that. It was true that the food – if that was an accurate word to describe what they'd eaten the previous evening – hadn't killed them; but made them stronger? She wasn't feeling stronger, not really.

She was feeling uneasy instead, a feeling that built in the pit of her stomach and made her want to run. She wasn't sure what was causing this sense of foreboding but she wasn't enjoying it at all. She thought for a moment it might be fear of getting poisoned, and she focused on that, but it didn't seem right. She had probably already been poisoned and it had not been that bad. It certainly hadn't compared to the way Martin had made her feel afterwards, with his sniping and unpleasantness. In fact, the way Martin had made her feel for years now. She wasn't even sure if she was safe with him and perhaps that was it. Perhaps finally her heart had caught up with her head on the subject of Martin.

The wind seemed to get up then, scraping across the bog and lifting Susie's coat. As it buffeted underneath her layers she shivered with the cold of it. Martin finished filling his carrier bag then turned towards Susie. He held out a hand. This was an uncharacteristic gesture from her husband and, at first, Susie looked at his hand as if she didn't know what she was supposed to do with it. Then she took hold of it and intertwined her fingers with his, but it didn't feel right. In fact, his hand felt cold and hard against her skin and something about holding on to him made her feel afraid.

They walked together as if they were the kind of couple who did this all the time. Her husband was swinging the carrier bag in a jaunty manner as they walked and the more she saw that, the more the regular rhythm grated on her. He smiled at her and she could hardly stand it. Then she slipped her hand from Martin's and rushed ahead, reaching to the ground as she went as if to make out she had needed to let go so that she could pick up something she'd seen.

They made their way across and back to the bothy, Martin increasing his pace to catch up, Susie sticking it out to keep ahead of him. She held her legs stiff and made them hurt with the effort of speed-walking that distance. Just before they made it back to the hut, she was rewarded for her efforts. A warm hand swept across her cheek, behind her neck. She turned, thinking that Martin might be closer than she had guessed. But he was lagging behind now, huffing and puffing as he double-stepped to try to catch up. It had not been Martin who had brushed her cheek.

It made her think. If Jules didn't want her to hold Martin's hand, how far did that go? Was it okay to talk to Martin, to sit in companionable silence? To touch him or curl up near him at night for the heat? Her gut told her answers to these questions that she did not like. Of course Jules would hate these things; he'd always been quite a jealous boy. She had liked that about him. It had been romantic. There was no way he would have been happy for her to squeeze up to her husband and hold on to him through the night. He wouldn't even like it that they shared a room.

That had been it, she decided, the reason that Jules had come and gone so quickly the previous evening. He hated it that she was there with another man. She had been lying with Martin too, their bodies touching, only for the heat, mind you, but that was no explanation for someone like Jules, she knew that. Jules had come and gone because he didn't want to be around while Martin was there. He wanted Susie to himself. She had to give him that if she was ever going to feel his touch again in the ways that she wanted to. She had no choice.

She opened the bothy door and Martin thanked her as he walked past. She watched the back of his head as he walked into the room, looking for soft spots, for places of weakness. She shook herself. She couldn't kill Martin. Even if she was entirely right about what Jules needed from her, there was no way she could harm her husband.

'You keep telling yourself that.'

The voice she heard was so clear she turned to look for its source. But there was no one in sight except Martin, and it was coming from the other direction. Anyway, it had not been his voice, that northern accent. It had been a much more exotic sound, one that made her think of sex. It was Jules who had been speaking to her.

The pan was steaming and fizzling as the food cooked. Martin had said that cooking the leaves and berries would kill any germs, make them safer to eat. Susie had made tea: black, no sugar. A few little touches and it would have been a scene of cosy domesticity. It wasn't, though, and almost as soon as Susie's nose had filled with the smell of cooking, her stomach had remembered yesterday's meal and how it had felt to lose the contents of her stomach so quickly and thoroughly. It knocked the edge right off her hunger. Martin didn't seem so bothered. He smiled from the cooking pot as if he was fixing them a real feast. She tried to smile back but her stomach turned and churned and she had to sit down. She sipped the tea, hoping it would calm these stirrings. It helped only a little.

As Susie watched Martin cook, she couldn't believe the thoughts she'd been having on her way back from their forage. This place was poison, she was sure of it. She wondered what it had done to Martin's parents. As soon as it came into her head, she felt a need to know more about what had happened. Martin was watching her from the fireplace. 'You look deep in thought,' he said.

'I was wondering what happened here, with your mum and dad,' she said, trying to sound casual. 'You never explained what happened before, when you came with your parents.'

A deep frown hit Martin's face and she wished she hadn't mentioned it. 'It's not fun to talk about. I'd much rather forget it ever happened.'

Susie was quiet for a moment, but then couldn't help but continue with the line of questioning. 'If it was so awful, why did you want to come back here? It doesn't make sense.'

Martin sighed and ignored the question. He stirred the contents of the pan furiously.

'Come on, Martin. Please, let me in. I just want to understand.'

'Fine. If you really must know, they rowed like animals when they were here and after we got back, my father started drinking. He accused Mum of having an affair. She denied it until she was blue in the face, but he wasn't having any of it. He wouldn't let it go.' He paused for breath, his face pinched tight.

Susie didn't want to make him angry but she needed to know the full story. 'But that's a problem they had before they came here. Like you said before, it must have been that you just heard their rows for the first time in the small space.' She breathed. 'It's nothing to do with the bothy itself.' She felt like she was trying to persuade herself of something.

Martin let out a snort, almost a laugh except a bitter sound. 'That was the crazy thing. He claimed it had happened here, on our trip. I mean, who with? That's why I needed to come back, I suppose. To convince myself he really was crazy and that my mum had done nothing. I mean, it's the middle of nowhere.'

A cold draught hit Susie's neck and she shivered. She felt chilled to the bone as she thought about her lover in the hut and wondered if she'd been his first. Was it the same thing that had come between Martin's parents? If it was, then it couldn't possibly have been Jules.

'God, Sue, he went literally insane. The more he

drank, the worse it got, and we all suffered for it,' Martin told her. His face looked drawn in the firelight as he spoke and his eyes were far away.

'Suffered?'

He raised an eyebrow and she knew somehow that he meant physically. No wonder Martin had behaved the way he had towards her those couple of times. It was a wonder he hadn't done worse, really. It was what he had learnt at home. She knew from her job that this was often how it worked. She felt sorry for her husband now. None of this was his fault. She felt bad for pushing him to talk about it, because she could see the dampener it had put on his mood.

'How is the dinner looking?' she said, trying to change the subject. With a flourish, Martin removed the pan from the fire. The way he moved she could imagine him as a TV cook with the apron and the sustainable ideas. 'What's on tonight's menu, chef?' she asked, as he emptied the contents of the pan on to the two small plates. Her voice was full of false cheer. The green-brown concoction looked as appetising as it smelt, which was not very.

'Wild leaves with wild berry coulis,' he told her. He was also trying to pick up the mood. His effort reminded her that he was her husband, and she stood up and walked over to him, placed a hand on his back.

'Wonderful!' she said. Martin turned and kissed her. She pulled back and looked at him. There were dark swollen circles under his bloodshot eyes. It looked like he might have been crying. She stared at him and wondered how much she knew about him, really. What a bizarre decision of his to come here, a place that had caused him nothing but misery. Even with his explanation about checking his mother's innocence, it didn't make sense to her that he would want to come back. It was so out of character for him to be illogical and it frightened her. She felt like she was there with a stranger. She tried to shake that feeling as he handed her a plate.

The food didn't taste so bad. She got it down and into her stomach without heaving and her tummy felt better for being full. She washed everything down with tea. She was getting used to taking it black now and quite liked the taste. On balance, you could have called the meal a success. Martin had this theory about making a meal, that to do the job completely you had to collect the pots afterwards and wash them up. It was something his mother had passed on to him. Not all of his role models were bad ones so there were only so many excuses for the way he was. He busied himself collecting up the cups and plates, then he headed down to the river with them.

The hut felt empty without him. No sign of Jules now. Susie sighed and looked round. What if she'd been right earlier? What if there was no chance of her lover coming back while Martin was there? There was nothing she could do about it, was there? She stood up and paced around the hut. She added more peat to the fire and jabbed it with the stick Martin had brought in for that very job. It was a good choice, a real find, and made the fire spark alight again in a very satisfying way. She played with the fire for a few more moments, until she got bored. Then she walked over to the hearth and grabbed the shiny metal that had been vying for her attention; the hunting knife Martin had bought in Fort William. Martin must have unpacked it and she wondered why.

Susie remembered how she had felt when they were in the shop and Martin had picked the knife up. They'd had a quick discussion about it, not a quarrel as such but it was heading in that direction. She couldn't see why he needed such a serious knife. He had dismissed her fears and spooked her even back then by buying it. Something about the potential of the thing. Not that she'd ever thought Martin would use it against anyone, not then. But you never knew who you might come into contact with. She'd read somewhere that people in the States who owned guns were much more likely to end up shot. It did cross her mind that he might grab the knife when he lost his temper and use it in the heat of the moment. She'd dismissed this idea – she was being a drama queen and it wasn't as if Martin was that volatile. But now she really wondered. It came to her then; the reason Jules had come. She couldn't believe she hadn't thought of it before. He wanted Martin out of her life. He didn't want her to live on that edge any more. He wanted her to get rid of the man who was capable of doing something terrible to her. She knew through her job; the most dangerous time for women like her was when they tried to leave their husbands. That was when they got killed. Jules must know it, too. The only way she'd be done with Martin was if she removed him in a permanent way.

She held the knife; ran her fingers along the blade. It resonated as her hand moved along its shaft, which made her start and drop the thing. She picked it up again. What had just happened? She tried once more, this time visualising the blade stuck right down the centre of Martin's shoulder blades. The knife vibrated again. The resonance shook right through her and set her teeth on edge. She looked up at the wall as if she might find the answer there. But the answers were inside her, she was sure of that. Jules was communicating to her through the knife. He was telling her she was getting it right.

The door opened then. Susie jumped again, just managing to keep hold of the knife this time. It had stopped vibrating in that strange way. She was glad of this; it would have taken some explaining and Martin wouldn't have believed her in any case, would have thought she was doing something to make it happen. He walked past her, completely unmoved by the fact she was holding such a sharp, dangerous object and had eyes filled with fear. He saw her as no threat whatsoever, that was the thing, and didn't even appear to note her at all. She stood frozen to the spot and watched him move. She could imagine walking up behind him and sinking the knife into the soft flesh under his lungs. She could picture it, feel the way each muscle would move and the resistance the knife would find as it hit major organs and popped them like balloons. But she didn't move in his direction at all. Instead, she placed the knife on the floor and sat down nearby.

Martin had picked up the fire-prodding stick and was having a turn at this himself. He stared intensely as the sparks flew in the grate and the fire picked up heat and Susie would have almost sworn he was angry, although she had no idea what could have sent him into that mood. He turned to Susie and frowned. 'Feeling better now your stomach's full?'

She bobbed her head by way of a reply but couldn't bring herself to say anything.

'Well,' he said, still pushing away at the peat in the grate even though the fire was going great guns again, 'the good news is that we'll be out of here before you know it. There's not a cloud in the sky and the river's already gone down some. I wouldn't say it's safe to cross yet but it won't be long. We should pack up so that we're ready and able.' He continued poking away and Susie thought his actions were beginning to put out the fire. He didn't look especially happy at the idea they might go home.

Something leaden moved inside Susie, threading

through her stomach and down into her legs. She shifted on the floor to try to shake it but it was no good. They couldn't come here and nothing change. It was not okay. They couldn't just go back and return to normal, this pretence at a happy marriage that had so much wrong with it.

It was not going to work like that. She was not ready to cross the river and leave all this behind, not yet she wasn't. She was not going to up and leave Jules even on the off chance it was him she had found after all these years.

She could not allow it.

Susie woke with a gasp and sat straight up in bed. It was still the middle of the night and pitch-black in the small hut. She caught her breath. What had made her wake with such a start? As her eyes adjusted to the dark, she saw that Martin was awake too. He was sitting beside their makeshift bed with the hunting knife, passing it from hand to hand and balancing it on one then the other, as if he was trying to work out how much it weighed.

'Are you okay?' Susie asked him. It was all she could do not to shudder at the sight of him there, holding the knife beside her. She thought about when he had pinned her down a few days ago, what he had said about the bog.

'Not really,' he said. 'I was thinking about what you asked me earlier, about my parents, and it's sent me into a spin.'

Susie sat up, pulling the sleeping bag hard around her to keep out the cold. 'I'm sorry I made you talk about that. I should have left the past in the past.'

Martin let out a snorting sound. 'No,' he said. 'It's me who should have done that. Coming here was a big mistake.'

She reached for him then, instinctively, her hand towards his shoulder, but he batted it away.

'I didn't tell you everything,' he said. 'There was a lot more to this story. Oh God, Sue, it was terrible. Truly the worst thing that ever happened to me.'

The cold ripped through the room as if the door was open and Susie pulled her quilt tighter. She didn't know whether to probe for the story or to wait for Martin to go on if he wanted to. She was sure he wanted to talk but she didn't want to push it in case he didn't.

'It doesn't make any sense but I'm beginning to

wonder if there is something about this place. My dad definitely changed when we came here. Hell, Susie, he was going to kill my mum. It was him that said that line, about the bog. I was just copying to see what it must have felt like to be him back then. She'd be out there in the dark and cold now, out there forever, if I hadn't persuaded him.'

'But he didn't do it. He probably never really intended to.'

Martin turned to her then, looked her in the eyes and the look went right through her with the cold. 'He did, Susie. He was going to. He told me all about it and asked me to help. I managed to persuade him . . .' Martin's voice broke up then and he was crying, a strange animal sound she had never heard before. Seeing him lose control was extremely unnerving. He was still holding the knife and she didn't dare reach for him again, half convinced he would hack off her hand if she went to comfort him a second time.

After a few moments, Martin calmed and began speaking again. 'I persuaded him to just scare and maim her, downgrade it. I persuaded him to do that because I said I'd help him. And I did help him. Oh

Sue, I helped him terrify my own mother and leave permanent scars on her.'

All sorts of things about Martin came together then. Susie remembered his mother, the scar on her face that she said came from a childhood scalding when she'd knocked over a hot pan of milk. She always wore long sleeves and polo necks or a scarf around her neck. There were scars there too, then. She had been a nervous woman, always looking behind her, startled by the slightest thing. And Martin had only been nine when he'd had to persuade his father to do this kind of damage instead of killing his mother. It explained so much about him.

'I helped tie her down,' Martin told her. He kept going but Susie didn't want to know. 'He scalded her, put out cigarettes on her in patterns. He did. No, *we* did. I helped him with all of it. He told her she was going in the bog and that no one would ever find her there. He strangled her to the brink of death, stopping just short, then kicked her in the head and knocked her out. Oh, Sue, it was fucking awful and I helped him. I fucking helped him.'

Susie felt like she might vomit. She tried to imagine how it would feel for your own little boy to turn on you like that. His mum can't have known it was an act of love, that the alternative was much worse. What a position for a nine-year-old child to be put in.

Martin wasn't talking any more and he wasn't crying either. He stood up with the knife, towering over Susie. His face had turned to stone. She looked up at him and held her breath. What was he doing? Then he began shouting. Fucking and blinding and throwing expletives around the room. He leaned against the wall behind them and swung the knife at it, hard and out of control. Susie moved away, trying to keep her movements subtle, but she was terrified, scared for her life. Martin pulled the knife out and started hacking at the wall. Bits of the dry stone were coming away in clouds of dust. The knife was a vicious piece of equipment.

In one final twist of anger, Martin jabbed the knife into the wall and it stuck there. He breathed, in and out, deep and long extended breaths. Again Susie wanted to reach for him, to help him, but she was too scared. He sat down on the bed then lay back.

'We should never have come here,' he said.

Susie knew he was right. Her instincts had told her so from the beginning. There was something in the bothy that played on your weak points and ruined your mind. Susie's loss, Martin's trauma, his father's insane jealousy. Whatever it was that haunted this place could pick these things out and torture you with them.

19

Susie lay awake, feeling sick to the stomach. She couldn't stop thinking about the things Martin had said and the anger she had seen flowing through him. The knife was haunting her, too. It had danced around her mind all night and made sleep impossible. Not for him, though. Very shortly after his outburst he had fallen asleep and he'd been snoring ever since. It was as if getting the story out in the open had drained him of life. She was terrified of what he might do when he woke up.

It was beginning to get light. A few days ago she would have been bounding down to the burn, desperate to see signs that she could go home, but now she didn't even get out of her sleeping bag. She sat up and stared at the dry-stone wall across from where she was sitting. She looked for any signs that Jules was still here, called for him with her soul. There was nothing. The feeling of not being alone had gone completely and there were just the stone walls, and their belongings, and Martin snoring.

It could have been hours she sat staring at the wall. She had no idea. Martin stirred and stretched, then went outside of the hut to take a leak. He came back in whistling. The sound cut through the air and set Susie's teeth on edge. It wasn't a cheerful sound, not this morning.

'How long have you been awake? It's really early,' Martin said.

Susie shrugged. 'I didn't really sleep, to be honest.'

'Did you check the river yet?' he asked her.

'No,' she said. 'It's your turn.'

He was wrapping himself back up inside his sleeping bag. 'What are you talking about? I went yesterday. Remember, I told you it was looking better.'

'I'm not going,' she said. 'I've been lots of times. You can go.'

He looked up from his nest. 'This is ridiculous. We're not children.'

'Then you go,' she said. She sat very still, her back as straight as the wall behind her. She wasn't going anywhere. She wanted to be gone, to be out of this place, but she couldn't rouse herself. She was frightened that she wouldn't be able to leave, that something would stop her feet as she walked through the door and pull her back in, no matter how hard she tried to escape it. She was so scared of this it was hard even to try.

'Fine, I'll go,' Martin said. He pulled his watch from under his pillow. 'Later. It's not really getting-up time yet.'

Susie turned her gaze from the wall to Martin's face. She expected to see anger there but didn't care. She was surprised, though. His face was blank, like it had been wiped of expression. It made her wonder if he didn't care about getting home either. Was something about this place keeping him here too, the same strange entity that had drawn him back here in the first place?

He caught her eyes and his glinted. It was a look she recognised and took her entirely by surprise. He emerged from his sleeping bag and made his way along the wall to her. For a moment he sat right in front of her, his face less than an inch from hers, staring like he was drinking her in. He looked possessed.

Her lips parted with perfect timing and Martin moved the centimetre he needed to make their mouths come together. He kissed her hard and she could tell there was no love left in what he was doing.

Susie lay feeling sleepy after sex, as if she had been drugged. There had been no tenderness between them, no making love, but instead they had both been wild like animals, taken what they wanted from it. Now she felt the warmth of satisfaction but it came with a sick feeling, like she had eaten enough cake to vomit. She slipped in and out of consciousness and a nagging voice inside said she had to fight that and get up and leave, but she couldn't.

Martin seemed drugged too, dopey and slow. Looking at him now, she couldn't imagine why she had been so scared of him. It seemed ridiculous again. She looked at him and remembered meeting him for the first time, in that bar, and how shy he had been. She recalled exactly how and why she ended up falling for him. She was not thinking of Jules at all any more, but of Martin, her husband and the man she loved despite everything.

It was the bothy that was doing this to her, to their marriage. She jerked herself upright as she realised and remembered its evil, insidious influence. It was coming after them both. She realised this with such clarity that she didn't want to spend a moment more inside the place. She put a hand to Martin's chest. 'I need to check the river,' she said. Her stomach was churning, although this time it wasn't a violent reaction to the food but to the situation.

There was a laugh from below her. 'Now you've come to that conclusion,' he said. He sat up too, shaking his head. 'Later, maybe. Or tomorrow, even. I'm not going anywhere yet.'

The way he spoke, like someone half drunk, she knew he was mesmerised by the bothy too. She couldn't believe she hadn't run out to check if the burn was passable the moment it began getting lighter that morning. It was as if the bothy had cast a spell on them both, making them turn a little insane. She couldn't believe the ideas that had been dancing in her head. She had thought Jules had come for her, which was ridiculous, because why would he come here now? She had thought that he would come back if she removed her husband from the equation. She shivered. Whatever it was that existed in the hut, it wanted blood. It wanted Martin dead and it probably wanted Susie's soul as well. It was more evil than anything she'd ever come across before. It sickened her to think she had associated that with the memory of Julian.

She wanted to leave more than anything in the world. She tried to get up. Martin pulled her down sharply and held her tight. She thought about struggling, running for her life, but she was afraid of the reaction that might prompt in him. Taken over by this place, he could be capable of anything. She lay down and tried to calm herself. She was breathing fast and hoped that Martin wouldn't note her panic. She needed to remember this state of mind. If she didn't, if she let this monstrous influence in again, she was sure that things could go very badly wrong.

The door rattled in the wind. She grabbed Martin and held him tight now, her heart racing. 'Relax,' he said, but he was barking it like an order and it had the opposite effect. His arms tightened further around her and it brought to mind a python wrapping its body around prey. She felt like she could hardly breathe.

Relaxing was a bad idea. The worst thing she could do was let herself fall into the same strange state of mind she had been in before. She was tired from a night without sleep but she would not let herself drift away because there was a big danger she would wake and have forgotten all that she had just realised. If she dreamed of Jules she would be back where she'd been a few hours earlier, holding their hunting knife and feeling it resonate in her hands. She tried to slow her breathing. She kept her eyes as wide open as she could, determined not to give in to the slow call of sleep. She kept turning her wrist to check the time on her little watch. Minutes passed and felt like hours. She wondered when life had started moving so slowly.

With a gasp and clenching of her jaw, Susie woke up. She was cold. Martin had moved away from her, his back curled in her direction. He was snoring again, the way he always did. He had turned right back into the husband she knew, and the one that she had conjured up before falling asleep, the one she thought she had forgotten; that husband was long gone. Just an illusion, she thought now as she tried to recapture him. Nothing.

She had been dreaming but it had been very abstract, ideas without images or action. There had been the feeling of Jules but no real sense of his being there with her. It felt like he was moving further and further away as time passed and Martin remained. And she had had sex with Martin so that, since this betrayal, Jules had receded as far into the distance as it was possible to be, just the essence of him waving at her from wherever he had found himself. He was ready to say goodbye for good and for ever.

The fire was out and, even though sunlight drifted in through the window, she was cold, so very, very cold. She felt empty. Sitting up, she allowed the sleeping bag to fall from her shoulders. She didn't care at all that the cold air inside the hut was welling around her neck and back; she didn't think she could feel much more of a freeze than the one going on inside her. She climbed out of her sleeping bag and stumbled blindly around the room. She knew what she was looking for and she knew where it was kept. Finding it without waking Martin in the process was the challenge now.

The floor was filthy as she crawled across and rifled through the pile of their belongings. She pulled out Martin's bag and unzipped it. Her husband made a slight moaning sound then, a low wail. *He must be dreaming.* She stopped stock-still and waited. Long moments passed but then he was snoring again. She dug in the bag for what she wanted, but she was disoriented. The light on this side of the hut was obscured and dust danced in front of her eyes and dizzied her. She began emptying its contents on to the floor. Martin would have freaked, she knew, if he woke up and saw her. *Best he doesn't wake up, then*, a voice whispered. She had got so used to the unusual goings-on in the hut she didn't even find it strange to hear a voice without an owner now.

She pulled things from Martin's bag: his clothes, phone, bits of camping equipment. Then something strange, an item she'd seen before, came out in her hand. It was the book she'd seen Martin holding, A5 size, bound and with a plain red cover. She opened it. She could see writing, Martin's writing, neat to begin with but getting spidery and scrawling as she turned the pages. It was too dark to read it but it appeared to be some kind of diary. She was shocked; she had never known Martin keep a diary or feel the need to write anything down. This was much more Susie's style. She closed the book and put it aside. She needed to know what he'd been writing down. She knew it must be important if he'd felt the need to make a record of something.

Finally, she found what she had been looking for. She pulled it from the bag and held it in the air. It shimmered; the hunting knife. He had packed it deep in his bag but not deep enough. She held it out in front of her and it sang. It felt right in her hands and now she was sure she really was back on the right track. She sat there for a moment, just looking at the knife, her heart beating fast. She couldn't believe she was sitting there with such power in her hands; the power to change her world.

She put the knife down and quickly repacked the rest of Martin's things, checking blindly around the floor to be as sure as she could that she hadn't missed anything. Then she crawled back to the middle of the room and the sleeping bags. She sat atop hers for a while, watching Martin, the movement of his chest. It was amazing really, the miracle of life, and it astounded her that it might be so easy to take it away. Holding the knife in her hands she felt more powerful than Martin for the first time in all the years they'd been together.

The knife was yet another presence in the room. She sat holding it and watching, imagining how it might work. A swift push just below the lungs. Or between a couple of ribs would ensure a quick and less messy death, right into the heart. She knew enough anatomy to work out the different ways she could use the weapon. She imagined the sound he might make, a swallowed sigh of last breath, although she realised this was pretty much modelled on the deaths she'd seen in Shakespeare's plays so not exactly realistic. She wondered how much blood there would be, how messy it might get.

Martin rolled over on to his back and it was like he was offering his chest to her. She held the knife, poised over him, and willed herself to push it down and into his body. She couldn't move, though. She sat for several minutes, looming over him, feeling like she was almost at the point where she could deal the fatal blow, but she didn't do it. Her heart was banging so hard in her chest she thought it might be making a bid to escape. Martin looked so peaceful. He smiled gently, as though he was having good thoughts in his dreams. She just couldn't bring herself to extinguish him.

Susie pulled the knife towards her chest and hugged it. It was cold against her body. She wanted out of her marriage badly, but not badly enough for this. There was no way she could follow through and stab Martin in the chest. She climbed into her sleeping bag.

She hadn't been able to do it there and then but she might change her mind. She held the knife close to her skin and lay on her back. If she woke feeling cold and lonely that might be enough, and she might make Martin sleep for ever.

It struck her then that she could just leave Martin. But she knew in her heart that if it wasn't what he wanted, he wouldn't let her. What she wanted was irrelevant to him and that was the problem. It seemed drastic to sever him from his life in the way she had been thinking about, but she knew deep down that it was the only way to remove him completely from her own.

20

Susie didn't fall back to sleep. She lay there, awake, feeling the cold steel of the hunting knife lying like a lover beside her. She wondered if life would ever be normal again, her and Martin in their two-up two-down house, doing their jobs, small roles in a big world, but important ones. She tried to imagine it but she couldn't. She wasn't sure she could forget about Jules again. The first time had been hard enough.

She lay there thinking about these things until sunlight made the room bright and warm. Martin was still sleeping, so she quickly took the knife and sneaked across the room. She was about to return it to his bag but changed her mind at the last moment. Instead, she packed it into her own rucksack. With a heavy heart, she took the other items she was responsible for carrying and piled them in there too, zipping it tightly shut. She knew Martin would want to head back today. It was time. He was due back at school. Whatever hold the bothy exerted on her husband, it could not be as strong as that of his job. She realised that now and already felt the pull of his will making her go in a direction she didn't want to, as usual.

A walk would make her feel better, she decided. She finished packing, then noticed there were a couple of things she hadn't replaced in Martin's bag so went over to that corner and began repacking them. It was then that she noticed the notebook she had put aside earlier. She had forgotten all about that. She dressed and put on her coat, placing the book in her pocket. She coughed and realised her throat was very dry; she was getting quite dehydrated. She wanted to make some tea, but that meant fetching water. She ripped open her bag again to get the pot, which she had packed, and decided to go to the river on her walk. She would read the diary later, find out if there were any secrets Martin was hiding from her. The book felt hot in her pocket as she walked. She knew it was wrong to steal it; a betrayal. But she had a feeling about it, in her gut. She was done ignoring those instincts.

As soon as she saw the burn she knew they would be able to leave today. The stepping stones rose from the water. It looked like the kind of river that had been marked on the map. Just a stream, really; nothing. It seemed unthinkable that it was the same stretch of water that had separated them from civilisation for so many days. She filled the pan and felt a light tug as she tried to remove it from the river, still strong but nothing like the torrent it had been.

She sat down on the stone by the burn. Her own theatre seat for the show that nature put on all around her. For all his genius, even Shakespeare couldn't compete with this. She listened to the birdsong, really listened. She realised that this was something she rarely did, that most of the time she took this beautiful music for granted. What a shame that was. It was a mild day, and she felt the slight breeze across her cheeks. It was the perfect kind of day to go home. She thought about a shower in the lovely hotel bathroom and a hot meal. A rare steak with chips, or even a burger. Away from the bothy, the idea of home began to appeal again. It had to be the place that was holding her back, whatever malevolence it was that lurked there. She would not set foot in it again. She wasn't going to let that thing take her over and use Jules to try to trap her there any longer.

Taking a deep breath, she pulled the notebook from her pocket. She looked towards the bothy: no sign of life. She opened up the book and read. As she read, fear hit her in waves. It filled every part of her, every blood vessel, bone and cell. She read and she understood the extent of her husband. She was overcome by a sudden nausea and threw up by the side of the river. She took deep breaths and tried to get back to normal. The sickness lingered but she didn't vomit again.

The book was almost brand new, purchased in Fort William like the knife, and everything written inside it had been put there since they came to the bothy. Its contents were the ravings of a madman. About the bothy, about his first trip there, horrible, vivid details of what they did to his poor mother. About trying to bring Susie here before and how she had refused. About this trip and the terrible things he planned to do to her, with diagrams and maps, X marks the spots. The idea about her body in the bog had not been born on his lips when

334

he'd said it, pinning her to the floor, but in that book, days earlier. She knew that for sure because everything was detailed and dated there.

Even when he had rescued her from the bog it had been with his own agenda. 'I'm damned if I'm letting the land take her. Her life is mine to extinguish and I won't be cheated.'

She read and reread the worst pages. It was hard to believe this was written by her husband, the man who worked as a teacher in Ealing. A person almost everyone she knew would say was a good man. And he knew about the thing in the hut, he knew what it was capable of. Despite all his logical denial about what he liked to dismiss as 'things that go bump in the night', Martin knew everything Susie did about heaven and earth.

And he planned to murder her, here at the bothy, and sink her body into the bog. She looked again at some of the things he'd written in the book and tried to take it all in. How was this possible? According to the book, he had wanted to kill her for years. And his reason? Distain and hate that had built over time but, mostly, just for the experience of it, because it was something he hadn't done. He wanted to see what it would be like to extinguish a life, squeeze it till gone between his hands, and how that kind of power over something, anything, would make him feel. It wasn't even personal.

The sun was bright as Susie sat on her stone watching the river flow by. She threw the book into the water. She didn't want to read any of it again and, anyway, she figured the most dangerous thing would be if Martin found her reading it. At that stage, he'd have nothing to lose. She needed to leave, she knew that. She needed to cross the river and get out of the place before Martin woke up and had the chance to carry out the terrible things he'd planned. She knew she should and yet she couldn't move. She looked across the river. She should just walk on to the stepping stones and get away. But was that the best thing? She would be vulnerable, on her own walking ahead of him towards Fort William. He could move faster and he was stronger. Going back for the map was too dangerous and he knew where he was going much better than she did. He would definitely catch her on the scramble, if not before. If she ran off, he'd realise that she knew. If he had any doubts about his plan, him finding out she knew would seal her fate. As she sat and listened to the birds and watched the water flow it became clearer and clearer. The only way out of this was to kill Martin. 'Me or him' were the words that went through her head, although she found it hard to take them seriously. She decided to head back to the bothy and do what she had to do.

The bothy loomed dark in the daylight as Susie walked towards it. She didn't want to go inside to her husband. She was very afraid, not just about what Martin might do but what she would have to do to save herself. She steeled herself, balling her fists and squeezing hard, and she walked into the hut.

There was a little peat left and she added most of it to the grate and got a fire going. No need to get more now. This activity shook Martin from his slumber and she heard him stirring behind her. Susie was a person who woke up piecemeal; snoozing her way to full consciousness. Although Martin generally woke up much later than she did, once he was ready to get up he was completely in the world and would jump from his bed and spring into action. This morning was no exception; he threw the sleeping bags off and dressed, then wandered out and away from the hut to find a place to relieve himself. She had noticed them both getting more casual about this the longer they stayed in the bothy. At first, they'd been prepared to walk some way off to ensure a kind of privacy but that had gone by the way as their stay was extended. Susie imagined that, if they stayed much longer, soon Martin would just turn around and unzip his flies, do it where he was standing.

'You're making tea,' he said, sounding slightly surprised.

'Yes,' Susie said. 'I'm dehydrated now and I figured it was a good idea for us to drink before the long walk. We can fill our water bottles at the river but I'm not so sure about drinking the water unboiled, personally.'

'Oh, it'll be fine,' Martin said, batting at the air with his hand as if to knock away the possibility that she might have a point. 'I'm sure it's better than what comes out of the taps in most big cities.'

His self-assurance was utterly annoying in light of what she knew about him now and Susie felt a moment of terrible spite, wishing she'd been able to ram the knife down into him when she'd had the chance. It seemed that nothing could dent this self-assurance, though, perhaps not even death. She thought about all the things he'd been so sure about over the years of their marriage but that had turned out to be wrong. Coming to the bothy, that was a huge one, getting stuck in the dark on the way here and getting trapped for days in this dangerous place. It hadn't even finished with them yet, that mistake. She remembered how he'd refused to have a child with her. That one stung deeply. She would only need to think about that to raise enough anger inside her to do whatever it took.

The water began to boil and the handle of the pot became hot. Susie managed to keep hold of it and pour the bubbling liquid into the mugs she'd got out from Martin's packing. She pushed the teabags around in the water until they made a muddy looking infusion, then she passed a cup to Martin. He began by taking a big sip but then coughed and pulled a face when the liquid's heat hit his throat and mouth. 'Jesus, Susie,' he said, as if it had been all her fault. Surely it should have been obvious the drink was hot when she poured the boiling water into the cups?

They sat blowing on their drinks and sipping them carefully. The day outside was promising to be fine and its brightness was lighting the small square window that Susie had looked at for encouragement so many mornings. She didn't feel encouraged now, though. She shivered despite the sunshine. Their marriage was never what she'd thought it was. The quiet coffees and pleasant dinners with friends were not real. It was the other part, the being pinned down and hissed at, pushed around and threatened, that was the truth. It chilled her so much it was hard to care what he might do next.

Finally, Susie had finished her drink. She shook the cup over the grate of the fire to get rid of the last drops of liquid and took the mug and the pot to pack it away. Martin didn't finish his tea and, pulling a face, he threw it over the fire. 'I'm looking forward to having milk again,' he said, as if it would be the biggest pleasure of all when he got back. He passed the cup to Susie and set about stamping out the fire. She packed and watched him. He looked a bit ridiculous, banging his foot up and down on the smoky peat, but eventually his efforts stopped the burning. He surveyed the room. She followed his eyes from the layer of peat to the small pile of sticks and kindling they'd collected as a bonus when they were foraging.

'Should we tidy?' she asked, thinking that they really ought to.

Martin shrugged. 'Nah,' he said. 'It might all be quite handy for the next guests at the hut so we'd be doing them a favour.'

She watched Martin as he made ready to go and wondered when he planned to strike. She felt certain after what she'd read that he would. She didn't see escape from that. But she had the knife. She had packed it in her bag and that was her salvation and his big error. Martin grabbed his rucksack and set it on his back, turning to Susie with raised eyebrows. Now was the moment; they were going to leave. She should do it now, take the knife from her bag and stick it in his back. Inside her head, she pictured herself digging in the rucksack and then lunging towards him, but the Susie who stood in that cold bothy room did nothing of the sort. In fact, she hoisted her own rucksack on to her back and got ready to leave too.

Martin headed out into the bright of the day. Susie found she had to squint to protect her eyes as they walked towards the river and civilisation. She couldn't imagine being there now, back in their own lives. The disconnect she always wanted from a holiday had finally come but, instead of making her feel relaxed and happy, it had a totally different effect. She felt sick inside and uneasy. She felt displaced. She remembered this sensation really well. It was familiar from years before, when she'd lost Jules. There would be those moments, every day, when she would wake up and have forgotten he had gone. For just a small bubble of time, everything was okay. Jules wasn't dead. Then all the knowledge of the weeks before would come flooding back and she would be devastated all over again. But it was the transition she was remembering most strongly, the moment when the sense of unreality began to burst and the first feelings of something not being right had crept in. That was how she felt now.

To make matters worse, Martin was marching off ahead with a spring in his step. He was not the man he pretended to be, not by a long way. She watched him walk off. She still couldn't imagine him trying to harm her despite everything she'd learnt about him. She began to doubt herself now, doubt what she'd seen with her own two eyes. It was just Martin and he was the sanest person she knew. Was it possible he'd changed his mind, or that the diaries were some strange fiction he was writing, his idea of originality? Had he dragged her out here to fulfil some strange fantasy but it was all in his head and he planned to return to his normal life afterwards with no one any the wiser? And what about the things he'd said about the bothy? That hadn't been like Martin talking at all. He didn't usually engage with anything spiritual; in fact, quite the opposite, he would always deny anything like that. This way, he kept the things he feared at a distance and could remain breezy. She had envied and resented him that.

As she followed him towards the river, she thought of the knife in her bag. She fancied she could almost feel it vibrate into her spine, remind her it was waiting there. She watched the jaunty Martin as he strode back towards life and noticed the spots in his head where the skull seemed to join. Weaknesses. She imagined taking one of the large stones she could see on the side of the path and bludgeoning him with it. She shook herself. She had never had thoughts like this before she came here; it just wasn't in her character at all. Something evil had risen from the bothy and taken her over. She could feel it in her bones and muscles. It had increasing control over her and she wasn't at all sure she could remain responsible for her actions. Whatever or whoever it was, it wanted Martin gone, and it would do pretty much anything it could to achieve that. That was when it struck her; that perhaps the presence in the bothy was responsible for the book and it wasn't Martin at all. It had looked like his handwriting but then, when she thought of all the other strange things that had happened since they had arrived at this place, anything was possible.

Susie stopped walking and found she was frozen to the spot. She was paralysed by the decisions she didn't know how to make. Martin marched on a little while, then seemed to notice she wasn't the constant she had been just in his wake. He turned and waved. 'Come on, Sue,' he called to her. He walked back towards her. 'You okay?' Then he was close enough to touch her and moved his hand towards her shoulder. She jerked away. 'I know you must be tired but you'll be back soon and you can have a hot bath and a good meal then.' He smiled at her and she wished she hadn't read the things he'd written so that she could still love him. She really and truly would have swapped everything else in her life, all her successes, for his voice not to bring to mind the words written on those pages so vividly. She didn't care that she would have been in danger. She would have known nothing about that and it's true that ignorance is better sometimes.

Susie tried to smile at him but she couldn't. He frowned, then looked off into the distance. Grey clouds were gathering, looming over the loch. 'Looks like rain,' he said. The promise of the day seemed to fade from view right in front of them. She dragged herself up from the low place she found herself in and stood upright. Martin continued along the mud track and Susie followed as best she could. She did everything she could not to think about Martin's diary or the knife in her bag. She told herself she was in control of her own mind and limbs and wouldn't do anything bad to Martin unless she really had to.

'Not long now and you can relax in a lovely hot bath,' Martin said. He was still sounding ridiculously cheerful.

Step by step, Susie watched the river get closer. She looked behind her; the bothy looked small now, like something she could pick up and carry in her arms. There was an emptiness inside her, a feeling that she didn't care what Martin did to her after all. She couldn't stop thinking about the knife inside her rucksack. She felt like Martin was pulling her onwards but that something darker, something completely black, had a greater hold on her.

Then they were there; right by the river and ready to cross. Martin stopped and put his rucksack down for a moment. He pulled his water bottle from its holder on the front of the bag and dipped it into the river. The water bubbled around the bottle and his hand, looking like it was boiling to his touch. He took a long draught from his bottle and let out a breath, then smacked his lips. He put the bottle back in the water to refill it, then replaced the top. He turned to Susie. 'Aren't you going to fill your bottle?'

The thought of drinking the river water without boiling it turned her stomach. She knew it was from a fresh source, flowing down from right up in the mountains, but that wasn't the point. Reeds grew in that water, and fish excreted there. It wasn't clean enough to drink the way Martin was choosing to. She wanted to tell him to stick that but found the words didn't come. 'I suppose,' she said instead, and found she was filling up the bottle. She was astounded to see herself doing it. She really couldn't be in control of her own body because it was doing the opposite of what she wanted it to.

The sun went right behind a rain cloud and she knew the fine dry weather they'd had was on its way out. Grey clouds stretched across the landscape for as far as she could see. Maybe he wouldn't do anything. He looked like the Martin she knew and he looked like he was set to go home. He had school to go back to and he would never compromise that. She suspected he would have crossed the river at this stage no matter what the danger. She could come up with all the arguments she wanted to about how they couldn't do much when they'd discovered he really had got trapped here and how they would understand, but it would be useless against the strength of his commitment to the job. Duty called and when Martin heard it calling, he was there. She knew she should admire this in him, was sure she once had, but she found she couldn't help resenting it as just one more thing that came above her needs.

A cold rush of fear washed through her. Martin took hold of his rucksack and swung it on to his shoulders. He faced the river and looked across its width. 'No problem,' he said, more of that confidence of his shining through. She gritted her teeth and watched as he moved his foot towards the first mossy stepping stone, its top surfacing from under the fast flow of the water. His boot moved and she knew this was the first action of them leaving, well and truly departing the bothy. She couldn't move to follow him. He stood there, his foot resting on that mossy stone, as she finished filling her bottle, and she pictured herself pulling the knife from her rucksack and thrusting it hard into his ankle.

Instead, she turned and attached her water bottle to its housing in the side of her rucksack.

As she looked up, she realised Martin had turned towards her and away from the river. He was still smiling but there was something wrong with his grin. He looked the same way he had when he'd been pinning her down and trying to scare her. That was when she saw what he was holding. He must have got it out of her bag when she turned to fill her bottle, or before they had left. She had no idea how he'd realised it was there but there was no mistaking the knife, glinting in the mid-morning sun.

She moved on pure instinct, something primal taking over. She pushed him, hard, unbalancing him from his footing on the wet stones. He turned, a look of complete incredulity on his face. She had surprised him and, despite his superior strength and size, he almost toppled forward and into the water. He regained his balance, and she heard the metal sound of the knife as it came close past her ear. She grabbed for his wrist and held it tight. He pushed the knife towards her. She was losing her footing on the stepping stone and was sure she would fall into the water any moment. She clung onto her balance. Martin was gaining ground, and the knife brushed her cheek. She was never going to win this wrestling contest; he was so much stronger than her. She would die here, in the middle of nowhere, and no one would have a clue what had happened to her.

She held him back, just, and the knife stayed cold against her face for several moments that felt stuck in time. She had no idea what to do, no way of getting out of this. She stared into his eyes and they stared back, steely and cold, so that she couldn't imagine he had ever loved her. Then there was a minor miracle. Martin slipped, and fell forwards into the water. She watched him fall. It was like slow motion as his mouth opened and his body hit the surface of the burn, splashing water in a great arc above them both. She clambered fast into the water; it was freezing cold but she pushed forward, feeling an almost superhuman strength. Within moments, she was on top of her husband. She didn't let him get back up on his feet before she leapt on to him, and added to the weight of his overfull rucksack to push him under. She took the back of his head and pushed until his nose and mouth were submerged. He kicked and bucked against her, but couldn't get to his feet to fight back properly.

The river flowed past them as if nothing was happening. Its casual observation of what she was doing encouraged Susie. It was nothing this place hadn't seen before and nothing it would not see again. It was not her but whatever she had brought with her from the bothy that was holding her husband down. She would not be strong enough to do this otherwise. Martin bucked and fought against her, trying to raise his head. But she managed to keep his face submerged until he was breathing water. She saw the knife, spinning into the river as he released it and sinking to the bottom. She did not let go.

He struggled a little longer, holding on to life by his fingernails. She didn't want to kill him, and looked down at her hands, holding him there as he weakened under her touch. She could feel his life ebbing away as she held him. She couldn't let go now, though. If she did, she was done for. Martin would rise from the water and come after her and he would make sure he did it right, the way he had planned to all along. Slow, painful, with her tied up in the hut the way his mother had been.

So she held him there, and waited until he stopped trying to live. Even when his body went completely limp she hardly dared let go. She stood there in the river, getting wetter and wetter. Martin lay face down, floating. He reminded her of a goldfish that had died in her tank when she was a little girl. What did you do with those? You had to flush them away, that was it. You had to send them away down the drain. That was what she needed to do with Martin.

She looked at her husband floating face down in the water and wondered if she was dreaming. It didn't seem possible or the least bit real. It started raining then, small sharp drops hitting her face and head. She pushed Martin towards the middle of the river, as if he was a raft or a canoe. He was very heavy now; she supposed that was what they meant when they talked about a dead weight. She guided him away from the stepping stones to a rapidly moving eddy and she pushed him into its flow. It felt like launching a ship.

The dead weight of Martin began to move and then the current took his body and he was off downstream. Susie saw the hunting knife glinting from the bottom of the burn. She had hated that knife but now she felt she needed to have it. She needed the security of knowing where it was so that no one could come after her with it. It didn't make sense as there was no one around for miles except her dead husband but she didn't care about what made sense any more. The world had proved that you couldn't rely on sense and logic and it had proved it over and over again. She retrieved the knife from the riverbed and immediately felt better.

Susie climbed out of the water. She was shaking so hard that the world was blurred with it. She felt incredibly cold.

21

After Martin's body floated away down the burn, Susie went back to the bothy. She dropped her bag to the floor and fell where she stood, and her blood ran colder and colder. She was wracked with tremors. She kept seeing the back of his head, his body underneath, bucking and kicking and fighting for life. Then the difference as it floated away down the stream like a balloon in the air. The difference between life and death was as huge as she remembered it, if not bigger. Martin's body had turned into nothing more than an object after she had squeezed the life from it. What had she done?

For hours she sat shaking and thinking about this. Of all things, she felt hungry again, although she hadn't when she'd set out for home with Martin. Being stuck without food had worked out to be a bizarre situation, and her hunger had waxed and waned in the same kind of cycles as it did when she satisfied it with eating. Psychologically, after what had happened, she felt she should lose all her appetite but she hadn't. She began to feel ravenous. She was so hungry that she looked at the pile of kindling, the dried-out peat, and she could almost imagine filling her mouth with these things. She didn't but filled the fireplace with peat instead, glad there was some left, hoping a good, hot fire could stop the shaking.

Making the fire kept Susie's hands busy and helped her to avoid thinking about Martin's cold, lifeless body in the water somewhere, getting bloated and being nibbled at by fish. There was still most of a box of matches they hadn't packed, and she lit one, enjoying the sound and the feeling as the end of the match exploded. She put kindling on the peat then threw on the match and poked around with the wooden stick, the way she had seen Martin doing so many times. It was completely surreal, the idea that he wouldn't just come back, walk in through the door and take over. That she would never hear his theory on this or that again, his slightly arrogant take on life that had always annoyed her but that she would give anything she had in return to hear again. What had she done? She had had to, though. No matter how bad she felt she had to keep reminding herself; it had been down to her life or his. She tried to cling to this reality but it was hard to believe in.

The fire had got going. She pulled her sleeping bag from the bottom of her rucksack, where it was tightly rolled, and she laid it out on the floor. She tried to imagine sleeping without Martin's warm bulk beside her. It would be waking up that would be the worst thing. Waking and feeling the cold and remembering what had happened and that he wasn't there. She began to cry then, at first just a gentle flow of water over her face but increasing in intensity. Before she knew it she could hear animal sounds, real sobs and squeals, and she realised that she was the one making these noises. She tore at her hair and kicked the walls and swore. She took Martin's name in vain over and over. It was all his fault. He had brought them here, back to a place he knew was possessed. He'd had terrible things planned for her and if she hadn't pushed him under the water then it would be her who was cold and dead now, sinking deep into the wettest part of the bog. Or worse, maybe not that, not yet. He might not have put her out of her misery. More likely, if what he'd written in the book was to be believed, she'd still be tied up in the bothy here, suffering at his hands, his knife making patterns on her bare skin.

It struck her how her life was going to be from now on. Living on her own in their Surrey house, waking up with no one to hold, no one to talk to. Cooking for one, eating for one. When she had imagined leaving Martin before, she had found the idea glamorous. She could get cats and act strangely, like other single women her age did. It would be fun. But now her life spread out in front of her as a succession of days spent alone and nothing about it seemed like fun at all. It was almost too much to bear. She curled herself up and rocked back and forth and thought about these things. Hours passed and all she did was rock and think.

The shaking stopped and Susie sat still for the first time in hours. She should head back to the hotel and get help. She should report Martin missing. She could say that the burn had washed him away; they were hardly likely to suspect someone like her of killing him. She wondered what the time was. It must be late afternoon, she figured, because the sun had started fading and the square of window had turned a darker shade of blue. There was no way of telling; her watch had stopped working since her escapades in the water and her phone was as dead as her husband.

It was only then that Jules came to mind. She thought about him, and it sent pains into her arms and legs. She had so wanted to believe that it was Jules coming back for her, that this was why she was having such bizarre experiences at the bothy. Now she couldn't. Jules had had a kind heart, had been quite pure in his way, and so young. She knew with all the surety that she could muster that Jules would never set out to harm anyone. Whatever had been haunting her, haunting Martin all these years and dragging him back here, it used people as its instruments of destruction. No, it could not have been her Jules. Instead, it was something twisted and sick, a malevolent force that had ruined her life and Martin's entire family's before that. Now she was here on her own with that to deal with. It didn't bear thinking about it. She should not have come back.

Susie's jeans were still very wet from the climb into the river, and her T-shirt and fleece were not much better. She opened up her rucksack and unpacked her second set of clothes. She had not made an effort to dry them, presuming they would be back at the hotel soon so that she wouldn't need these again. They were still damp from the first river crossing and smelled musty. They were a better option than the clothes she had on, though, and so she stripped and changed. All the time, she looked around herself, at the walls, at the door and window. She felt like she was being watched by a pair of greedy eyes. She did not feel alone but, this time, the sense of a presence in the hut was not something she welcomed at all.

She climbed into her sleeping bag now shaking so badly again that she could hardly do up the zip. She closed her eyes and tried to pretend she was some-where else. A much better somewhere. The hotel before all this had happened, lying next to her husband as he snored his head off. She screwed her eyes up tight and willed herself there. She wondered; if she willed it hard enough, could she take herself there, back in time, and stop all of this from happening? She wished for it with every cell in her body.

But when she opened her eyes she was still in the bothy, and Martin was still gone.

The sound of something crashing against the bothy wall outside woke Susie up. She sat bolt upright. She wasn't sure when she'd fallen asleep or how long she had been gone. She was terrified. Who or what could have made that noise? There was no one around for miles, of that she was sure, no one except Martin and he was dead. Wasn't he? Could he have pretended, though, and pulled himself out of the water further downstream and come looking for her? She remembered the times they'd gone swimming together, when they were younger. Martin could swim a long way under water, hold his breath for ages. She moved to the corner of the room and tried to make herself as small as possible.

She stayed like that, bent over and shaking, for ten minutes, but no one made any attempt to get into the hut. She figured that there wasn't any immediate danger and decided to investigate. She pulled her sleeping bag tight around her and hobbled to the hut door, opening it. Outside was a strange kind of light, bright from the moon despite the night. She turned and looked to see what it was that had crashed against the outside of the bothy. Sat there lying on its side she saw Martin's rucksack. She screamed and looked around for her husband, but he was nowhere to be seen. She tried to calm herself by taking deep long breaths. She muttered, 'There's no one here, no one here, no one here' over and over but she didn't believe it.

The knife. She needed to have hold of the knife because if Martin's rucksack was here then someone must have brought it. She thought about the possibilities. Someone else, someone here in the middle of nowhere, that didn't seem likely. The presence at the bothy didn't appear to account for it, either. She hadn't felt anything outside the place, by the river or in the bog. Whatever was in the bothy belonged there, inside, and it couldn't carry a rucksack back from a river and throw it against a wall. *When you've eliminated the impossible, whatever remains, however improbable, must be the truth*. She thought about this hard. It was Martin. He was alive; it was the only possibility. He had pretended to drown. She rushed inside to find the hunting knife. It was where she'd hidden it, next to the fire. She pulled it from its hiding place and put it deep into her jacket pocket. She placed one of her gloves on top and around it to keep it hidden.

She sat on the floor then and waited. She knew he was coming for her and she prepared herself. She would have to kill him again. But she was tired, so tired. She tried hard to keep her eyes wide open while she waited for her husband to come back but she was quickly losing the battle.

Susie woke to firelight. The room was different and she couldn't work out why to begin with. As she came to properly, she realised it was candles, carefully placed around the hut. Lit like this, it resembled a fairy grotto. She remembered that candles had been just Julian's style. He had owned a load of them. His friends had teased him about it but it had worked a charm with the ladies so they had eventually changed their minds, and learnt from him about the art of seduction. In fact, Jules had been a bit of a sod before he met her, flitting between one girl and the next, messing them around a little. She had calmed and settled him.

The room was warm in the candlelight and Susie let her sleeping bag slip from her shoulders and on to the floor. *Am I dreaming?* she wondered. She wished she could be sure. It felt completely real. She pinched herself and it hurt in just the right way. She searched the room for signs of that absence of logic you get in dreams. She prodded things. They were as real and as solid as she was and yet it still felt like a dream. It was as if she had woken into a different reality.

And Jules was there. She felt him strongly and was certain it was him. Her Jules. She sat up and reached for him, turning towards the wall where she felt him most strongly. She started as her arms met someone solid, someone wet and cold but as real and alive as she was.

'Hello, Susie.'

Martin's hair was plastered to the side of his face it was still so wet. Being soaked through didn't seem to bother him. He wasn't shaking like Susie had been and didn't look cold. He stared right at her and his eyes looked blank and void of all emotion. They were the most frightening eyes Susie had ever seen. She had discovered on this trip that Martin was much more capable than she had ever imagined but she had never believed the things she'd read in the diary, not really. Now he looked capable of anything. He grabbed her and held her, too tightly. Was he trying to squeeze the air out of her, to kill her like a python would? But then he stopped. She wasn't sure if he'd changed his mind or run out of strength. He pulled her upright and pushed the sleeping bag down then over her feet, on to the floor. She had no strength to fight him, nothing anywhere in her body. She would have fallen to the floor if he hadn't been holding her. He dragged her by her hair over to the window.

'I have something to show you,' he said. 'More pretty lights.'

The candles went out then, one by one, around the room. She tried to turn to see who or what was putting them out but Martin wouldn't let her. He held her fast and hard and made her stand by the window. Then the last of the lights was gone and it was completely dark and very cold. Martin's arms pinned her own to her side and his hands moved to her face and held it tight. He made her look into the dark outside.

'Can you see them yet, the pretty lights?' he said.

Susie's throat was dry. She tried to shake her head but Martin was holding her too hard and fast.

'Can you, bitch? Can you see the pretty lights?' His voice was calm and kind of sing-song; it didn't tally with the words he used.

She looked at the window and something wasn't quite right. Stars were sparkling in its glass, making regular constellations more like a kaleidoscope than the sky. She looked right into the glass and stared and stared as the patterns danced. She was fascinated with where they might have come from, and the way they moved, tracing intricate circles and always moving exactly in sync with one another.

And then she saw it, just like Martin had described in his boarding-school story. This wasn't just one creature on the other side of the glass with eyes like headlights, dancing its intricate dance, but lots of them. A whole swarm of ethereal dancers with eyes that shone. She screamed. She tried to get away from Martin but he was too strong and held her tighter and tighter. She thought about the knife in her pocket but there was no way she was going to be able to reach it considering how fast he had hold of her. She could hardly breathe but let out several yelps. Martin wrapped his hand over her mouth and pushed her closer to the window but she closed her eyes. Something on the other side of the window was knocking against it. She could hear the tapping against the glass. Martin pushed her right against it. It was freezing cold on her face and she could feel the vibrations as whatever it was knocked and scraped its surface.

'Can you see them now, Suuuusssieee?' Martin

asked her. He pulled her head back and bashed it hard against the glass. She could feel the heat of a bruise forming on her right eye socket. 'Of course you can. You're so fucking weak and suggestible you'll see whatever I tell you's there.'

'No!' She was shouting. 'No, I won't look!'

'What the fuck?' Martin turned her head towards him, yanked it hard. He grabbed at her eyes, pulled her eyelids roughly open. 'You will fucking look.'

In grabbing for her eyes, Martin had let go of Susie's arms. She knew she only had a short window to save herself. She was so tired, so weak from not eating properly for days and from fighting him in the river. Her arms were sore from how hard he had squeezed her and she could hardly move them. But she made herself. She pushed against the fatigue and found her pocket, throwing out the glove and grabbing hold of the knife. Martin didn't even notice the glove fall to the floor. The knife was in her hand and she felt it vibrate, the way it had before. It was on her side.

She plunged the knife as hard as she could, backwards towards his chest. He made a sound like liquid and she felt his grip loosen on her head. He fell to the floor, wheezing. She turned and looked at him. Blood bubbled from the wound in his lungs and shone from the corner of his mouth. He was trying to tell her something but he couldn't speak. And then the gargling and rattling from his chest stopped.

Susie walked over and placed a hand across his mouth. She pushed fingers into his neck, where she knew the jugular passed. No pulse. She was making damn sure he was dead this time. She remembered the lights at the window. She turned to look again but they were gone.

She went to investigate where the candles had been around the room but there was no evidence of anything physical having ever been there. No stump, no silver-foil tea-light case, no burn mark on the floor. What had he shown her? It wasn't her sort of ghost story but his. She wondered if it had been some kind of clever illusion. He had wanted to terrify her, the way his dad did to his mother, and he had told her that ghost story before. But she had seen it with her own eyes and she had felt the window pane vibrate next to her skin.

Martin lay looking up at her, his chest still leaking blood but very slowly now. The shock at being stabbed was still there in his eyes. She closed the lids so he was no longer looking at her. She needed to get rid of his body but she was so utterly exhausted. She felt trapped between one world and the next, in limbo.

It was cold when Susie woke again. Something subtle had changed, like when a fever breaks or a migraine wanes and it feels like waking up. She wasn't sure exactly what had happened but she knew something had burst.

She remembered the eyes she had seen at the window, the monstrous creatures attached to them and moving inches from her nose. It was their proximity that had been the most frightening thing about them. They could have reached through the glass and put their hands around her neck, poked out her eyes.

She sat up. Her skin was covered in a film of water, a proper cold sweat. She held one hand out in front of her and saw that it was shaking. It was light in the bothy now, full-on day, and it looked like it might even be sunny outside. She reached around for her bag and grabbed a mirror; something in her needed to see the state she was in even though she'd not looked at her own reflection for days. She pulled the small compact from the side pocket of her rucksack.

The face that met her in the glass was a complete

mess, although perhaps not quite as bad as she'd expected. She was a little thinner around the jaw and cheeks but she still looked like herself, which was what surprised her. She wasn't sure what she had been expecting; would murdering someone change the set of her eyes, the strength of her nose? There was some blood on her face, and on the clothes she was wearing, but other than that no other signs of her crime. The bruise around her right eye was already fading. Her skin looked jaundiced and her curls were stuck to the side of her face and the top of her head like a helmet. She tried to bush them out a little with her fingers but they were too heavy with dirt, grease and river water, and so she pulled her hair back instead and tied it with a band she had found in the same pocket as the mirror.

She was going back, now, that much she had decided. Jules was not coming here for her. It had never been Jules. That was just a convenient way to get her attention and control her. There was something in this hut and it was dangerous and she wanted away from it. Even now, she felt a presence looking over her shoulder, eyeing up the back of her neck with bad intentions. She shivered and turned and could see nothing, but she knew there was so much more than the things you could see. She had always known that. Even Martin had known that, it turned out, in the end.

She looked at him now, his face twisted with a permanent expression of shock. A practical mood came over her now. She needed to get rid of the body and the knife, clean the blood from herself and the walls of the bothy and dispose of the wet, bloody clothes she was wearing. They could all go in the bog. Martin had told her; no one would ever find the things that would incriminate her if she made them sink into the peat. It came to her with clarity, what she had to do.

The body was very heavy and it took some effort to drag it across the floor and out through the door. It was even harder work as it snagged on the grass and heather as she pulled it along outside. She had to keep stopping to catch her breath and recover but she was determined, and started again as soon as she could. It took her close to an hour but eventually she was at a part of the bog she remembered; the place where it glistened with water. It was as damp as it had been in the worst of the wet weather and Susie figured it was always this way. She pushed down hard on Martin's stomach. He began to sink, slowly. It didn't matter. No one would be passing by this place that soon.

Down at the burn, she scrubbed herself hard to get off all the blood and changed into Martin's spare set of clothes. They were almost dry but far too big for her. She had to roll up the jeans and make a new hole in the belt so she could tighten it far enough. The T-shirt and fleece hung down almost to her knees but that kept her warmer anyway. She was dressed and ready to go but took one last walk out to the bog with the knife and her bloody clothes. Martin's body had sunk significantly since she'd seen it last and was almost completely under the peat. She pushed the bundle she was carrying into the soggy ground, pulling the cloggy mud up over them in a mound then stomping on it. She inspected the site. She wasn't happy that she was leaving anything on display, never mind the tip of her dead husband's nose and the tops of his shoes. She walked over and sat on him, pushing down these extremities. He sank easily. She stood up quickly, not wanting to join him stuck in the mud. She pulled her coat tight around her shoulders and walked back to the bothy to get her rucksack.

She picked up her bag and looked around the room one more time. She tried to imagine the lights, the sense of evil she had felt before. She couldn't feel a thing now. It just felt like a cold, empty room. She couldn't understand how she had ever thought Jules could have come to her here. She knew one thing for sure; there was nothing here for her now.

22

The river welcomed Susie the way it always had. It was not judgemental despite the things it had seen her do. She wondered what she looked like. Possibly just like any other hiker coming this way from a distance. A complete mess if you looked close, of course, in her oversized clothes and with hair that hadn't been washed for over a week. And perhaps somewhat lost, although she knew where she was going. The problem had much more to do with where she'd been and what had happened while she was there. She certainly didn't feel like any old random walker. Her insides were sore and she was battered and bruised, physically and psychologically. She would never be the same again.

The river had dropped so low that the stepping stones cleared the top by inches now. She mounted them carefully, crossing tentatively and trying not to look downstream. She was nervous even now that Martin might rise up from the water, back from the dead a second time. As it was, the river was easy to cross. It had seemed like such a barrier just a few days before but she could hardly believe now that it had ever been. So much had happened since she'd come to the bothy and so much of it had been surreal, she began to wonder about Martin. Could she have dreamed it all? She wasn't sure if she had been raving with the fever or if it was something more sinister, more supernatural, that had given her such bizarre and frightening visions. She was just glad to be away from the place and whatever strange influence it held over her.

She would have liked to go to sleep and wake up to find the whole experience had been a long, bad dream and that she was back at the hotel with the man she loved who had never planned to kill her. She wanted him to be alive and the person she'd believed she'd been married to more than she could say. Now she was away from the bothy and heading back towards normality, the idea that Martin had been any danger to her seemed ridiculous. She wished she had kept his diary instead of throwing it into the water so that she could keep looking at it and remind herself what he'd really been like. The only evidence she had was memories, which were so unreliable, and she'd had plenty of good times with Martin that contradicted what he'd been like the night she killed him. She didn't want any of it to be true but it lurked in the pit of her stomach that it was, that it had all happened. As much as she wanted to believe otherwise she knew it would only be delusion.

She walked along the path and towards the loch. In the light of day it was a very different place, not at all cold and frightening the way it had appeared on the route here. In fact, in the sunlight, it was rather beautiful, the water glassy and clear as it spread smooth towards the hillside. The air was fresh against her face and, although there were a few clouds, it hadn't started raining. She might have enjoyed the walk in different circumstances. As it was, though, she was bone-tired and every movement sent shocks through her muscles, which were sore from being on the cold, hard floor for so many nights. She was hungry too, a dull ache that filled her up and made her want to walk faster, except she couldn't because she was just too worn out.

Each step was an effort as she made her way across the land and back towards Fort William. As she walked, she thought about how long they'd been gone. She was surprised, really, that no one had come looking for them. She supposed they were both grown adults and could do what they wanted. Still, it was so out of character for Martin to miss school and unheard of that he would have been absent without phoning, so that must have raised some alarm. And their stuff would still be in the room at the hotel. They hadn't checked out when they were due to, or paid the bill, or moved their belongings. Surely someone had thought that strange? Perhaps the problem was the vast nature of the Scottish hills. Who would know where to look for them, when it came down to it? They hadn't left their itinerary or travel plans with anyone. She made a mental note not to go anywhere without doing that again, no matter what Martin said about it. Then she remembered there would be no Martin to tell her what he felt, to complain or bark at her for bothering. She wanted to feel bad about that and she searched inside her for the guilt she had felt before but it wasn't there. All she could feel was a gushing relief that she had escaped him.

Stopping for a moment, Susie dug into her rucksack and retrieved the map and compass. She pulled it out, playing with the compass for some time, orienting it with the map in the plastic case and trying to work out what lay ahead. She saw the steep hill they had scrambled up and remembered that challenging part of the journey. She really didn't feel up to that and examined the map for an alternative route. There was a very clear and evident substitute involving following a Land Rover track up and over the edge of the valley. It was a little longer but it was pretty well flat all the way. Susie wondered why they hadn't gone that way in the first place. She remembered she had wondered at the time if he'd taken her up the scramble to scare her and now she was sure of that, too. She was glad she'd killed him. For a moment, that feeling came to her clearly but then it faded, and she felt only a terrible fatigue.

As she walked, Susie noticed that the quality of the light was exceptional. She wasn't quite sure how it worked, but the contrasts of the colours and the sheen of the water were all quite stunning. It was as if she had been given a new pair of glasses to see the world. Everything looked clearer and sharper, more intense than it usually did. Super-real, she would have said to describe it if she'd had to. She wasn't sure she liked it. She would have been more comfortable walking with a pair of sunglasses to tone everything down; it hurt her eyes a little in its intensity.

One foot went in front of the other and she walked. She wondered what time it was, what day it was. She wondered if civilisation still existed. Anything could have happened while she'd been gone; a nuclear bomb, an alien invasion, anything at all, and she would have been none the wiser. She glanced at the map again. The first sign of life would be a large house on the other side of the valley, one of those homes big enough to have outbuildings and a groundman's cottage. She was looking forward to seeing ordinary things like lights in the windows, neatly trimmed lawns and wooden fences.

She kept looking out for the house but it didn't appear for a long time. It felt like she had been walking for ever. Her sense of time was warped. She wouldn't have been able to say with any surety if she'd been walking for hours or days, except that she knew it had been light all the time so that it couldn't have taken nearly as long as it felt like it had.

At last she could see the big house getting closer. Its drive was lined with conifers and there was a dog running in the garden. Her heart leapt as she heard its bark and saw in the distance the random way it ran and ambled around its grassy home. There were no lights on in the house. It was too early maybe. She walked on and on, towards the building, the sight of it giving her a new impetus. When she finally got there she stopped and rested for a moment on a large stone conveniently located by the side of the path, as if it was supposed to provide rest for weary travellers.

It was here she wished she had some sandwiches, or a flask of tea to drink. Thoughts of such ordinary things came so close to normality and civilisation. At the bothy, the idea of a sandwich had seemed somehow surreal. Sandwiches had nothing to do with survival, so why should they exist at all? The idea of the kind of food she usually bought, the ready meals and quiches and suchlike she got from Marks & Spencer, all of that had seemed quite ridiculous. Now she could almost smell that kind of food on the air. She was looking forward to getting back to meals she could trust not to poison her or make her throw up. As civilisation approached she became conscious of the state of her hair. The grease had built up and sent it two shades darker, as well as making it hang heavy around her face. She felt dirty through and through and was looking forward with renewed vigour to a very hot shower. And then even that thought was spoiled. After what she'd done to Martin would she ever feel clean again?

The state of her legs became such that walking was a real effort. She had shin splints like a million knives digging into her bones and each step became an agony. She stopped for a moment and consulted a map, measuring the distance left in fingernails and working it out on the scale from there. Two kilometres to go. She couldn't imagine that she could walk that far. She thought about giving up then, walking away from the path and finding a nice bit of woodland or undergrowth and lying down there. She would let the plants and trees grow over her body, reclaim her for nature.

As tempting as becoming one with nature was, she didn't stray from the path. In fact, she got up and carried on walking with new determination. She decided that the only answer was to power through and get herself back down to the hotel in Fort William as fast as she could manage. She walked quickly, and her legs began to feel like they belonged to someone else, like she was floating. She could almost have believed she no longer had legs if it hadn't been for an excruciating pain that came from underneath her waistline exactly where the things should be.

The rhythm of her walking took over and she let herself switch off from everything except placing one foot in front of another. She went into a trance-like state and she walked, watching the steady horizon and letting her eyes go out of focus. The countryside around her was pretty constant: grass, sheep, hills and water in the distance. The air had turned damp now, the way it had been when they first set out, and droplets of water framed her face and kept her alert.

Then, finally, it was there in front of her. Houses and streets, the wind and the clouds of Fort William. As usual, it wore its damp, miserable face for her. She had never seen it any other way. It was typically British in its dull, grey light and constant threat of rain. The very normality of it made the last few days she'd had in the bothy seem especially ridiculous. Had any of it really happened? Was Martin about to catch up and grab her hand so that she realised none of it had actually passed and they were just wandering around on holiday, their second honeymoon to celebrate ten years together?

She savoured that idea for a moment. An alternate reality where there was more time with Martin, further anniversaries and Christmases and birthdays and things to celebrate together. Not the Martin in the bothy, the one who had attacked her on 'the weekend', but the man she had thought he was, eminently practical but loving with it. A reality, perhaps, where they'd had children and she'd been more fulfilled and satisfied with her lot. Hell, if she was going to make it up, she might as well create something better than she had.

She knew, though, as she walked through Fort William and towards the hotel where their car was parked, what was real and what was not. It was time to face up to the terrible thing she had done.

23

The hotel looked different from when she'd left it, Susie thought. Bigger and cleaner, more shiny. She knew that it couldn't have actually changed so that it must have been her that had changed. She had certainly got dirtier, if not smaller. And she had got rid of Martin. The facts of this, its irreversibility, shook through her and she waited for the guilt again but it never came. She hesitated as she looked at the hotel's doors. She had lost the hang of being part of civilisation, turned into some kind of wild creature. She wondered if she even needed food any more, never mind soft sheets or good movies. She told herself she didn't deserve these nice things, not after what she'd done to her husband. She hadn't even been satisfied with killing him once but had done it a second time. But it hadn't been a choice. She would be sinking deeper and deeper into cold peat herself if she hadn't acted in her own defence.

The front entrance to the hotel had revolving glass doors. Susie's legs felt like they must be bloody stumps as she walked towards them. The doors moved as she neared them, sensing her presence and starting up. She stood back, waiting for a safe gap. They seemed to be going too fast, making her dizzy. She wasn't sure that if she stepped in she would ever manage to get out again. She could imagine being trapped there, going round and round in an incessant circle, for eternity. Like the eternity of a wedding ring, the round and round of that trap. She held her breath and jumped into the moving stream of the doors. They spat her out on the other side.

The lights in the hotel lobby were unbearably bright; she didn't remember them being like that. She shielded her eyes from the glare and tried to walk. Her legs had weakened to the point where she could hardly move them. Blood was rushing from her head, as if she had stood up too fast. She tried to move forward but her body didn't respond. It was like wading through treacle. She pushed and pushed against the sticky substance that seemed to be surrounding her legs but she hardly moved. She began to feel desperate then. All she wanted to do was to lie down, close her eyes and make it all go away. To go back to a time before they had come on this bloody trip to Scotland. When Martin was here and he was normal and they were both safe. He hadn't been perfect, not by any stretch, but he had been hers. And now he was no one's, nowhere. He was nothing and never had been the man she'd thought he was; it was all a lie. His body was just a shell, sinking into the peat where it would never be found.

She could feel that she was all over the place now, staggering, her feet hardly able to hold her body upright. She looked for something to reach for but there was nothing at the right height. The marble floor of the reception area went on for what looked like miles to her tired eyes. She was skidding on its surface and very disoriented. She saw the concierge clock her from his place behind the desk and a look of disgust twist his face; she could only imagine how she looked right now.

Then his face changed; there was some recognition there. He was heading towards her and reaching for her.

She fell just before he got to her, skidding across the floor and hitting him in the legs, sending him flying. The room had gone paler; her eyes weren't working properly, but she hadn't passed out yet. He got up then grabbed her under the elbows and looked down kindly at her, a small smile on his face as he spoke with that soft Highland lilt. 'We were getting very worried,' he said. He continued to talk but his voice got further and further away.

Then everything faded out altogether.

The room where Susie woke up was very bright and white. It looked like it had been scrubbed clean over and over again just to make a point. She had been cleaned too, when she was out of it. Her skin felt soft and smelled of lily of the valley and the covers felt lovely against her cleanness. It reminded her of bed after bath time when she was young, the feeling of clean pyjamas against clean skin. She couldn't work out at first where she was or how she'd got there. It took her a few moments to orient herself and remember the bothy, but, even then, she wasn't sure whether it had been real or a dream. She blinked her eyes against the brightness of the walls and sat up. All her muscles ached from the long walk home and the more conscious she became the clearer she felt that it had all happened.

She wondered if they had found him. Once she was back inside herself, it was all she could think about. She knew even then that she would deny any involvement and say that the river had swept him away. She had lost so much; she wasn't prepared to lose her freedom too. The evil of the bothy had taken her husband and it had taken her peace of mind, stripped them both from her as if she never possessed them, and she was damn sure she wasn't going to let it ruin her entire life. She would fight for her freedom, damn right she would.

There was a sound from outside the room; the door opened and a nurse came through it pushing a trolley. Of course; she was in hospital. Now she understood. She tried to piece things together. She had been walking back to Fort William. She remembered arriving in town and how tired she had felt, how it had been by sheer force of will she had continued to walk, her legs sore and buckling but her mind refusing to let them stop. Had she made it to the hotel? She pictured the place now, its revolving doors and marble lobby. She had vague memories of a man helping her, but they weren't at all clear. Yes, she had made it there and then, nothing. She must have collapsed.

The nurse smiled at her and pushed the trolley across to the bed. 'You're back in the land of the living then,' she said. Susie looked at the contents of the trolley. There was a bowl of soup and lots of bread. It smelled good, not like she remembered hospital food being at all. But then, she had eaten only sporadically over the last week or so and, when she had had food, it had been those mouldy leaves or, at best, tinned beans. In comparison, this was a gourmet offering. She reached for the spoon and saw that her hand was shaking like mad, which was strange because she hadn't noticed the tremors at all before. Now she checked, and could see that it was not just her hand but her entire body. She was shaking and she couldn't stop.

'You're in shock,' the nurse told her. She reached for her hand and guided it to the spoon. In normal circumstances, Susie would have hated this, but she let the nurse help her. She picked up a spoonful of the soup and pushed it into her mouth. It was hot and tasted very rich. She grabbed bread and tore it. The shakes began to subside and she was able to eat. In fact, she was ravenous. As soon as she put the food into her mouth she wanted more, and soon she had torn up and dipped all the bread, and lifted the bowl to her mouth to drink what was left.

'Can I get you some tea?' the nurse asked. Susie nodded. It was only now that she noticed the woman had an unusual accent; Northern Irish, and not from these parts. She also saw her name badge which said 'Sue'. This reminded her of Martin and, strangely, made her throat tighten and her eyes well up. It was weird how these things worked; she had hated him calling her Sue and yet the name suddenly brought him to mind vividly and she felt her loss keenly. The nurse must have seen her distress and rushed over to her side.

'My husband . . .' Susie's voice trailed away. She wasn't at all sure what she wanted to say about him.

'They've been asking. The police.'

Susie sat up straight and looked alarmed.

'He didn't turn up with you at the hotel. They had noticed you both gone and alerted the authorities. When they realised who you were, they had expected to see him pile in behind you but you were on your own. Did he walk with you back to Fort William?'

'No,' Susie said. She let out a sob. 'He was

washed away,' she said, right through her own wailing. The crying was completely sincere and the lie, when it came, came easily. Strictly speaking, she supposed, it wasn't a lie, even if it wasn't the end of the story.

The nurse's hand reached for her arm and held steady there. Susie was shaking again, as bad as if she was in withdrawal from a drug. She was, in a way, she thought; withdrawal from Martin and her life with him. She wondered if she could really live with it. It had been hard enough after getting rid of the baby but this, a full-grown man, a man she'd always believed had loved and trusted her, and she had taken his life knowingly and actively. All of this raced through her head, repeating over and over, and she sobbed and she sobbed and she sobbed.

It was as if her surroundings disappeared while she was crying. She literally couldn't see the room through the mist of tears but she couldn't even picture where she was either. That was the thing about crying; the physical intensity of it, when you got it right, made everything else go away. *That's why we need it*, she thought. When she stopped, the white of her surroundings hit her vividly, and she screwed up her eyes against the harshness of it.

She felt the nurse's hands, on her arm and her shoulder, and she brushed them off. She didn't need anyone's sympathy. She didn't deserve it; it just made her feel worse.

'I'm sure they'll find him,' the nurse said. 'He probably climbed out of the burn just a little further down. The rivers aren't so deep around here. You need to tell us where you were.'

'The burn was deep.' The lies came quick, one after the other, and she looked up plaintively at the nurse. 'We had walked up over the top of the valley and to that bothy by the loch, the one just north of here.'

The nurse looked confused. 'I don't know where you mean,' she said.

Susie was almost too tired to explain in any more detail. She lay back down for a moment then gathered her strength. She had to sort this out. She wanted it all to be over, one way or another, she didn't care, but she didn't want it hanging over her any longer. 'The map in my bag,' she said. 'Where's my bag?'

The nurse leaned down, opening a locker in the cabinet next to the bed. Her half-empty rucksack had been crammed inside and it was an effort for the woman to pull it out. She dug around inside the cupboard and persevered and, eventually, it came loose.

'The front pocket,' Susie told her. Her voice had gone dry and raspy. 'You said something about some tea?' she said, every word feeling like sandpaper in her throat.

The woman nodded, and passed her the plastic case which contained the map. Susie took it from her, leaning back against the hospital bed. The nurse made sure she was propped up comfortably and left the room. With some effort, Susie unzipped the bag. Her fingers were shaking like crazy, and covered in scratches and cuts. It hurt to use them but she kept on, unfolding the map as best she could over the trolley and the residue of the soup. She found the bothy on the map, conveniently marked with a blue-biro cross: Martin's work. She wondered if that had been the last mark he'd made on paper. But, no, she remembered his diary and the things he had written there. The last entry had been a few days before he'd died. She should have kept the book. It would have been evidence if they found his body. As it was, she had no proof that he'd meant her any harm, no real defence at all. She let go of the map, too tired to keep hold of it while she waited for the nurse to return. It dropped into the soup bowl. She knew this would stain the underside but didn't really care. She would not be going walking in Scotland ever again. She closed her eyes and waited.

The nurse came back with a mug in her hands, which she handed carefully to Susie. The familiar smell was very comforting. She sipped; it had been made milky, not the way she liked it best but strangely soothing. Martin had always steadfastly ignored her preferences, making Susie's tea milky like this, the same way he liked it. How could Susie possibly know better about how she would enjoy her tea? She was glad these kinds of memories came readily, and not the good times they'd had together.

Putting down the tea, Susie reached for the map again. She pointed at the cross Martin had made. 'There's a bothy there,' she said. 'Martin had been to it years ago and wanted to go back. We got trapped. This burn here,' she indicated on the map, 'it was in spate and we were cut off. The other side is all bog.'

The woman looked at where she was pointing. 'I go up that way walking a lot,' she said. 'I've never been to the bothy there.'

Susie was getting tired. 'See the biro cross,' she said. 'The bothy is there.'

The woman nodded, staring at the map. 'And you say you couldn't cross the bog?' She stopped and grabbed the map, pulling it right up to her face. 'But there's a path right the way past –' she was pointing '– here. Look so.' She held the map out for Susie to see. There was a track marked right where the woman was pointing. She tried to work out where it would be. Not visible from the bothy, that was true, but a short walk away. How had she not seen that when she mapped out her route back, that day when she'd insisted on trying and got stuck in the mud? Martin must have known. He could read maps like no one she'd ever met before; it was like he could look at the contours and see the land they represented. He knew they weren't trapped. It had all been part of the same game. She felt angry with him all over again until she realised it was wasted emotion. What was the point in being angry with a dead man?

'This was the burn that swept him away?' the nurse asked her now, carefully pointing to the map and holding it out to her.

Susie nodded. 'A few days ago,' she said. 'I didn't dare cross after that so I waited until the water level dropped. It was terrifying, being there alone, my husband gone and not knowing if he was alive or dead.'

The nurse patted Susie's hand. *There, there,* the gesture said, as if something so trite could make anything better. It was to shut her up, she realised. That was okay, though. She really didn't want to talk any more. She drank some more milky tea. She was tired. Her head throbbed and she felt weak and dehydrated, like she was hungover. She put down the tea and closed her eyes. She didn't think she could ever sleep enough to feel anything like awake again.

When Susie woke up next, there was someone new waiting by her bed, a young man dressed in a smart blue uniform. A police officer. It was true what they said: the police were getting younger. She knew that thinking this was the first sign of middle age. She wondered if they had found Martin yet. Had the policeman come to arrest her, or just to find out more information? She smiled at him, and hoped that her nerves didn't show. She couldn't imagine, though, that she looked anything other than tired.

'Mrs Crannock,' he said. 'We're still trying to ascertain the whereabouts of your husband Martin.'

She nodded. Why did the police always insist on talking like this, as if real life was one of their carefully worded statements? She frowned at the young-looking man. 'He was swept away,' she said. 'I told the nurse earlier.'

'Yes,' he said. 'She passed on your story. We just wanted to check a few of the facts with you.'

'Go ahead.' She cleared her throat, which was still feeling rather dry. She saw there was a jug of water on the table across from her and she reached for it. The policeman saw her struggling and got up to help, pouring a drink for her and handing her the beaker. She felt truly useless; unable to pour herself a glass of water! Her eyes were tearing up again.

'I know this is very hard,' the young man said, misinterpreting her tears.

She nodded through them, then began to speak. 'We went to the bothy. I showed the nurse on the map. We got trapped by the swollen river and neither of us realised there was a route over the bog. I even tried, but I got stuck.'

'And your husband?'

'He was happy to sit it out, for a few days, but then we ran out of food.' She sniffed, and gulped involuntarily. She wasn't sure what she looked like to this youngster. A pathetic, frazzled and slightly overweight middle-aged woman, she supposed. She hated the way her age made her appear to those who were still in their prime. 'We ran out of food and so we tried to get over the river. It was desperate, really. Flowing too fast. Martin was swept away. I tried to grab for him . . .' Her voice trailed off. She couldn't sustain her own lie.

Now it was the policeman's turn to hold and pat at her hand, that *there, there* gesture. She didn't mind this so much. It was good to feel the touch of a man, even in this context. She didn't know how long it would be before someone reached for her again. 'We have a search party out looking for him. I'm sure we'll find him soon.'

'You will?' Her voice squeaked a little at that idea.

He stroked her hand and nodded.

'Officer?' she asked. She couldn't help herself, even though she knew the answer to the question would make the man uncomfortable. She wanted more of him, of his sympathy and token affection. If it was all she could have right now from a man, then she wanted it. 'Do you think there's any chance at all that you'll find him alive?'

The young man looked at the floor and shrugged. He squeezed Susie's hand. 'I'm really sorry,' he said.

His hand moved over hers in a stroking movement and she relished it. She stared up at him with puppy-dog eyes so that he would carry on. She couldn't have love now, or desire, she knew that. It was too much of a risk and could only lead to horror, the way all her love affairs had. She would take what she could get.

Epilogue

Two months had passed since Susie came back from Scotland but the trip felt an entire lifetime away. She had worked hard to get on with things, to put it all behind her. She still had half her life to live, as her mother and sister kept reminding her. She had been down to the RSCPA and rescued a cat called Coco. He was a lovely little thing; a tabby cross with brown and grey stripes and she had fallen in love with him. Of course, like all cats, he was independent and ever so slightly superior. Like most widows of a certain age, she admired those qualities.

Widow. It is one of those words you can never imagine applying to yourself when you are young. There is too much tragedy in its syllables, too much of a sense of age inherent in the term. She was hardly young any more but, as widows went, still youthful. She tried to work out if she actually missed Martin. She could no longer believe in the marriage she'd thought she had and the only thing that hurt her soul was at night-time, the hole where there had been his warm, soft shape. She got an electric blanket and kept her bed well covered so that she wouldn't feel this. She didn't want to miss him in any way. She tried hard to feel guilty about killing him, like she felt she should do, but whenever she thought about it she remembered that last night in the bothy and the ice in his eyes. She could only feel relief that he was out of her life.

They never found Martin's body in its resting place in the wet peat. She had worried about it at first, convinced they would find some sign of his presence there in their fingertip search. But they believed her story and had looked in and near the river. *No sign*, they told her with regret. She acted bereft when they said that but that's what it all was: an act. The real Martin had been a world away from his day-to-day persona. He had come through to the surface on a few occasions, notably that weekend away when he had pinned her down and tried to strangle her.

There was no part of her that made excuses for him now. Martin's father had a lot to answer for but, then, so did Martin. He had been a violent bully. It was only now he wasn't around that she fully realised this was true. The threat had hung over her ever since 'the weekend' and it had surfaced in his eyes and in the tone of his voice whenever he had needed it. It had never failed to shut her up. Now she could say what she thought about anything, she really remembered that feeling of being silenced and she resented it. No one made him turn into the man he became. It wasn't what everyone with abusive fathers did and there was always a choice. She had come to despise the part of her that had made excuses for him; the victim inside her that had attracted Martin in the first place. She would never be that person again, thank God.

Although her memories of events at the bothy had become a little cloudy even in the short time she'd been back, they were clear enough for her to know that something very strange had happened there. There was no doubt in her mind that a supernatural force had been at work in that strange little shelter, something that drove her to unimaginable actions. Even Martin had seemed to know this, towards the end. She'd talked to a close friend about the things that had happened in Scotland, although she'd not told her everything. She'd missed out the incriminating parts and stuck to her story about Martin being swept away. Anna had said she'd known for years that Martin was a bully, that everyone had seen it except Susie. She told Susie that the whole thing was probably a psychiatric break, her mind creating a world that helped her escape from her abusive husband. Susie had almost laughed when she heard this. It was just the kind of explanation Martin would have come up with and it was nonsense. Even Martin, in the end, had conceded that, if only in his notebook.

Her main regret was not keeping that book. While Martin's scrawls made uncomfortable reading, she felt that having them would have helped her remember. It would have been good to see in black and white that she'd had no choice but to do what she had done to her husband. She would never forget the things she'd read on those pages, the hate he'd felt towards her and the damage he'd wanted to do. So much for her logical, sensible husband. He had been hiding such a big part of himself from her.

She would never forget either the terrible force that had pulled her around in the bothy and twisted the knife into what was left of their marriage. This force had conned her, brought back her lover from the grave and messed with her head. It had made her collude with its evil plans and it had killed her husband, in the end. She had been powerless against something so potent. She had no idea why the bothy had wanted Martin so badly. It had dragged him back, across the years.

Beside her bed, she kept the rucksack full of her things from the trip. She had not thrown them away immediately the way she had expected to. The bag was stained with peat, and it smelled of the bothy. She would hold it to her face at night before she went to sleep and pull back some of the memories. She could whisk herself off there in a moment, if she tried hard enough.

Once there, she would wait. She was alone and it chilled her to the bone but she knew she wouldn't be lonely much longer. He would come for her, her Jules would come, he hadn't forgotten her, he couldn't have. He was biding his time and then she would feel his touch again, his breath against her neck. She could reach an arm out from under the covers or leave her back bare out of the quilt and feel the cool whisper of him there; every night she tried to feel it.

The problem was that Jules never came. The only thing that did was bad dreams. A couple, young and hopeful and new, the way she and Martin had once been, turning up outside the bothy. Walking in and finding the gas stove and the cooking pots, all the things she'd left behind. The pair settling for the night and telling ghost stories. The creatures that had lights for eyes, dancing outside the bothy window as the couple slept and the hunting knife glinting in the corner of the room too, although how that had found its way back into the hut from out of the peat bog only made sense in the logic of dreams and that of the bothy.

She would wake then, in a cold sweat, her arms and legs all aches and pains from the adrenaline. The dream felt too real; it felt like being there again. Some nights she wanted to get in the car and drive all the way up to the bothy to satisfy herself she'd find the place empty.

Other nights were even worse, though, and she woke to total emptiness. All she could do then was fall into the cold. The freezing cold of being alone.

THE DARKENING

Stephen M. Irwin

The dark trunks stood like a row of black teeth, endlessly huge, stretching into the night. Waking as they scented prey . . .

After his wife's sudden death, Nick Close returns to his hometown in Australia. He is still haunted by the murder of his friend Tristram thirty years ago, and a strange sense of foreboding now overshadows his arrival. Soon after, a child's body is found in the woods at the edge of town, a death
that closely echoes Tristram's.

Quietly probing into the town's secrets, Nick uncovers a string of unexplained disappearances and brutal killings, some decades old. Every single one leads him back to the twisted maze of the woods. But there is one other connection, and Nick suddenly realises that it hadn't been Tristram who was meant to die all those years ago . . .

'Brilliant . . . A gripping rollercoaster journey that you'll remember for days – and nights – to come' *She*

978-0-7515-4396-4

THE BIRTHING HOUSE

Christopher Ransom

They were in the house a week before it came for him . . .

When Conrad and Jo move to the historic Victorian house, it seems like a new start for them. With its fairytale porch, wooden floorboards and perfect garden, it feels as though they have finally come home.

But when Conrad is given an old photo album, he begins to discover what dark secrets the house is harbouring. Looking through the cracked, hundred-year-old pages, he finds a photo of a group of Victorian women standing outside his house. The women look fearsome, angry; they are all dressed in black with their arms folded.

And then his heart nearly stops when he sees that one of the women – raven-haired and staring at him with hatred in her eyes – is his wife . . .

'A stunning debut – swaddling the reader in dread from the very first sentence, and spiraling into a heart-stopping climax' Michael Marshall

978-0-7515-4171-7